The C

Man Overboard

(Michaela McPherson Book 3)

Books by Judith Lucci

Michaela McPherson Mysteries
The Case of Dr. Dude
The Case of the Dead Dowager
The Case of the Man Overboard
The Case of the Very Dead Lawyer
The Case of the Missing Parts

Alex Destephano Novels
Chaos at Crescent City Medical Center
The Imposter
Viral Intent
Toxic New Year
Evil: Finding St. Germaine
RUN For Your Life
Demons Among Us – Coming 2020

Dr. Sonia Amon Medical Thrillers
Shatter Proof
Delusion Proof
Fool Proof
Tamper Proof – Coming 2020

Artzy Chicks Mysteries
The Most Wonderful Crime of the Year
The Most Awfullest Crime of the Year
The Most Glittery Crime of the Year
The Most Slippery Crime of the Year

Other Books
Beach Traffic: The Ocean Can Be Deadly
Ebola: What You Must Know to Stay Safe
Meandering, Musing & Inspiration for the Soul

The Case of the Man Overboard

A Michaela McPherson Mystery

A NOVEL BY

Judith Lucci

Bluestone Valley Publishing

Harrisonburg, Virginia

ISBN-13: 978-1981594023

Chapter 1

The Mediterranean Sea glittered like diamonds and gemstones while good Southern Rock music filled the air. Dancers in bathing suits swayed poolside to the sounds of Lynyrd Skynyrd and Greg Allman. A light breeze filtered across the ship and the sun shone in the faces of hundreds of very happy, slightly intoxicated passengers. White-jacketed waiters passed trays of tall, cold drinks with an umbrella and a cherry on top.

Two men sat below the pool on the Promenade deck of the Mediterranean cruise ship and gazed at the Mediterranean Sea. One man was older, short, stocky, and bald while the other man was in his forties, with dark oily hair, well-built but thin and wiry. The younger man had a snake tattooed on his right hand. The inked area was vicious and evil - a lot like the man. Both men were on their third drink.

"Now, this is living," the first man declared as he gazed at the crystal blue water and clicked his fingers at a waiter who walked by their chaises. The waiter stopped immediately and smiled at the two men, his perfectly white teeth gleamed against his darkened skin. He pulled out his pad, ready for their order.

"Gimme another vodka on the rocks," the older man barked in deeply accented English. "And be quick about it," he added with a scowl.

The waiter nodded and glanced at the younger man who shook his head and waved him away with a flick of his hand.

The older man, Vadim, gave Snake an incredulous look. "What's up, numb nuts? You quit drinkin' for the day?" He sneered. "You a lightweight? Don't tell me those assholes hooked me up with a sissy, lightweight boozer." Vadim shook his head, leaned forward in his chair, and smacked Snake on the hand.

Snake felt his blood pressure jump as a red light flashed before his eyes. He remained calm. "Yeah. I need a clear head for tonight." He surveyed the distance between his chair and the turn in the Promenade deck. He pointed and said, "That's the place to do it. There's no visualization at the turn and we have the metal staircase to block us. No cameras either. No one will see."

The old man snorted but said nothing and continued to stare at the sea. "Piece of cake, baby play," he said with a snort as he lifted his glass to his lips, drank deeply, and savored the taste of the clear liquid.

Snake kicked his companion on the foot and said, "Listen to me, old man. I wanna do this right. I'd like to hook a few more assignments like this, particularly at this rate of pay, so I can disappear somewhere forever, maybe to my own private playground."

"Yeah, no kidding," Vadim said. "This place ain't bad though," he added as he looked around the ship. "I loved the homeland and then New Orleans, but I think I may buy me a big boat and live at sea. I like the feel of it." He paused for a moment, shut his eyes, and continued, "Yeah, a big old cabin cruiser with a cook… and a butler to round me up some native girls when I get the urge."

Snake looked over at Vadim and shook his head. The man was ugly. He had scars on his face and a long jagged line down his right arm. His left shoulder had obviously encountered several knives and/or bullets, possibly both.

He could see the scars running up his arm where his muscle shirt ended. The man also sported the biggest nose he'd ever seen on a human. His face was permanently flushed from vodka and a network of circuitous red veins paraded around his face in angry red patterns.

Snake turned his head away. He figured no one ever looked Vadim in the face. He was too ugly and it was easier not to. He ran his fingers through his oiled black hair and changed the subject. "How do these doctors get all this money? I heard nobody got rich these days practicing medicine."

Vadim turned, gave him an incredulous look, and snorted, "Ha, are you crazy? Ain't none of these doctors paid for this cruise. It's a big, fat reward from Blake Pharmaceutical. The doctors got this trip for free. They act like whores for these drug companies and do anything they ask them to do. They talk up the drugs and prescribe them… even if you don't need them," he said in an angry voice.

"Free? Are you kidding me?" Snake asked with a sneer on his face. "These doctors are here for free?"

Vadim rolled his eyes. "You don't know nuthin'. Yeah, dumb ass. Free. They do it all the time in New Orleans. Blake Pharmaceutical paid for this cruise, trust me," Vadim assured him, as he spat his words at the younger man, an angry edge to his voice. "You know those medical assholes don't pay for anything."

Snake felt anger building in his chest, but held his tongue. "Are most of them from the US?" He asked in a neutral voice.

The man looked at him as if he was stupid. "Hell yeah, dude." The Russian squinted at him and then shaded his eyes with his hand. "Where the hell you from, fool? Are you stupid or what?" Vadim asked. "What have you been doin'?

Twiddling your thumbs? Have you done your homework for this assignment?" He asked as his beady, reddened eyes stared at Snake.

Snake's ears burned in anger. He'd killed people for calling him less. His fingers blanched as he gripped the aluminum rail of his lounge chair. He turned toward Vadim. The look in his eyes was deadly. "I've been in Siberia testing sarin gas, asshole. That's where I've been," he said as his eyes burned into those of his companion.

Vadim cut his eyes toward his almost-empty tumbler of vodka. He could swear the ice cubes melted under the heated gaze of his companion. A few moments passed before he asked, "How'd that go? The testing, I mean, the sarin?"

"Fine, it went good," Snake said as he gave Vadim a cool stare. "I have a few small canisters with me just in case someone gets in my way." He rested his cold eyes on Vadim, the threat clearly implied in his voice.

Vadim nodded as his hand tightened around his glass and he looked at the water. I may have to kill this son of a bitch before I get off this boat.

Snake stared at him, but Vadim avoided his eyes. He felt the urge that always got him in trouble. The urge to kill. Better not go there yet; it was too early in the voyage. He willed himself to calm down.

Snake continued to glower at him, but Vadim ignored him and looked out to sea. "The sea sure looks pretty," he said as he avoided Snake's angry face.

Snake remained silent and sucked on his ice cubes.

Vadim reached for his shades and stole a look at Snake's hand as the man grasped the aluminum rail of his lounge chair. The snake eyes on his tattoo rippled over the tendons in his hand. The inked snake looked as angry as Vadim felt. He sat quietly behind his sunglasses and watched as Snake's anger continued to fester. There was no way the younger man was gonna get in his way during this trip.

Vadim made a decision. After they'd done their work, he'd steer clear of him. He felt the hairs rise on the back of his neck in anger. He was sick of these pieces of shit who thought he was less talented, less able, or less dedicated to the cause just because he was older. He longed for the peaceful days in New Orleans with his daughter and her husband. But of course, she was gone, killed by an ignorant US bitch doctor. He felt a flush overtake his body. He hated doctors. Maybe he'd kill a bunch of them after their main job was over. He felt his face redden with anger as he reflected on the last year. It had been a painful one for him; hence, the overindulgence in alcohol and sometimes the other stuff just seemed to be necessary for him to keep on keepin' on. A second later, the Russian threw his glass over the side of the ship.

Snake noticed Vadim's reticence... and his anger. "We got everything straight for tonight? I don't want there to be any trouble," he said in a voice that irritated Vadim to his limit. What the hell was this kid doin' bossing him around? He was far more superior in every way. Why had the bosses put him in charge of the mission and not him?

Vadim nodded and said, "Yeah. All set. Everything's okay. The plan ain't changed since we set sail two days ago."

Snake nodded. "Yeah, okay," he said as he struggled out of the chaise. "I'll meet you here tonight an hour and a half after midnight like we talked about, got it? That's when our target takes his nightly run." He stood and stared down at Vadim who remained comfortably seated. Snake noted how truly ugly the man was. Not even a mother could love a face like that. He shook his head and wished for next week.

"Yeah, I'll be there. See you then." Vadim said as he held the man's eyes with his. "Remember, I'm in the stairway and you're in the doorway. No cameras," he reminded him.

Vadim watched the man depart, and noted the slight limp in his walk. Who the hell was this man and why have they hooked him up with him? Vadim was tired of having these crap partners. But, he said to himself, this is the way this organization works and I can't complain about the pay. He accepted a fresh vodka and continued to sip his magic liquid and people-watched from his secluded chair on the ship's deck. He fell asleep and awoke several hours later. Vadim's 'fresh' vodka had collected several gnats. He stood up and stretched. He felt great. This was an easy gig and he got to cruise the Mediterranean as part of the deal. Life was good… even for the bad guys. He picked up the glass and drank the vodka in one gulp. Gnats and all.

Chapter 2

The Countess Dorothy Borghase sat in the Captain's private dining room of The Regina Roma Mediterranean for High Tea. She looked around appreciably at the décor in the dining room and nodded. She admired the ornate moldings and the beveled marrows. The silk wallpaper was a lush teal color and beautiful. The private dining room was filled with Italian art and artifacts and was fit for a king and certainly fit for her, an Italian Countess and part owner of the Mediterranean Cruise Line. Dottie and her husband, the late Count Borghase, had invested heavily in the Mediterranean Cruise Line over fifty years ago and the cruise line had grown to a fleet of twelve large, well-managed, and highly successful ships. Mediterranean controlled most of the ocean liners and cruise ships in the Mediterranean. She allowed herself to dream and reflect as she remembered her honeymoon aboard a much smaller, but similar ship many years ago. She was in a suite with the same number on this voyage and her best friend, Michaela McPherson, was next door with Angel, her retired police dog. They'd been traveling for over three weeks and the cruise was the highlight of the trip.

Dottie looked up and smiled graciously at the Sommelier as he entered the quiet dining room to retrieve a bottle of wine. Her attention turned to the door of the Captain's dining room. The ship's First Mate passed through on his way to the dining executive offices. He smiled at her and waved as he passed through the dining room.

Such a good-looking man, she thought to herself. The man was tall - probably greater than six-foot-three. He reminded her of Count Borghase, her husband, who'd died years and years ago. Dottie's thoughts about Borgy made the eighty-two-year-old Countess' heart beat madly. The pair had been the toast of Europe back in the fifties. He was tall, dark, and handsome and she was his beautiful, tall, brunette Olympian wife. Dottie had won a Gold Medal for Italy in the 1955 Olympics. She still missed Borgy, even after all of these years. They'd had fifteen playful, often reckless, but incredibly happy years together until the Count died suddenly and tragically. Dottie, a widow at forty and fabulously rich, had moved to the United States to handle her husband's US investments in Virginia. She'd found she liked the States, loved the south, and stayed there to start a new life.

Dottie reflected on her journey to Europe and to her husband's ancestral home, The Villa Borghase, with Michaela. They'd left Richmond almost a month ago and spent three weeks at the Villa Borghase outside of Rome. Dottie hadn't been to the Villa in fifteen years and it was wonderful to see all the relatives. There were dozens of cousins, nephews and nieces, and all of the Borghase offspring, down to the newest baby, a tiny little girl who had been born to her favorite grandnephew or maybe it was her great-grandnephew. She couldn't remember… she was older than dirt and she knew it, but of course, she'd never admit it. The tiny infant had been named for her. She'd even tried to make peace with the sullen, egotistical, and selfish Borghase woman who would inherit her title when she died. That had been painful. She sighed as she remembered that dreadful afternoon. It was clear the woman was pissed because Dottie was still alive. Screw her, Dottie thought as she reached for her glass of cream sherry just as an attractive young couple came into the private dining room.

Dottie eagerly studied the couple. She loved trying to figure people out. The woman was a tall brunette with beautiful blue eyes and a lovely dress the same color. The woman smiled at her and spoke. Dottie nodded her head slightly to acknowledge their presence.

The couple seated themselves on the aft side of the dining room and quietly discussed the drink menu. Dottie wondered who they were as only a few people had 'anytime' access to the Captain's dining room. They were an attractive couple and appeared to be American. She noticed the woman ordered a mojito while her husband, a forty-something guy selected a craft beer. She eavesdropped as best she could on their conversation. After a few minutes, she'd learned that he was a physician guest of Blake Pharmaceutical, a large US pharmaceutical company that had booked practically half of the cruise ship.

Dottie raised her little finger and a waiter immediately appeared and asked her if she'd like another glass of sherry. Dottie shook her head and asked him to send a bottle of Moet Chandon over to the couple on the other side of the room. Dottie was like that. She was generous and she gave lavish gifts, but God help anyone who got in her way or crossed her path. At eighty-two years of age, and an aristocrat to boot, she didn't take anything off anyone and she did exactly what she pleased whenever she pleased. Well, maybe she did take some stuff from Michaela but after all, they were business partners. In truth, Dottie had ordered the champagne for the couple because she was bored and the couple looked interesting. She was also angry because Michaela hadn't bothered to show up and she wanted someone to talk with.

She watched as the maître d' delivered the bottle of sparkling wine and smiled at the surprised look on the couple's faces. The waiter swept his arm away from his body and said, "Champagne for you, compliments of the Countess Dorothy Borghase."

The man looked confused and didn't quite understand the waiter's accent. "I'm not sure what you said. Could you please repeat it?" He asked in a pleasant voice as he eyed the bubbly.

The waiter nodded. "Of course, sir. The Countess Dorothy Borghase, who is seated across the room from you, sent you this champagne with her very best wishes," he repeated as he pointed toward Dottie and smiled.

The couple turned to Dorothy and the woman smiled widely as her husband stood and approached Dottie's table. He extended his hand and said, "What a lovely surprise, Countess. Will you join us for a glass of champagne?"

Dottie looked into the man's friendly eyes and said, "I'd be delighted, sir. Or, perhaps you would like to join me since I have a larger table," she suggested as her well-manicured hand swept across the deep mahogany dining table.

"We would be delighted to join you. It's so kind of you to send us the champagne," he said with a smile that showed crinkly laugh lines in his face. Dottie was immediately drawn to him and felt there was something special about him.

He extended his hand and said, "My name is Ian Pennington. Let me go and retrieve my wife, Alana, and I'll be back in just a second."

Dottie smiled and watched him return to his table, assist his wife out of her chair, and guide her toward Dottie, with his hand at the small of her back. The waiter followed them with the champagne in a silver stand and crystal flutes.

Ian introduced Alana who took Dottie's hand and said, "Thank you so much, Countess. How lovely of you to send us a bottle of champagne. I hardly know what to say."

Dottie smiled at the woman and noticed the vivid blue shade of her eyes. For a moment, she was taken back to her own self as a young woman. She'd looked very much like Alana Pennington. "You don't have to say anything, just join me for a glass," Dottie encouraged her. "As a matter-of-fact, I'll propose the toast," she said grandly as they each took a fluted champagne glass and held it as the waiter filled it with the sparkling beverage.

"To my new friends and the Mediterranean Sea," she said as she raised her glass and clinked it with Ian and Alana's. "May you have a wonderful cruise." Alana smiled and said, "Thank you, Countess Borghase. We hope that you do as well. How is your cruise going so far?"

Dottie smiled as she swept a piece of white hair back into her chignon. "It's been lovely. I've traveled from the US with my wonderful friend, sort of an adopted granddaughter, Michaela. We've just spent three weeks at my villa outside Rome where I visited cousins, nieces, and nephews I haven't seen in years." She paused for a moment, took a sip of her champagne. "How are you enjoying things?" She asked pleasantly as she looked at Ian and Alana. "Have you been on a Mediterranean cruise before?"

Ian spoke and said, "I've not been cruising, but my wife has been here many times. She taught at the University of Malta for several years before we married. I'm a physician, a psychiatrist actually, and I have a practice outside Washington, DC, and we're here as guests of Blake Pharmaceutical."

"Oh, I see," Dottie said. She was impressed. She turned to Alana, "How did you end up teaching at the University of Malta?" She paused for a second and then added, "Malta is such a special place," she ended a dreamy far-away look in her eyes. "The Count and I used to vacation in Malta."

Alana smiled and said, "I spent a summer there when I was in graduate school. I'm a speech pathologist and I did a student exchange with a University of Malta graduate student. I loved it. Then, after I got my faculty position, I returned to Malta as part of a faculty exchange. I taught in Malta for a year and she taught in my place at George Washington University."

"What a lovely story and a great opportunity," Dottie said pleasantly as she surveyed the young woman.

Alana smiled and continued, "Well, it didn't end there. I loved Malta so much, I decided to stay a few more years and teach. Then I returned to the United States and met Ian... and well, here we are," she said with a giggle. "Now, we're the parents of two children, two-year-old, Hannah, and five-year-old, Brent. This is sort of like a honeymoon cruise for us. My parents volunteered to take the children so we could vacation."

Dottie noticed how Ian put his hand directly over his wife's and said, "Fortunately for me, Alana hasn't wanted to go back to Malta to teach. So, I'm a lucky guy."

"Yes, you are, Ian," Dottie said as she flashed her beautiful smile at the young psychiatrist. "Yes, you are," Dottie raised her eyebrows, "I'd say you're both pretty lucky to have each other."

"You said you traveled from the US, do you live there?" Alana asked.

Dottie nodded her head and said, "Yes, I actually live in Richmond, Virginia, in the US just a couple of hours from you. I've lived in the states since shortly after my husband died. I love it there."

Ian smiled and said, "Richmond? I love Richmond. I went to medical school at the Medical College of Virginia at

Virginia Commonwealth University. I've spent lots of time in Richmond. I'm amazed at how the city has grown. It's a great place to live."

Dottie nodded in agreement. "Yes. It is a wonderful place to live." She paused for a second and asked, "Would you two like to join Michaela and myself for dinner this evening? We'll be dining in here at eight o'clock. I'd love to have you as my guests."

Alana flashed her husband a look and said, "I'm not sure we can. I think Ian has to…"

Ian interrupted and said, "I have a previous commitment with Senator Peter Bostitch from the state of Maryland. But I'm sure we can reschedule. We'd be delighted to have dinner with you, Countess."

Dottie smiled and said, "Please invite the Senator to join us, or better yet, I'll have the ship send him an invitation. We'll have a jolly time," Dottie promised as her blue eyes danced with delight.

Alana was thrilled, "I'd much rather have dinner with you and your friend than a bunch of pharmaceutical people," she said softly. Ian shot Alana a dark look and she smiled brightly. "You know what I mean, Ian. Some of those pharmaceutical executives are a bit over the top," she said as her eyes held him for a moment.

Ian nodded, "Countess Borghase, in that case, we'll be delighted to see you and your friend, Michaela, at eight o'clock," he said grandly, a pleased look on his face.

"That's wonderful," Dottie said as she stood. "I apologize, but I must go. I'm meeting several gentlemen in the library for a few hands of bridge. I'll see you this evening."

Ian stood next to Dottie. "We'll see you at eight and thanks again for the champagne. I'll see that it doesn't go to waste," he assured her.

Dottie smiled at the young couple and said, "My pleasure." She left the dining room, her back ramrod straight with every strand of her beautiful white hair in place.

Ian looked at his wife and said, "Wow. What a lady! She's pretty unusual, don't you think?"

Alana nodded. "She sure is. I bet she has a life story we wouldn't believe," she guessed as she looked into her husband's eyes. "How old do you think she is, Ian? She's still quite beautiful for an older lady," she mused.

Her husband smiled. "I've got a feeling we're gonna hear a lot about her and her life tonight," Ian assured her. "But I bet she's in her eighties."

Alana giggled and clinked her glass with her husbands. "No doubt, now, let's drink the rest of this bubbly. I've only had this twice in my life," she said with a bright smile.

Ian grinned at his wife. He loved her more than life itself. This was the honeymoon they'd needed for years. Life was so busy, his practice, their family. He hoped for a perfect cruise. Life was good, wasn't it?

Chapter 3

Michaela was totally relaxed. She floated on a raft in the private adult pool on the ship's Lido deck. Her mind wandered as she reflected on the past year. It had been full and busy, and a bit scary at times with that crazy perp in her house. She really needed a break. Finally, she drifted off to sleep, something she rarely, if ever, did during the day. Angel stood guard over her from where he lay under the umbrella, watchfully checking his mistress and watching the people around her.

"Michaela, Michaela, Mic. Get up," Dottie said in an irritated voice. "For heavens sakes, you were supposed to meet me for High Tea well over an hour ago."

Mic struggled to open one of her eyes and saw Dottie, perfectly attired in the latest cruise wear, standing over her on the side of the pool. Angel stood beside her.

"Oh, Dottie. Sorry. I fell asleep," she said with a yawn, "and for some reason, the alarm on my watch didn't go off."

Dottie remained silent and scowled down at her. "Perhaps," she said icily, "that's because you don't have your watch on."

Mic rolled off her float and stood in the water. "Well, how was it?" Dottie remained silent as Michaela pulled her body out of the salt water. She spoke again and asked, "Did High Tea meet your expectations?"

"Humph," Dottie snorted and ignored her. "I didn't stay. I waited for you and when you didn't come, I came down here," Dottie said angrily. "Do you really expect me to believe you just fell asleep and didn't come?"

Mic toweled her hair, "Yeah, that's exactly what I expect."

Dottie gave her an icy look. "Come on. You didn't wear your watch on purpose," she said as her blue eyes flashed angrily.

"That's not true," Mic defended herself. "I had every intention to join you for tea. You know how much I loved those scones yesterday. It would be worth leaving the pool for the scones," she admitted as she stood by the pool and looked up at her perfectly coiffed friend and her dog who licked Dottie's hand and looked at Mic with adoring eyes.

"Well, it's too late now," Dottie said acidly. "However, I met a nice young couple, a psychiatrist, and his wife, in the Captain's dining room. They're joining us for dinner tonight, along with Senator Peter Bostitch. It'll be an interesting time," Dottie said happily.

Mic nodded. She knew Dottie scoured the ship every day for people she'd like to have dinner with. Mic supposed that was okay as long as they weren't boring and tedious people, like the ones they'd eaten dinner with the first night after leaving Rome. That had been, at best, painful and the longest dinner she'd ever had.

"Sounds good," Michaela said as she looked over at the pool bar. "Let's have a piña colada. Go over there and save us that larger table under the umbrella and I'll order the drinks."

Dottie smiled, "Okay. Make mine with double rum and less of the sweet stuff. I don't want to whack my blood pressure or my blood sugar from the sweet drinks you consume that are like Kool-Aid," she complained as she turned to walk toward the umbrella table.

"Oh, did they take the sugar out of the rum?" Michaela asked, her voice a tad sarcastic, as she picked up her sunglasses, bathing suit cover up and hat, and wandered over to the pool bar. She ordered their drinks and as she waited, her eyes wandered over to the two men sitting at the pool bar. One man looked familiar, but she couldn't place him. He had oily black hair and a sinister look about him. Her stomach constricted in pain for a few moments as she watched the man. Where have I seen this guy? She asked herself as she pulled her ship charge card from her pocket.

"Here you go, ma'am," the bartender said as he returned her ship charge card. "I'll carry the tray over to your table," he offered.

Mic smiled, nodded, and led the way to where Dottie was seated on the aft side of the adult pool. The waiter left the drinks on the table and Michaela sat down and looked at Dottie. "So… tell me about these people we're having dinner with."

Dottie motioned for her to be quiet and nodded her head toward the table next to them. "Hush," she said in a loud whisper. "Those two people over there are arguing about the new Blake Pharmaceutical drug. One of them insists it gave one of his patients a heart attack and caused another one to commit suicide."

Mic stole a look at the table next to them. Her eyes rested on a young man, his face was white with anger as he stared at an older man. The young man had bright red hair. The older man wore a Blake Pharmaceutical nametag, but Mic couldn't read his name. The conversation was heated.

The young man's voice was loud and agitated, "I'm telling you, the drug wasn't tested well enough. I've read the research studies. Your company never tested the drug independently, and that never should've happened. You're the vice-president in charge of research, and you know this drug needs to be recalled for testing," he continued furiously in a slightly lower voice as he hit the table with his hand to make his point. Drinks splattered the table. "The drug is unsafe," the man insisted.

The Blake representative looked around the crowd. He hoped no one had overheard the crazy psychiatrist he had reluctantly agreed to meet. "Will you shut that Irish trap of yours? People are staring at you," the Blake Pharmaceutical representative hissed. "You may be a physician, but you're not a researcher. This drug is safe. It met all of the US pharmaceutical requirements with flying colors."

The physician was flushed, "Yes, I am a physician and a researcher, and the drug isn't safe. You've received thousands of complaints. Tell the wife and the husband of my two patients that are dead that this drug is safe."

The pharmaceutical representative shrugged his shoulders. His demeanor was one of apathy.

The physician was furious. He glared at the rep and said, "The autopsies confirmed my suspicions. Both victims had the residual chemicals of Quelpro in their bodies, chemicals compounded in the United States.

The rep's eyes burned with anger as a slow flush traveled up to his neck. "That's two patients... two people out of thousands who've taken the drug and gotten better. Two deaths mean nothing statistically," the man said loudly, a look of contempt on his face.

The physician stood and glared angrily at the rep. "The drug isn't safe, and I intend to tell my colleagues tomorrow during my talk." He looked at the check on the table and grabbed it. "Screw you; I'll pay for my own drink. You and your damn company aren't buying me," he snarled as he headed for the doors separating the pool area from the rest of the ship.

The pharmaceutical representative shook his head and cursed under his breath. He moved toward the pool bar and took a seat. Mic heard him order a double whiskey. The bartender hopped to attention.

Mic watched the corporate guy and thought he was gonna have a stroke. His face was beet red and she could swear that smoke came out of his ears. He finished his drink in one long sip and ordered another. Then she noticed the Blake representative was sitting with the man with greasy, dark hair who seemed familiar to her.

"Well, that was pretty interesting," Dottie snorted. "I don't think that drug rep, or executive, whoever he was, agreed with the doctor."

"No kidding," Mic opined, as she watched the pharmaceutical representative signal the waiter for another drink.

"That's the cat's meow for me," Dottie said. "That's exactly why I don't take all those pills my doctors want to give me." She kicked Mic's leg under the table to get her attention. "You know all those damn pills have side effects?"

Mic didn't respond as she continued to watch the man quickly consume his second drink.

"Hey. You. I'm talking to you, Michaela McPherson," Dottie whined.

Michaela grinned and said, "Yeah, really. All drugs have side effects. But sometimes you gotta take the risk and take the drug," She gave Dottie a stern look. "Either way, did you take your heart pill this morning?"

Dottie nodded briefly and reached for her drink, "Dammit, Michaela. I may be old, but I still know to take my medicine."

Mic nodded, but her eyes returned to the two men at the bar. The pharmaceutical representative and the guy she thought she knew had struck up a conversation. She looked back at Dottie and said, "Now, what were you saying?"

Dottie gave her a dirty look. "Nothing. Absolutely nothing."

Mic laughed. "Okay, Countess. Don't get uppity with me."

Dottie glared at her and said, "I told you. I met a nice young couple and we're having dinner with them. If you'll pay attention to me, I'll tell you about them."

Michaela smiled and listened to Dottie's story, but her eyes jumped back and forth between Dottie and the two men at the bar. They gave her an uneasy feeling.

She hated it when a feeling came over her that something bad was gonna happen. She picked up her piña colada, savored the taste, and pushed the two men out of her mind.

Chapter 4

Snake cursed as his cell phone vibrated on the dresser in his small inside cabin. Who in the hell could be bothering him now? He hoped it wasn't that damn, drunken Russian idiot. He gritted his teeth and barked into the phone, "Yeah. What? This better be good."

There was no answer on the other end so Snake entered his passcode. His bosses contacted him on the secure line. He heard the phone ring and a familiar voice said, "Yeah."

Snake grunted and lay against the pillows as the voice continued, "How's life on the Mediterranean Sea?"

Snake smiled to himself. He'd never seen the man on the other end, but knew he had a sense of humor.

He replied sarcastically, "Just great, just bloody great. Why'd you hook me up with this Russian asshole?"

The voice was quiet for several moments and then replied, "He's a good man. He's been loyal to us for over forty years. I'd advise you to not mess with him. He can be a rather bitter enemy," the man warned him.

"Yeah, yeah, I've heard that before." Snake replied sarcastically as he waited to learn the reason for the call.

"I've got new business for you. Three more packages," he said in a low voice. "You'll find out who later this evening."

Anger sparked Snake's temper. "You gotta be kidding. I'm not sure that jerk-off can handle anything else," he complained as his tattooed hand clutched the cell phone and dug his fingertips against the phone.

"Just get it done," the voice said. "Don't screw it up. Your partner's good. And he's lethal. Give him a chance."

"Yeah," Snake said wearily as he studied the ceiling tiles in his room.

"Check the same place for our message. You'll have to re-plan some of this. Things have heated up," the voice reported in a flat tone.

"What's new?" Snake said sarcastically. "Things always heat up where I am. You got me trapped on a damn boat, and I can't even get away," he complained. "I hate being trapped somewhere. It's a disadvantage."

"Figure it out," the voice said angrily. "Figure it the hell out and shut up."

Snake heard the phone click. He took one long stride to his bathroom and splashed water onto his face. His head throbbed from drinking all day. He opened the small closet in his cabin and searched his backpack for Tylenol. He popped two in his mouth and reached for the room service menu. He scanned it briefly it, picked up the phone, and ordered a six-pack of Budweiser. There was nothing like a few beers to cure a hangover.

Chapter 5

Ian Pennington looked down at his sleeping wife. Alana was so beautiful. He'd never understood why she'd been interested in him. Of course, all of that was history now. He scribbled a note to her on the ship's stationery and then quietly left their stateroom.

He climbed the steps to the bar at the very top of the ship. It was empty and the view was stunning. He ordered a beer and took a moment to enjoy the panoramic view of the Mediterranean Sea. The water was crystal blue and reflected like diamonds in the late afternoon sun. He turned his head when a voice behind him spoke softly.

"Hello, Ian. Thanks for coming on such short notice," his colleague said with a thin smile.

Ian noticed the lines of stress on the face of James O'Leary. The young man was tired and distressed. "Let me get you a beer," he said.

Ian grinned at his friend. "You're welcome, James. I hope this is important. Alana and I are pretty much on a second honeymoon and you did interrupt my nap," he said with a smile as he warmly shook James' hand.

James opened his mouth to apologize, but Ian waved him off. "No, no, it's okay. What's up?" He asked as his green eyes studied his friend.

James O'Leary, an academic psychiatrist at the University of Maryland, offered up a tight smile "Unfortunately, nothing good. I've tried to reason with the head corporate henchmen, Jeff Baldridge from Blake Pharmaceutical, and to say he blew me off isn't an exaggeration."

Ian nodded as his stomach clenched with pain. "So, Baldridge wouldn't listen and has nothing to offer?"

Both men were silent as the waiter served them their beer.

James chuckled; he was an attractive young man, younger than Ian was, probably in his early thirties. In addition to being a psychiatrist, he also had a PhD in neurological research. "Oh, Baldridge listened for a couple of minutes and then pretty much told me to get my head out of my ass. He assured me that Quelpro was perfectly safe. He said their research findings were impeccable, and there was no way that the drug could be responsible for any deaths or increased morbidity," James said as his hand clutched his beer.

Ian shook his head as he picked up his beer. The chill of the glass soothed his hands, which were hot with anger. He took a swig of his beer and said, "Well, truthfully, we never expected for them to own up to the catastrophic outcomes. Was he amenable to any further research testing?"

James shook his head vigorously. "Hell, no. And that's an understatement." James' face almost matched the color of his hair. "He didn't want to hear anything I had to say. He's standing solidly behind his company's research and he's not willing to listen to anything we have to tell him."

Ian nodded. "It's not sounding good, is it?"

"Nope." James paused, signaled the waiter for another beer, and continued, "I know we're right about this, Ian. Here, look at this data on my phone. It's unrefuted and ironclad. It suggests, pretty much concludes, that the chemicals in Quelpro have killed at least seven patients that we know of, three of them at the University of Maryland."

Ian reached for James' iPhone and scrolled through the screens. The evidence damaged the integrity of the drug.

His heart rate picked up as he reviewed the irrefutable evidence that all but guaranteed Quelpro was a bad drug. He nodded his head. "You're right, it's a bad drug. We need to try to talk with them again, perhaps all of us at the same time. This data is alarming," he concluded as he handed James his phone.

James nodded, "No argument from me. If they don't listen, I'll take my findings to the FDA and ask them to pull the drug from the market until we can test it further for safety and efficacy."

"Do you have the data from the original testing?"

James reached for his beer. "Yeah, I do. The statistics were manipulated to suggest the drug was safe." He sighed and said, "Trust me, it's not."

"I was afraid of that," Ian said softly. "There are other physicians here that have questions about the drug's safety, at least among the people we know. Some who have grievous concerns about Quelpro. Perhaps we can meet with Baldridge and their head of Research and Development and persuade them to do further testing. In the meantime, the drug needs to be delisted and pulled from the market."

James raised his eyebrows and gave Ian a short laugh. "No can do, my friend. These pharmaceutical executives don't want to hear anything negative about anything they do. We can moan and groan until the cows come home, but we'll get nowhere with these folks."

Ian shook his head as the waiter handed James his second beer. He shrugged his shoulders and said, "We need to talk with Senator Bostitch, see what he suggests. At least he's a physician and understands what we're talking about."

James nodded, "Yeah, he's a good man. I was talking with Toby from NYU and he agrees the drug isn't safe and needs further testing. We can invite him."

"What are you planning for tomorrow? In your talk?" Ian asked. "Are you going to report the data findings you have?"

James nodded vigorously and said, "I am absolutely gonna report my research findings. And the serious implications they highlight concerning complications and safety of the drug. I told that to Baldridge and I thought he was gonna have a stroke."

Ian nodded and picked up his beer. "Well, your research is rigorous and the statistics don't lie." Ian paused for a few moments and said, "You know I'll back you, man, don't you?"

James smiled grimly. "Thanks, Ian, but I can tell you, the going is gonna be rough. They're gonna be more than pissed because what I reveal in my keynote speech will cost them millions of dollars, not to mention the cost of potential lawsuits against Blake."

Ian nodded his head slowly. "I'm having dinner with Senator Bostitch tonight. I'll tell him what's happening and ask what we need to do to prepare. He's our direct line to the FDA. I'm sure he'll liaise for us."

James shrugged his shoulders and smiled across the table at Ian. "I wish they'd listen to me. I've given them every opportunity to reevaluate their position on the drug." He looked into Ian's eyes and said, "Who in the hell ever thought a cruise on the Mediterranean Sea could be potentially devastating?"

Ian laughed, picked up his beer, and downed the remaining liquid. "Isn't that the truth? Who would have thought?"

Chapter 6

Michaela examined herself in the floor length mirror in her suite. She turned to the side and smiled in satisfaction. Her workouts in the pool and at gym had paid off. She looked great. She wore a dark green formal satin gown that made her green eyes sparkle brighter than usual. Her dark hair gleamed in the low light and her short curls were shiny. I look pretty good for a middle-aged gal, she thought to herself. She moved closer to the mirror, inspected the fine lines around her nose and mouth, and decided they were 'experience lines' and wouldn't worry about them. Then she reached into her safe for Dottie's emerald necklace. She clasped it around her neck and the beauty of the jewels stole her breath away. I hope I don't lose this necklace or that no one knocks me out and steals it before I can return it to my safe. Dottie will never get over it if I lose this emerald necklace.

She reached for her cell, snapped a picture, and texted it to Slade. Then she picked up her glass of champagne and walked to the sofa. Angel was asleep in his orthopedic bed but opened his eyes as she sat down. She spoke softly to the dog, and he closed his eyes as she scratched his ears.

Mic hadn't known a cruise stateroom could be so plush. She had a king-size bed, an enormous bathroom with a whirlpool tub, a large sitting area, a huge closet, an outside deck and balcony, a small kitchen, and the most romantic lighting she'd ever seen. She smiled to herself and her heart jumped a little when she thought of Slade McKane, the number one man in her life. Mic was excited about the cruise. She and Dottie had shopped for months in preparation for the long trip to Dottie's home in Italy and the Mediterranean cruise. Her three weeks in Rome had been fantastic, as had her time in Venice and Tuscany. It was a trip of a lifetime for her and sort of a Swan Song for Dottie because at eighty-two years of age, Mic wasn't sure she'd make it to Europe again to see her family, most of whom she didn't like. At any rate, Michaela was now the owner of four formal evening gowns (Dottie had been appalled when she'd suggested wearing the same one twice) that she wore to dinner on the ship. Each night, they dined for several hours in the Captain's Dining Room with the passengers du jour. It'd been fun the past several evenings, but tomorrow night she'd decided to put her foot down and tell Dottie she was eating in her room. She wanted room service and she wanted to wear her favorite sweatpants. She laughed and thought of how angry Dottie would be.

Angel startled as the stateroom room phone rang. Of course, it was Dottie. "Where are you, Michaela? It's almost eight o'clock. The Captain is escorting us to dinner and we'll knock on your door shortly. Are you ready?" She impatiently asked.

"Take it easy, old lady" Michaela said happily. "Don't have a conniption fit. Of course, I'm ready, but remember, the Captain works for you because you pretty much own the cruise line."

Dottie hesitated. "Well, that's true, but still, I'm not so old that I don't want to be wined and dined by a handsome man in a uniform - even if he does work for me. Be ready," she growled. "It'll be fun."

Michaela's phone signaled a text. She picked it up and smiled at the digital display. "Miss you. Are you sick of lobster and filet mignon yet, beautiful?"

Mic typed in, "Almost."

"I'm just hungry for you," Slade texted back.

Mic's heart jumped in excitement and she sent him a sad faced emoji.

"Have a great night, gorgeous. I've gotta go cook my hot dog."

"Good night, Slade. I miss you."

Michaela's eyes widened in delight as Slade texted her two hot dogs on coat hangers. She laughed. He was such a great guy. They'd been together for about eight months now. She was feeling that nesting instinct, which frightened her because she'd never wanted to settle down. She imagined Detective Slade McKane in her mind. Tall, dark, Irish, and handsome. Her heart hammered as she thought about him. Her daydream ended when Dottie rapped sharply on her door.

Michaela slid into her heels, opened her stateroom door, and smiled into the eyes of the ship's Captain. Captain Frederick Wodensen was devastatingly handsome in his full dress uniform. Dottie stood next to him and was dressed in a lovely flowing raspberry silk dress. Her silver hair was arranged beautifully in a chignon. Gorgeous crystals hung from her ears.

Dottie kissed Michaela on both cheeks and said, "You look lovely, dear. I may leave you those emeralds when I die."

Mic laughed and said, "You're never going to die, Dottie. We all know that." Her eyes admired the elderly lady. Dottie was amazing and could easily pass for fifty, not eighty-something.

Seconds later the ship's First Mate, Gustav Hensen, appeared and offered Michaela his arm. Mic accepted with a smile, called to Angel, and then she, Mr. Hensen, and

Angel followed the Captain and Dottie to the private dining room.

This is the life, Mic thought to herself. What could possibly go wrong on a Mediterranean cruise? She closed her eyes, excited about the remaining seven days before they departed Rome for Richmond.

Michaela was too excited about the evening to notice the angry man near the elevator watching her.

Chapter 7

Vadim drank steadily all day. He was depressed and angry. As he watched the happy people around him, his foul mood exacerbated and he decided to gamble in the ship's casino. He returned to his small stateroom, showered in his tiny bathroom, and put on a suit and tie. He checked himself in the mirror, pleased he looked as well as he did. He took out some makeup filler and covered the two jagged scars on his face. Satisfied with his appearance, he grabbed his ship charge card, shut the door of his cabin, and took the elevator to the eighth floor where the casino was located.

The Royale Casino didn't open until nine p.m. With nothing else to do, Vadim stopped at the piano bar in the lobby and ordered a double vodka on the rocks. He watched the passengers walking by. Some were dressed in formal wear for dinner; others were more casual in cruise attire. He noticed a group of young people who were downright nasty looking with their dyed black hair, white skin, and multiple piercings. He studied one young woman in particular. She looked about nineteen years old. Her hair was short and dyed jet black, but she had the most beautiful blue eyes he'd ever seen. Her teeth were straight and white, most likely the result of expensive dental work. She was beautiful, but the Goth look repelled him. If she were his daughter, he'd make her wipe off the makeup and yank the rings and hooks out of her ears and nose. She looked like garbage, cheap, and tawdry.

The young woman saw him staring at her and flipped him off. Vadim was enraged and stood. He walked over to her and grabbed her face with his hand. The woman twisted away from him and quickly walked down the corridor surrounded by her equally offbeat friends.

Vadim cursed to himself as his heart remembered his beautiful daughter, Ana. She'd been so beautiful with a similar look of this young woman but clean and wholesome. Long naturally dark hair, vivid blue eyes, and a natural, joyful disposition described his now-dead daughter. He clutched his heart as the pain raced through and took his breath away. He waited until the pain subsided, reached for his vodka, and signaled the waiter for another. He continued to people- watch until the casino opened. By this time, he had consumed three double vodkas and had no pain at all. He entered the casino, pushed his ship charge card toward the gated cashier, and asked for five thousand dollars US in chips.

The casino cashier turned her security camera on and rested it on his face. His name, face, and cabin number appeared on her computer screen. He'd been approved for ten thousand dollars. She shoved the chips at him, smiled, and said, "Good luck."

Vadim nodded curtly and headed toward the blackjack tables as he grabbed a vodka off the beverage tray.

Chapter 8

Dinner was delightful. The mood was romantic, the cuisine excellent, and the company interesting. A harpist played softly in the background. Michaela enjoyed the best company she'd encountered at any dinner aboard ship. The crystal chandeliers reflected beautifully in the mirrored ceiling and everyone at the table was beautiful or exceedingly handsome. It was a collection of beautiful people. Mic had a lovely conversation with First Mate Hensen, a handsome man from the Netherlands. Dottie had happily been the center of attraction for the Penningtons, Captain Wodensen, and Senator Bostitch.

Mic had finished her dessert, Bananas Foster, a recipe straight from the Big Easy, when she overheard Ian speak to Senator Bostitch.

"Peter, if you have time after dinner, Dr. O'Leary and I would like to speak with you about our concerns with Quelpro. James O'Leary has credible research that seriously questions the drug's efficacy. Do you have a moment?" Ian asked with a serious look on his face.

Senator Bostitch nodded his head, "I've heard rumblings that tomorrow's conference could be disappointing for Blake Pharmaceutical." He gave Ian Pennington a grim look and continued, "Is this part of that reasoning?"

Ian nodded and said in a low voice, "I'm afraid so."

"Are you all talking about that 'dirty drug,' or whatever you call it?" Dottie piped up from across the table. Her blue eyes were bright with interest.

"Countess, whatever do you mean?" Ian asked with a smile and a look of surprise on his face.

"Well," Dottie said as she settled back in her seat for a bit of gossip. "What I mean is that I heard two men at the pool arguing this afternoon about some drug that one man considered to be unsafe."

"Oh, interesting. What else did you hear, Countess?" Senator Bostitch asked as he leaned his head towards Dottie to hear better.

Dottie shrugged her shoulders. "That's about it. They argued. That's what I mean. The man from the drug company was quite angry," she added. "And I do mean angry," she reiterated.

Ian nodded his head. "I'm sure. What else did you overhear?"

Dottie looked over at Mic. "Did I miss anything?"

Michaela shook her head. "I overheard the same conversation as Dottie and it was quite heated," she assured them as she watched the Senator and Ian Pennington's faces carefully.

Alana interrupted and said, "Oh, Ian, is that the antidepressant you've been so worried about? The drug you think caused the death of two of your patients?"

Ian smiled grimly and nodded at his wife. He continued, "Did one of the men have red hair?"

"Indeed he did," Dottie said excitedly. "His hair was as red as a fire engine. He was very upset. There's no question about that," she said with authority. "He was very insistent the drug be tested further. He thinks it's unsafe, and the angrier he got, the more red his face became."

Ian shot a look at Senator Bostitch and said, "That's Dr. James O'Leary. He's a staff psychologist at the University of Maryland Medical Center. He's also a clinical researcher. Dr. O'Leary has both a medical degree and a PhD. At one point in his career, he worked for the FDA. So, he knows the procedures for drug approval fairly well."

Senator Bostitch nodded, his silver-white hair shined in the candlelight. "So, Dr. O'Leary is the man you want me to meet with in a little while, is that correct?" he asked as he picked up his dessert fork.

Ian nodded. "Yes, James is an expert researcher and he has compelling evidence that Quelpro, the brainchild antidepressant medicine released by Blake Pharmaceutical, isn't safe.

Senator Bostitch nodded and said, "I imagine this is going to be a pretty sticky situation. At this point, Quelpro is their signature drug. They've invested millions of dollars in it, hours of time in research and development, not to mention marketing."

"Humph, I heard something about this medicine on a morning television show a few weeks ago. Isn't this the antidepressant that's been implicated in several unexpected deaths in patients?" Michaela asked.

Ian nodded his head. "Yeah, it is. Dr. O'Leary has credible information that Quelpro is quite dangerous – bottom line, he believes it should be recalled and further testing be done. He doesn't want it prescribed until the deaths and side effects can be tested, explained and/or minimized."

Senator Bostitch fiddled with his dessert spoon and was silent for a moment. He knew the Quelpro dilemma was an explosion ready to ignite. "And you, Dr. Pennington, what is your opinion? Tell us your experience with Quelpro since you've eloquently discussed Dr. O'Leary's opinion."

Ian picked his words carefully. "I, too, have concerns about the drug. A number of people in our local psychiatric group have significant concerns. At the very least, we believe Blake Pharmaceutical needs to further examine Quelpro – test it some more."

"Well, if you ask me, I think all those damn drugs need to be taken off the market," Dottie huffed. "People take way too many drugs. Honestly, I feel ten times better when I don't take all that damn medicine," she blurted. "I hate the crap."

Michaela rolled her eyes and said, "Dottie, you know that..."

Michaela's sentence was interrupted by seven short blasts of the ship's alarm and a voice on the PA system that repeated, 'Charlie, Charlie, Charlie', over and over At the same moment, a crewmember entered the dining room and whispered into the Captain's ear.

A look of anger flashed across Captain Wodensen's face and he hastily stood, "I'm afraid I must leave. There's something I need to immediately attend to." He turned to Dottie and said, "Thank you, Countess, for a lovely evening." He leaned down and kissed Dottie on both cheeks. Then he looked at the rest of the passengers at the table and said, "Carry on. Enjoy yourselves and thank you for being our guests for dinner." Then he gave a curt bow and left the dining room just as the ship's communication's area re-broadcasted the 'Charlie, Charlie, Charlie' alarm.

Senator Bostitch looked concerned. "What does 'Charlie' mean? What the hell is going on?" he asked as he looked at his tablemates.

Michaela shrugged her shoulders. "I've no idea, Senator." She turned to Dottie and asked, "Do you know, Countess? You've cruised more than any of us, I imagine. Plus, you do own most of the cruise line."

Dottie shook her head, her blue eyes pools of dark ink. Her face was pale. "I don't know, but it can't be good. What I do know is that it takes something very serious for the Captain to be disturbed at dinner," she said in a worried tone. "Especially when he's dining with me," she added.

"You mean something like an iceberg or collision with another ship?" Alana asked, a note of fear in her voice, her eyes wide.

Ian smiled and put his hand over his wife's hand. "I hardly think there's an iceberg in the Mediterranean Sea," he said with a wink. "Whatever it is, I'm sure it'll be under control in several minutes."

Senator Bostitch nodded his head, his silver hair gleaming in the light. He smiled at the women. "Ian is absolutely correct. Everything is fine. The ship is practically brand-new and I'm sure nothing serious could go wrong," he assured them. "In the meantime, I think I'll order a Drambuie," he said as he signaled the waiter.

"Good idea, Senator," Dottie agreed, always the gracious hostess.

"The Titanic was new as well, and look what happened to it," Mic grumbled. "That story just doesn't hold water, Senator," she said as she challenged him.

"I suggest we enjoy our after-dinner drinks," Senator Bostitch suggested. "If something bad happens, I'm sure we'll hear about it."

Michaela reached for her Drambuie and took a sip. It burned all the way down and took her mind off the potential danger. "Let's have a toast. To the Countess Borghase. Thank you for this lovely dinner," she said.

The sound of the glasses touching was almost musical. Michaela stared at the ceiling and looked at the happy faces reflected in the beautiful mirrored ceiling, but she knew that somewhere on the ship, things weren't nearly as lovely. Once again, the feeling that something wasn't right passed through her. It gave her chill bumps, but she decided to ignore the feeling and savor the moment.

Chapter 9

Captain Wodensen entered the closed door of the Royale Casino. Fortunately, his casino manager had sent the passengers who'd been in the casino to the bar next door with the promise of free drinks while staff worked on an equipment breakdown. The casino staff had thrown a green, velvet cloth over the body. His staff assured him most people didn't know what had happened.

Wodensen and First Mate Hensen stared dumbly at the body. One of the ship's blackjack dealers lay on the floor. His throat was slashed from ear to ear. Bright red blood covered the victim's freshly-pressed white shirt and tuxedo jacket. His eyes were opened wide in death, shocked at what had happened to him. The Captain and casino staff were appalled at the sight of the body.

Captain Wodensen controlled his emotions and asked in a calm voice, "What happened here?"

The casino manager nodded for a second blackjack dealer to respond. The man, about forty years of age, spoke in an accented voice, "It was so fast. It happened so fast I can hardly remember. Dietrich was dealing blackjack to a customer who appeared quite drunk. The passenger had lost heavily and accused Dietrich of cheating, and before anyone knew it, he pulled a knife and slit his throat."

"Then what?" The Captain asked in a low voice. "Where'd the man go?"

The blackjack dealer looked uneasy, "I… I don't know. It was so fast. It all happened so fast. I leaned down to help Dietrich and I when I looked up, he was gone. I reached under the gaming table and covered Dietrich with the blackjack table cover."

Captain Wodensen turned as his head of security touched him on the shoulder. "Sir, we've identified the murderer, but we haven't located him. We have him on camera from the cashier. He's not in his stateroom. My security team has been briefed and we're searching the ship for him."

"How quickly can you find him?" the Captain asked in an angry voice, a deep scowl on his face. The reality of a murder aboard ship infuriated him. There was going to be hell to pay. Lawsuits, a crazed passenger group, and whatever else found its way to torture him.

The security chief looked at the floor and then back into the eyes of Captain Wodensen. "We hope to find him quickly, sir, but this is a very large vessel."

Anger shot through the Captain. "I know how damn big the ship is," Wodensen snapped. "Just find him." He turned to the First Mate and said, "Make sure this mess is cleaned up. Re-open the casino as soon as you can. The least said about this the better," he instructed. He looked at the casino staff that had surrounded the game table. "Keep quiet about this. The cruise line doesn't need to pay out millions in lawsuits. If I hear of any gossip among the crew, you'll be punished," the Captain said in an irate voice as he left the Royale Casino.

The casino staff stood transfixed as they stared at the body on the floor and the bright red blood on their friend's crisply starched shirt. Dark blood pooled on the floor under the table. A young woman gasped at the sight and held onto the table for stability.

Captain Wodensen looked around at the crewmembers and asked, "Is that understood?" He watched as each casino dealer, barmaid, and casher nodded his or her head and then he turned abruptly and left the area.

Chapter 10

Vadim left the casino, found the closest stairway, and rushed down to deck four. Several minutes later, he was in the hall beating on Snake's cabin door. "Open the door, open the door, dammit," he said in a quiet, breathless voice.

Snake cursed. He'd ordered room service and was watching a movie. He slid off the bed and moved to the door.

"What the hell do you want, man?" Snake hissed as he opened the door. "Can't you just leave me the hell alone?"

Vadim pushed Snake out of his way and went into the small stateroom. That's when Snake realized something was wrong. "What's up, man? What do you want?" He asked as he glared at the older man. He paled when he saw the blood splatter on Vadim's shirt. Snake's eyes widened, "What the hell have you done?"

Vadim's face was black with rage. "I'm in trouble. I just offed a man up in the casino. The guy cheated me in blackjack and I lost my temper," Vadim said, his voice seethed with fury.

"You did what? Did I hear you right?" Snake asked in an incredulous voice. "You killed some son of a bitch?"

"Yeah, yeah, you heard me right. I killed a dealer in the casino. The bastard cheated me. It's exactly like I said," Vadim repeated with defiance in his voice as his eyes glinted with fire.

Snake couldn't believe his ears. "What the hell, man! We're supposed to do the killing later. How the hell are you gonna get away? This affects both of us, or have you noticed?" Snake boiled with anger.

Vadim shrugged his shoulders, unconcerned. "That's your concern. Give me the key to our other cabin. They know who I am because I used my ship charge card to get money. Ship security is probably all over my cabin by now."

Snake shook his head. "I'd like to kill you. Do you have any idea what you've done? How badly you've screwed up?" Snake was livid with anger.

"Yeah, I know," Vadim snarled. "The guy pissed me off. Bastard tried to cheat me. End of story." He waited a moment and hissed, "Give me the damn key. I need to get in there, clean up, and get some sleep."

Snake was incredulous at Vadim's lack of concern. "Man, I got a call today. They've beefed up our workload. And, now you've put a target on your head."

Vadim ignored him and held his hand out for the key.

"We got one tonight and a couple more tomorrow. Now, you've gone and fucked everything up!"

Vadim was losing his patience. He could feel the blood pulsing through his head. He took a step toward Snake and pushed him back onto the bed. "I messed nothing up. Give me the damn key to the extra cabin and I'll go change. Then I'll meet you upstairs on the Promenade deck just like we planned." He paused for a minute and stared down into Snake's face. Vadim's eyes glinted with rage. He was furious.

Snake sat up on the side of the bed. "You're a crazy bastard, a lunatic. I'm not gonna give you the key to nothing. Now, get the hell out of my room before I call security on you," he threatened.

Vadim crossed his arms in front of his chest. He was powerfully built. His upper arms rippled with muscle through his bloodied clothes. "I'm gonna ask you once more for the key. If I don't get it, I'm gonna tear you apart limb by limb and feed you to the sharks. Then, I'm gonna find the damn key," he threatened as he stared at the younger man

Snake stood and locked eyes with Vadim. "What are you gonna do, man? Where're you gonna hide? They gotta be tearin' up the ship looking for you. You'll never get away with this," he insisted as he shook his head.

Vadim shook his head. "They'll never find me. I'll go to the safety stateroom. I'll change my appearance so much that even you won't know me."

Snake shook his head and scoffed. "Yeah. Sure. You're full of shit. You don't have a ship credit card or any other means of identification you can use. It's only a matter of time," he smirked. "They're gonna get you and we'll be screwed," Snake said as he banged his fist on the wall.

Vadim slowly shook his head again. "You're wrong. They're not gonna find me. I have another stateroom you don't know about. It's on deck three. I boarded the ship twice, with two different IDs. I'm traveling under two passports, and two identities. If need be, I'll exit and board again in Rhodes with another passport. Oh, and by the way, I've got access to other passports as well, so screw you," he said, a look of triumph in his eyes.

Snake stared at him, a bewildered look on his face. Is this guy smart or is he full of shit? His mouth fell open and he said sarcastically, "Yeah. Sure, you will. What are you? Some kinda magician or something?"

Vadim's face was blank. "Surprised you, didn't I asshole? You thought you was traveling with some old, washed up son-of-a-bitch."

Snake nodded as his face registered surprise. "So, what you want to do?" For a few seconds, Snake felt positive. Maybe the old man hadn't messed it up.

"Give me the key to our other cabin. I got stuff in there. I never moved it into the stateroom that's under my Russian passport."

Snake moved over to his safe. He was impressed. He'd never given the guy credit for being as smart and cunning as he obviously was. He unlocked his safe and handed the key to Vadim "Here you go. Now take it and get the hell out of here. I'll see you upstairs in a couple of hours." He stopped for a moment and searched Vadim's eyes. "We're still on for tonight, just liked we planned."

Vadim grabbed the key, "Hell, yeah. Yeah, bozo. I'll be there. You got a sweatshirt? I need to put something on over my shirt; I don't want anybody to notice the blood on me."

Snake opened his drawer and threw a sweatshirt at Vadim. He watched as the short, stocky man wrestled himself out of his suit jacket and slid the sweatshirt over his head. It was skintight and Vadim's muscles rippled through the thick knit fabric. Snake had to admit the guy was powerful. He opened his mouth to speak, but Vadim raised his hand to object.

"No more talkin'. This'll do. I'll see you upstairs in a couple of hours. After that's done, you can fill me in on what happens tomorrow." Vadim dropped his bloodied coat on the floor in Snake's room. He turned his head and said, "Pick the jacket up and bring it with you later. I'll take care of it then," he ordered.

Snake watched the stocky Russian leave his stateroom. He wondered how many other ways the Russian would screw up the job in the next few days. Snake was a loner. He liked to work alone. He'd dreaded this gig from the get-go, and now he knew why. He set his cell phone alarm for two hours and lay on his bed. It was gonna be a long voyage. He closed his eyes for a few moments and awoke at ten minutes to one in the morning.

He rose from the bed and put on his last dark colored sweatshirt with the hood. He picked up his ship charge card and left his stateroom, heading for the Promenade deck where he'd meet Vadim.

Chapter 11

Dottie pulled on the sleeve of the dining room waiter to get his attention and asked, "What was that emergency call we just heard?" She asked, as her inky blue eyes demanded his attention.

The waiter looked surprised and said, "Oh, you mean the Charlie announcement?"

"Of course, that's absolutely what I mean," Dottie snapped. "Has there been another emergency call?"

Michaela wanted to slap Dottie for her arrogance. She hated it when Dottie got on her Countess high horse, although admittedly, it generally brought closure to whatever had caused her anger. She reached down, patted Angel, and interrupted, "We were having dinner and the Captain had to leave unexpectedly. We thought it might be a serious emergency," Mic said as she searched the waiter's eyes. "Could you tell us what happened?"

The waiter shook his head and said, "I don't know what happened. They sounded the all clear a couple of minutes ago. The Charlie signal is the code for a security threat."

"A security threat?" Senator Bostitch said loudly. "What kind of security threat?"

The waiter shrugged his shoulders. "I don't know," he repeated. "I'll check with the dining room manager. The managers are notified when something is wrong. But, as I said, they sounded the all clear, so whatever happened is over."

"Would you please tell the dining room manager that we'd like to see First Mate Hensen at his earliest convenience?" Dottie asked in a nicer voice. Mic shot her a look of approval.

"Yes, ma'am, I will." He picked up the cordial bottles and offered to refill everyone's glasses. Alana Pennington put her hand over her glass. She'd had quite enough alcohol.

"I'm a lightweight, I'm afraid," she said apologetically. "I hardly ever drink."

"You're probably smarter than the rest of us, Alana," Mic assured her. She looked up at the waiter, smiled and said, "I'll have one more."

Dottie looked over at Ian Pennington. "Okay, so tell us more about this dirty drug. I do love a good story," she said with a conspiratorial wink.

Ian looked uncomfortable and said, "Oh my, Countess. I'm sure it would bore you. It's a lot of medical jargon you probably aren't interested in."

"Oh, but I am," Dottie said as she turned her intense blue eyes on him. "I love controversy, especially when it's on my very own ship. I saw how mad that pharmaceutical guy was today. I thought he was going to either blow up or have a stroke. So," she continued as she batted her eyelids at the psychiatrist, "do tell..."

Ian cleared his throat. "Well, basically Blake Pharmaceutical has released a generic antidepressant, and I'm of the opinion, as are many of my colleagues, that the drug doesn't work."

"What do you mean it doesn't work?" Mic asked. "Aren't generic drugs the same as brand name drugs?"

Ian shook his head and a shadow crossed his face. "No, not exactly. The chemical structure may be different. In fact, in most cases, it is different," he honestly admitted.

Mic arched her eyebrows and looked confused. The emeralds from her necklace shone in the mirrored ceiling above. "Oh, I never knew that. I've been under the impression the patient received the same thing as the name-brand drug," she said, a look of misunderstanding on her face.

"Most folks think that," Senator Bostitch said, "but they don't take the same drug. The generic prescription drug market is enormous and obviously created to save the government money."

"But they are good drugs, well-researched drugs, aren't they?" Michaela persisted.

Senator Bostitch hesitated and then nodded. "For the most part, they are. The government and insurance companies spend billions of dollars every year on generic drugs," he added. "Usually, the drugs work well and there are minimal complaints. Sometimes, they don't. Many of us believe this drug, Quelpro, may have some issues and that's what we plan to examine," Peter Bostitch admitted as he stared into his empty glass. "I'm sure you realize the manufacture and sales of generics is a huge business."

Michaela nodded. "Undoubtedly." She paused and then added, "I still can't get my head around the concept that they're not identical, that they're not the same drug," she said, a frown on her face.

Senator Bostitch smiled. "I'm sure it's hard to understand but they're not the same; they're definitely not identical, although the FDA website leads you to believe generic drugs are identical. But they aren't. Their chemical structures vary and the way the drug works may vary as well."

Alana Pennington frowned. "But I don't understand. I agree with Michaela. I always thought generic drugs were the same. Now, I'm confused… and a little frightened," Alana said as she turned to her husband.

Ian patted his wife's shoulder. "Senator Bostitch is correct. The drugs are different. They have the same chemicals, but the way the chemicals are structured in the generic pharmaceutical may differ. We're actually operating under a system of 'equivalence' when we talk about generic drugs.

"This is just getting worse… and more confusing," Dottie snapped. "Equivalence?" What do you mean by equivalence?" She paused a moment, "Are the drugs the same or not?" she asked Ian, as her eyes locked with his.

Ian sighed. "I know, guys, it's pretty confusing," he said as he looked around the table at the uncertain faces. "The drugs are not the same and they vary in their production, or at least that's the easiest way to explain it." He was perplexed when he noticed every eye at their table was focused on him.

"So, what exactly do you mean by equivalent?" Mic asked. "Equivalent how? In what way?"

Ian cleared his throat and said, "Name brand drugs and generic drugs are not identical, but they must be biochemically equivalent. Drug companies are given leeway on how close the generic drug's structure is to the brand drug…"

"So," Michaela said, "A brand drug could be like Cheerios on the grocery shelf and the generic drug could simply be like any toasted oat cereal, the much cheaper version, down the aisle."

Ian nodded and said, "Yes, exactly. Good analogy, Michaela."

Senator Bostitch agreed. "Well, unfortunately, that's pretty much it. Your oat cereal example is a good one. The generic drug could have more oats, or more sugar, or more flax, or more of whatever chemicals go with the name brand. Basically, the same chemicals are used, but the chemical structure is different."

"I can hardly believe what you're saying," Alana said in disbelief as her eyes searched Senator Bostitch. She turned to her husband. "Is this true, Ian?" she asked, with outrage in her voice. "I've had lots of generic foodstuffs in my life that were nothing like the brand name. I certainly hope that's not true of pharmaceuticals, particularly psychiatric drugs that already have so many dastardly side effects." Alana was shocked and her face showed it.

Ian patted her hand and said, "Unfortunately, that's true and, it's legal. Bio-equal or bioequivalence means the generic drug must show that the drug releases an active ingredient in nearly the same - but not exactly - concentration as the brand drug."

Dottie looked over at Mic, a look of triumph on her face. "I told you Michaela, and half the drugs I take don't work, maybe this is the reason." Dottie played with her napkin and mused, "Maybe I won't take them anymore since no one seems to know if they work."

Mic shook her head, rolled her eyes, and said, "Most of the drugs you take don't work because you take them every now and then and most definitely not how they're ordered. I think we're talking two different issues here," Michaela said as she glared at Dottie. "This is no reason to stop taking your heart and fluid pills."

Peter Bostitch laughed. "Truthfully, Countess, I feel the same way. Sometimes, I'm not sure my meds are working at all," he said with a grin. Dottie couldn't help but notice how handsome the Senator was.

Mic's mind raced a mile a minute. "Ian, I don't know much about medicine, or pharmacology, but it seems to me that this could be very, very dangerous. I've always thought, and assumed it was critical that all drugs were titrated equally. Am I wrong in thinking that if a drug delivers an amount of chemicals differently than the name brand drug, it could be very dangerous for the patient?"

Ian nodded his head and said, "Yes, Michaela, you're absolutely correct. It's very scary and trust me, can be a real problem for us, the clinicians who practice medicine. We depend on good research. Basically, people react differently to different drugs. There have been lawsuits against drug companies where people who are taking generic drugs have died, committed suicide, or become very ill. That's why monitoring people on generic drugs, or any drugs for that matter, is critical."

"I'm stunned by this," Alana said as her face reddened with discomfort. "Doesn't the FDA regulate the generic drugs? It seems to me that if they're regulated and clinically tested, there shouldn't be a big issue."

Ian looked at Senator Bostitch. "This question is for you, Senator," Ian deferred. "It's a policy and compliance question," he said, happy to bypass the hot seat for a moment or so.

The Senator shook his head. "Unfortunately, the FDA doesn't independently test generic drugs. In truth, the FDA doesn't know if a drug is bioequivalent or not. It's impossible to have this information if the drug is not independently tested."

"But, but..." Michaela's voice faltered as knots of fear jumped around in her stomach. "Isn't the FDA the agency that assures the safety and efficacy of all drugs and pharmaceuticals? I can hardly believe these generic drugs are released and prescribed by medical practitioners without being independently tested by a government agency." She tried to rub the knots out of her stomach. She felt impending doom.

Ian's face was dark with concern. "Well, it's the truth. In a perfect world, we would expect the drugs to be tested in a rigorous and unbiased manner. Fortunately, the more you know about statistics, the more you understand how statistical results can be changed, manipulated even, based on the research question. That's why it's critical that there be independent testing of any medicine by someone other than the drug inventor - or the company that holds the generic drug patent before it's released to the public."

"Appalling, this is appalling," Dottie spat, concern on her face. "We can't... well, you guys can't," she said as she looked at Ian and Peter Bostitch, "practice medicine with medications that haven't been tested."

Ian nodded at the Countess. "But we must remember that a lack of efficacy or usefulness of a high dose antidepressant drug is a safety issue. It's not an issue with the drug manufacturer. It's a safety issue that could be remedied with independent testing."

Senator Bostitch interrupted. "I must remind all of you that there are hundreds of generic drugs that do work extraordinarily well and save the government and insurance companies, and consequently, the consumers hundreds of thousands of dollars every month. It's much easier for a patient to pay $20.00 for a generic drug than $165.00 for the brand-named drug."

Michaela nodded. "I'm sure, and I agree with you. But this is still a surprise to me." She paused for a second. "So, I guess that's why it's important for physicians to report side effects, correct?"

Ian's face was flushed. "Yes. No doubt. That's very important. Quelpro, the antidepressant in question, concerns many psychiatrists. We've reported our concerns to the company and have pleaded with them to gather more data and to test it further. We would like to see expertly designed, controlled studies that measure the drug's usefulness and worth."

Dottie sniffed, "That's certainly reasonable. What's the problem, then?"

Ian sighed. "Blake Pharmaceutical refuses to test the drug even though they've had numerous complaints about the drug not working… its lack of efficacy. As a matter of fact, The People's Pharmacy, a well-known syndicated radio and newspaper column that gathers data from patients, has received hundreds of complaints about the drug. There have been at least seven deaths of people taking Quelpro as well as several hundred people who have developed severe blood diseases linked to the medicine. Still, no one listens," he said angrily, his face stained red.

"What about the FDA? Can't they do something?" Mic asked.

"The FDA has been notified, but has turfed the problem back to Blake Pharmaceutical, and they've chosen to do nothing."

Mic shook her head, "This is shocking, absolutely shocking. I'm sure most Americans… anyone… think they're getting the same drug. I especially feel bad for people with psychiatric issues because my guess is people blow them off because they have 'mental issues.'"

Ian nodded. "Yeah, you're exactly right. Add to that the fact that a psychiatrist - at the very best - often guesses about a patient's diagnosis. We make hunches, simply by the nature of what we do as psychiatrists. Behavior diagnosis is often non-scientific. There's no blood test to measure for bipolar disease or major depressive disorder. Certainly, the practice of psychiatric medicine is not as scientifically based as diagnosing cancer or heart disease where a tissue cell or a biopsy could offer the practitioner a definitive diagnosis. Consequently, since a lot of what we do is guesswork when we diagnose, it's imperative that the drugs be safe and efficient."

"Now, that's the truth," Mic acknowledged. "I hadn't thought of psychiatric practice as a string of guesses or hunches. It's essential you get the correct medicine," she said as she looked over at Dottie who nodded at her.

Alana shook her head. "I've spent quite a few years of my life doing social science research which measures what human beings do. Sometimes, social science research is hard to control, but bench science or the kind of science they use to develop pharmaceuticals, is an exact science. Ian's correct. The testing must be rigorous, controlled, and monitored. This shouldn't even be an issue," she scoffed.

"I agree!" Michaela said firmly and boldly. "There's no way we can expect large corporations to police their own medicine. They wouldn't do it! It's costly and there's no short cut. In my opinion, letting the government give up oversight of independent testing as a safeguard for the American people, or people anywhere, for that matter, is a cop-out."

"You're both correct, Alana and Michaela," Senator Bostitch said as the door opened and the Captain returned to his private dining room.

Michaela noticed, even in the low light of the room, that the Captain's face was flushed, and his behavior restrained. Something bad had definitely happened.

"Captain Wodensen, have you come to tell us about what's happened?" Dottie asked with a smile. "Do tell what was so serious that called you away from dinner," she insisted.

The Captain sighed deeply and said, "Unfortunately, we've had a murder on board. It occurred in the Royale Casino. A passenger had lost quite a bit of money and accused the blackjack dealer of cheating. He killed him."

Michaela heard a gasp from Alana Pennington. Her husband reached over and put his arm around her.

"A murder?" Dottie asked as her eyes lit up. Have you caught the man that did it?"

"We know who he is and we'll apprehend him shortly. My security team is quite good," the Captain assured them. "But, please keep this quiet. I need to leave again to return to the Bridge, so I came to bid you all a good evening," he said with a smile. He turned around again, smiled and said, "There's nothing to worry about."

Ian and Alana stood. "We must leave as well. Thank you, Countess, for a lovely evening. It was delightful to be your guest."

Alana circled the table and gave Dottie a kiss on the cheek. "Thank you, Dottie. It was wonderful."

Dottie nodded and said, "You're welcome my dear. Perhaps I'll see you tomorrow for a round of bridge?"

"Of course," she said with a smile. "I'd like to play bridge with you."

Peter Bostitch stood and offered Ian his hand and said, "I'll meet you and Dr. O'Leary about 11:30 in the private bar on the eighth floor. Will that work?"

Ian nodded and shook the Senator's hand. Michaela smiled and waved at Alana who was on the way out.

Bostitch looked at Dottie and said, "No reason to be alarmed, Countess. The Captain will get the killer within the hour."

Dottie sniffed and said, "Well, Senator, this is an enormous ship, and you've only seen a part of it. If they don't catch the man, Michaela and I and Angel, of course, will get him," she said as she pointed at the massive dog that stood between her and Michaela's chair.

The Senator gave the Countess a benevolent look. "That'll be fine, Dottie. You two can have at it," he said as he grinned at Michaela. "Don't worry. "We'll keep this quiet. We don't want the passengers alarmed."

The Senator smiled and kissed Dottie on both cheeks. "I'll see you tomorrow, Countess. Get some rest, ladies, and many thanks for a lovely evening."

Dottie turned her head up for the Senator's kisses, nodded, and waved. The Senator cut a fine figure as he left the dining room. Then her vivid blue eyes locked with Michaela's green ones. "We got ourselves a job, Michaela."

Michaela laughed and said, "I'm sure the ship can handle this without us. Besides, we're on vacation. I don't want to work. I want to sunbathe and go to the spa," she declared. "This is my vacation of a lifetime."

Dottie frowned and said, "I'm not so sure. Security is pretty good, but I think we're probably better," she said as she reached down and ruffled Angel's ears. He looked at her expectantly.

Mic nodded, "Who in the world has the audacity to murder someone in a casino aboard a ship in the middle of the sea?" she wondered out loud. "That's one hell of a perp," she added.

"Yeah, sounds like a rage killer to me," Dottie said. "He's dangerous. We've got our work cut out for us, Mic," Dottie opined as her eyes gleamed with excitement.

Mic's feeling of knowing overtook her. She knew Dottie was right. They'd have to solve the murder. She reached down and rubbed Angel's back. His fur had bristled. He knew something was wrong. Even her dog was on alert.

Angel whined and licked Michaela's hand. He knew something was up and he'd be ready to help them solve whatever they needed solved.

Chapter 12

It was after ten p.m. when Dottie and Mic left the dining room. Dottie was exhausted, pale with fatigue, Mic was dog-tired herself, and even Angel seemed to be missing his spunk. Michaela couldn't wait to hit the sack and said so as they headed to the elevators.

Michaela broke the silence. "Well, Dottie. You didn't tell me you were bringing me on a cruise where there'd be a murder. Thanks a lot. This may turn out to be a busman's holiday," she said with a laugh.

Dottie shrugged her shoulders and with a note of derision in her voice said, "I had no idea any of this would happen. But now that you mention it, lots of crimes do occur on cruise ships. It doesn't make the newspapers - at least for the most part, which is certainly good for my business."

Mic was surprised. "Really, I've never thought about crime aboard a cruise ship," she admitted. "I think of cruises as being happy vacations, certainly not people on board planning to murder each other." She stopped for a moment and began again. "Except, of course, for the newlywed wife who pushed her husband overboard a few years back."

"Yeah, no kidding," Dottie muttered. "That was a marriage made in hell."

"What kinds of crimes occur on ships?" Mic asked as they reached their staterooms.

"Let's sit on your deck for a few minutes," Dottie suggested. "I'm so wide-awake from the news of a murder, I don't think I can calm down and go to sleep quite yet. Maybe a little fresh air will make me sleepy."

"Sure, that's okay with me. But I'm taking off this evening gown and putting on my sweats. And, by the way, I'm not dressing for dinner tomorrow night. I think I'll order room service and eat in my jeans or sweat pants," she informed Dottie who rolled her eyes.

"Oh, whatever," Dottie said in a caustic voice. "I guess we'll dine al fresco if you like. Then, perhaps we can go to the Royale Casino and gamble for a bit. I haven't gambled on this cruise."

Mic was quiet for a moment and then asked, "Ah, the scene of the crime. By the way, is there someone on board who gathers forensic evidence? It'll be hard to find the killer if no one gathers evidence."

Dottie gave a short laugh and said, "Trust me, Michaela. There's no one to gather forensic evidence. Most likely, the murderer will never be found. If they don't find him in a few days, my guess is he'll leave the ship when we dock in Athens. Besides, no one has jurisdiction at sea. Very few crimes or deaths are even investigated."

Mic pulled on her T-shirt, picked up a bottle of brandy and two snifters, and motioned for Dottie to open the glass door that led to the balcony.

Mic poured them both a snifter of brandy. Dottie accepted the glass gratefully and said, "It's chilly out here. I thought the wind had died down, but I guess it's come back up." She looked over the balcony. "The Mediterranean is usually still but the wind has churned up the water." Mic stared into the dark water below and shivered in the darkness.

She stood and placed her brandy glass on the small table between them. "Wait here. I've got another heavy sweatshirt in my closet. I'll get it for you, Dottie."

Dottie nodded her thanks and said in a prim voice, "I've never worn a sweatshirt with an evening gown."

Mic went into her stateroom, grabbed the sweatshirt, returned, and said, "The last thing I need is your ornery tail getting sick aboard the ship. That would be a real pain in my ass," she snorted.

"It would be a bigger pain for me. The medical facilities here are limited. The cruise line offers immediate medical attention, for things such as heart attacks, but if someone is acutely ill, they'll order them off the ship at the next port, no matter what language is spoken," Dottie said with a frown. "The cruise line will transport the passenger to the closest hospital and that's about it. I have no intention of becoming ill at sea… or anywhere else," she assured her.

Mic nodded and said, "So, who has legal authority aboard ship?"

"Pretty much, it's the Captain, then the First Mate, and so on down. Anytime there's a crime reported at sea, the Captain may, or may not, decide to report it to authorities," she said as she paused to think. "Although, if an American dies at sea and it's suspicious, the FBI is notified and they may decide to investigate. The crime is reported to law enforcement officials in the next port of call and they can choose to investigate or not. They rarely do. And, from what I've heard, they don't really give a rip, so an investigation is pretty useless." Dottie shrugged her shoulders at the blistering look Mic gave her. "I know it sounds bad, Michaela, but I can't control any of it," she said as she reached for her brandy.

Michaela was disturbed about how crime was handled at sea. She sipped her brandy and it warmed her all over. She reminded herself to take two Tylenol before she jumped in bed to deter any potential headache she might develop the next day. Mic rarely mixed her alcohol, but she had that evening. "So, suppose an American is killed at sea. Certainly, that wouldn't go unnoticed. I'm still steamed up about the blackjack dealer who was killed. Will the cruise ship notify the family? Will there be an investigation?"

"We'll notify the young man's family about his death," Dottie said. "As you know, most crewmembers come from poor countries and make almost no money. They sign on for three to six month tours of duty and are barely paid minimum wage."

"Humph. That's not much," Mic said. "The service has been excellent."

"It gets worse," Dottie said with a sigh. "The minimum wage is terrible because the salary is based on the crewmember's country of origin and the ports of call the ship visits. Although truthfully, most of the money made by the cabin stewards, bar people, restaurant workers, and so on, is based on the tips you leave when you check out."

Mic nodded, "Yeah. That's what I heard. I suppose that's why there are no American employees on board."

"Pretty much." Dottie bottomed up her brandy snifter. "I'm tired, so I'm going next door to turn in," she said with a yawn.

Mic looked up at her standing at the rail. Dottie looked tired. "Do you need any help getting all those clothes off? I can come over and help you get your jewelry off," she offered.

"Hell no," Dottie snapped. "I put it on and I'll take it off, but thanks for the offer."

Mic shook her head and walked her to the door, "You're a stubborn old bat, Dottie. Get some rest; we've got a lot more traveling to do."

Dottie nodded briefly and Mic watched her enter her stateroom. She shook her head. Dottie could be one stubborn pain in the ass. No question about that.

Chapter 13

Snake stood in the shadow of the outside stairwell on the Promenade deck. It was cold, and he pulled his sweat jacket closely around him. He looked down at the inky sea and wondered how cold the water was. He knew the normal temperature in the Mediterranean approximated seventy degrees. He could see whitecaps on the water, which was uncommon for the usually calm sea. He figured they were most likely caused by the ship's propellers. He finished his cigarette, ground it out on the deck with his foot and threw it overboard. Then he sat on the bench behind the column to wait for Vadim. The lounge chairs they'd sat in yesterday were gone. The Promenade deck was clear and unobstructed. Fortunately, the wind had died down.

He checked his watch. It was almost one thirty. He strained his ears and heard footsteps. Someone was running. He smiled to himself as he recognized the size and build of their target from half a block away. Snake stood and moved into the darkness under the stairway. If Vadim showed up, they'd grab him on the next rotation. Snake had watched the man jog for several days, and knew he generally ran for about forty-five minutes. He watched as the man continued running down the deck. The man was tall, close to six feet. He would need Vadim's help to hoist him over the rail.

Several minutes went by and the sound of the jogger faded into silence. Then he heard a click, and the door across from him opened. A man the size of Vadim stepped out, walked over to the rail, and lit a cigarette.

Snake watched him from behind the column. His heart pounded in his chest. The light from the match reflected on the man's face, but it wasn't Vadim. His heartbeat accelerated. Who the hell was this guy? He could've sworn it was the Russian based on his size.

The breeze stopped for a moment and a voice said, "Okay, asshole, I see you behind the column. How much time do we have?"

It was Vadim. Snake couldn't believe it. How in the hell had he disguised his face? Snake walked out from behind the metal post.

"We've got about three minutes. Are you ready?" He asked as he scrutinized the face he didn't recognize.

Vadim nodded and inhaled deeply on his cigarette. "Hell, yeah. I'm ready. This is easy. Just a grab and hoist."

Snake nodded and said, "The dude's tall, man. Close to six feet. And, he's big."

Vadim shrugged his shoulders. "So what, it won't be a problem. You stop him and I'll grab him, and together we'll push him over the rail. It's a piece of cake," he assured him, a sneer on his face.

"It sounds like you've done this before," Snake said.

Vadim looked at him, his dark eyes glittering in the low light. "Nah, but I've done everything else," he admitted. He stopped for a moment and said, "Get up there near that doorway and stop him. I hear him coming our way."

Snake quickly moved into position and stood in the dark. He flattened his body against the doorway. He looked up, saw a security camera, and cursed quietly to himself. A few seconds later, he jumped out as their target ran right in front of him. Snake grabbed him and wrestled him to the ground. The element of surprise worked in their favor. The man was stunned and hardly resisted. Several seconds later, he and Vadim tossed the shocked man into the Mediterranean Sea.

They heard the splash ten stories down as the body hit the ocean.

Snake shook his head. "I can't believe the son of a bitch didn't even scream. I'd have been yelling my head off."

Vadim nodded. "My guess is he was scared shitless and the cat had his tongue," he said with a grin as he looked down at the water. "I don't see nuthin' going on down there," he observed.

"Let's get outta here," Snake suggested, "before all hell breaks loose."

"Good idea," Vadim agreed. The two men separated and walked quickly to their staterooms.

Chapter 14

Michaela sat straight up in bed when the first bell rang. Angel jumped from his bed and barked loudly. Her heart exploded with fear. The ship's alarm rang seven short bells followed by the ship's horn that made her skin crawl. Her mind was fuzzy and her heart beat frantically in her chest. Then the PA system sounded and a voice said softly, "Oscar, Oscar, Oscar." The horn blasted again and the noise seemed to last forever. She covered her ears with her hands to block out the blast. Mic knew something bad had happened. Seconds later, she heard noises in the hallway. She opened her cabin door and saw two stewards racing toward the elevator.

"What's happened? What's going on?" She asked.

"Everything is fine," the young cabin steward said. "Do not worry; you and your dog are safe."

Michaela looked and saw an alarm flashing in the hall. The alarm and light blasted in concert with her beating heart. Angel whimpered. Mic couldn't imagine how the sound affected him with his sensitive hearing. She reached down and patted him as she tried to calm him but Angel's eyes were bright with fright and uncertainty.

She heard Dottie's door open. "What's happened?" Dottie asked as she rubbed the sleep from her eyes. "I'd just dropped off to sleep."

Mic shook her head, "I don't know. They said 'Oscar' three times. The cabin steward said we were safe, but obviously there's some sort of emergency," she said with certainty as she watched passengers in all stages of dress migrate into the hall.

"Well, I'm gonna call the front desk and ask. I think a Code Oscar means a man has gone overboard. If the front desk doesn't know, you and I are going up to the Bridge and find out from the Captain," Dottie said as she struggled into her robe. "I think you're fine to go just like you are," she said, as she appraised the sweat clothes Michaela had worn to bed. "Come on in," Dottie invited, her face set and determined to find out what had happened. Mic and Angel entered Dottie's suite and Angel immediately put his head under his pillow bed. Angel had two beds on the ship. Dottie had a bed for him in her room.

Michaela sat quietly as Dottie called the front desk. They patched her through to Captain Wodensen. Dottie's face was grim as she listened. Mic heard her tell the Captain to keep her advised. "Captain, I need to know who it is as soon as you identify who is missing and recover the body." She clicked off and turned to Mic whose gut had constricted with pain.

"There's a man overboard. Just as we thought. Otherwise known as an MOB. They have pulled the rescue boats and they're looking for the person now," she said grimly as she watched Angel wrap his paws around the pillow to block out the sound. "The noise really hurts Angel's ears," Dottie said.

Michaela was surprised. "How do you 'fall off' a cruise ship?" she asked. "It looks to me like it's just about impossible. The railings are tall, above my waist. I honestly don't see how anyone can just 'fall off'."

Dottie shook her head. "Usually they don't just fall off. From what I can remember from my years of owning part of the cruise line, is that alcohol is generally involved, probably more than half of the time. Then, there's always the possibility of suicide. That occurs on cruise ships more than we like to think," she admitted.

Mic shook her head as she stroked Angel's back. "When will they stop those alarms? It's loud and tedious," she complained.

"Soon. Very soon, I'd think," Dottie responded. The purpose is a call to action and a way to alert the crew," she said.

"Well, if the crew doesn't know by now, they're dead! Let's go up to a higher deck and see what's going on. I'd like to watch the rescue," she said. "Is that the best place to go?"

"Let's look from the balcony first. The rescue boats should be in the water by now. There should be a lot of lights."

Michaela nodded, "I think they've slowed the ship. It seems like we're hardly moving," she noted as she followed Dottie through her suite and onto the balcony. Sure enough, there were half a dozen lifeboats and buoys in the water. Search lights beamed down from the ship into the general vicinity and crewmembers shined lights from the lifeboats."

"They've turned the ship," Dottie announced. "They always turn the ship in the opposite direction of a fall. That keeps the man overboard from becoming entangled in the ship's propeller."

Mic grimaced, as she scratched Angel's head. He seemed to have calmed down some. "That's a horrific thought. How do they know for sure that someone has fallen overboard?" she asked. "Could this be a false alarm?"

Dottie shook her head and said, "Apparently, a couple on a lower deck were on their balcony, saw the body fly by and heard it hit the water," she reported. "The man immediately called the desk and they initiated rescue operations."

"Oh, they're announcing something on the PA system," Michaela said. "Let me go listen."

The voice on the PA system repeated, "Oscar, Oscar, Oscar. All staff alert, all staff alert," over and over again.

Michaela returned to the balcony where Dottie continued to watch the rescue attempts. "They're still announcing 'Oscar, Oscar, Oscar' repeatedly on the loud speaker. Do you see anything?"

Dottie looked at Mic and shook her head, "I haven't seen anyone pulled out of the water. I don't know if they'll find anyone or not," she said sadly. "They hoisted the 'Oscar' flag so any approaching ships will look for the man overboard. I'm sure they've notified the Coast Guard and the Italian Water Fleet as well."

Mic nodded, "Sounds like they're doing all they can." Michaela was antsy and wanted to move. "Let's go down to the Atrium. I'd like to get closer to the action and hear what they're saying. I'm sure people have gathered there for news."

"Undoubtedly. Yes, let's do that," Dottie agreed. "Let me slip into something other than my bathrobe."

Mic nodded and continued to watch the rescue efforts. The crew knew their jobs, and the rescue effort was organized, non-chaotic, and well-orchestrated.

Several minutes later, Dottie tapped her on the shoulder and the two of them left the suite and took the elevator down to the Atrium, with Angel at Mic's side. Angel was calmer since the alarm had ceased.

The Atrium was located mid-ship and, as Mic had imagined, it was filled with people. Ship officers milled around frightened passengers and reassured them everything was being done to recover the man overboard.

"Let go over to the bar area and order some tea," Dottie suggested. "Needless to say, the more time that goes by, the less the chance of rescue."

Mic nodded and ordered tea and a pastry from the waiter. "I would suggest chances for a successful rescue are slim, almost impossible. I don't know the temperature, but I suspect the water is cold this time of year." She stopped a moment and added, "Besides, the winds were heavy earlier, and I suspect the sea is turbulent."

Dottie nodded. She picked up her teacup and looked around. She saw Ian Pennington and waved. He smiled, waved back, and stopped at their table.

The man's face was strained. "It seems I just told you two good night," he said with a smile. "Dreadful business… this man overboard, isn't it?"

Michaela nodded. "Yeah, it is. This cruise is certainly not typical. First a murder, and then a passenger overboard. That's a lot."

"How's Alana taking this?" Dottie asked. "It's a bit too much excitement for me."

Ian hesitated and said, "She's okay. Just rattled by the events of the past few hours. I'm taking her some tea and I picked up a couple of the seasick pills from the front desk. They should help her sleep."

Mic nodded. "I may pick up a few of those as well. I wonder how they'll determine who fell overboard. Do they do a roll count or something?"

Dottie nodded, "Yeah, if they don't recover the person overboard, or a body, they'll muster us and determine who's missing, that is, if no one reports a spouse or friend missing."

"Let's hope it doesn't come to that," Ian muttered. "I'm off to try and get some sleep. I've got to look smart early in the morning when James and I present our information about Quelpro," he said with a smile. "I'll see you tomorrow."

"Good luck. Get some rest," Mic said as Ian stood to leave.

"I'm gonna try," he said, "and Countess, thank you once again for dinner."

Dottie smiled, "You're welcome, Ian. Good luck tomorrow… or today, rather," she said as she looked at her watch.

Ian stood and said, "Thank you, Countess Borghase. I'm sure Dr. O'Leary will present his work proudly and he'll be able to defend his research. Good night to both of you," he said as he kissed Dottie on the cheek and flashed Mic a tired smile.

Chapter 15

Snake and Vadim sat in Snake's cabin where they toasted a good day's work.

The get-away had been simple. The men had parted ways and taken opposite stairways to Snake's room. They entered just as the ship's first blast occurred.

"Shit," Snake said as he smiled broadly, "that was the easiest hit I've ever done. No muss, no fuss, just a quick toss and that's it." He clinked glasses with Vadim, who gave him a wicked grin as he noted the vodka bottle on the desk. Maybe this guy wasn't so bad.

The Russian downed his drink and said in a pleased voice, "Told you, man. You stick with me and I'll teach you that killing is never work. It's a pleasure. It fills a need we both have. All you gotta do is think about it before hand and plan so there's no mess-ups." Vadim smiled as he reached for the vodka bottle.

Snake considered an angry retort, but held it in. They still had a few more days together. "Dude, let's do a shot each time the bell sounds and the whistle blows, and a double shot each time we hear them say 'Oscar.' It'll be a reason for us to reward ourselves with a drink," he suggested. "After all, we've earned it."

Vadim threw back his head and laughed, "Comrade, you ain't got enough vodka for that. My shots are this big," he said as he held out a water glass.

"Ah, you don't know that, Vadim. I got my own private storage…"

The Russian looked at him through his little squinty pig eyes and said, "Humph, I may like you after all…"

Chapter 16

Michaela and Dottie enjoyed a late breakfast in the Captain's dining room when Ian Pennington rushed in, obviously agitated, a look of fear on his face.

"Ian, whatever is the matter?" Dottie asked. "You look like you've seen a ghost."

"Do… Do you know if they recovered the body from last night?" Ian's face was pale with either fear or fatigue. He looked ill.

Mic's heart rate picked up, "Dottie and I talked to one of the executive officers a couple of hours ago, and he told us that the body hasn't been recovered yet."

"Oh, oh no. That's not good," Ian said as he slid wearily into a seat at the table. "That's not good at all," he murmured more to himself than to Mic and Dottie.

"He did say," Dottie continued, "that another ship and a Coast Guard vessel were en route to pick up someone stranded on an island." She looked at her watch and added, "They should be able to tell us who it is by now."

Ian was preoccupied with his own thoughts and didn't seem to hear her.

Mic continued to look at him. Beads of sweat framed his face and his breathing was irregular. Something was wrong. "Take a deep breath, Ian. Something's wrong. I can see it in your face."

Ian's face was bloodless, his eyes watery, and his hands were shaking. "I… I can't find James- Jamie O'Leary. He didn't show up at our lecture this morning. He was keynote speaker with plans to present the data on Quelpro."

Mic's stomach formed a hard knot and an uneasy feeling consumed her. She felt blood rush into her head.

"Now, now, Ian," Dottie soothed. "There are over three thousand people on this cruise ship. Perhaps your friend overslept." She looked at Michaela and said, "Mic and I certainly did, after being up half the night with the man overboard."

Ian shook his head. "No, I don't think so. I've had the ship's receptionist call him a dozen times and I've beaten on his door three times. I don't think he's in there," he said, his eyes fraught with concern.

"Let's not jump to conclusions," Michaela said. "I know you're worried, but there may be a logical reason for his absence."

"Yeah," Ian said in a soft voice. "I think they killed him. I think they threw him overboard so he wouldn't screw up the marketing of their killer drug..." Ian said as he covered his face with his hands.

"I'm gonna call up to the Bridge," Dottie said. "If they haven't identified the man on the island they believe might be our man overboard, I'm sure the Captain will order a muster."

"A what? Order what?" Ian asked as Mic signaled the waiter for a cup for Ian.

Dottie nodded. "A muster. Yes, a muster. Everyone will be required to check in with the security so they can identify who, if anyone is missing."

Ian nodded. "It's James. It must be James. I know he would never miss a keynote address; especially about something that concerns him as much as Quelpro. He's been working on that presentation for months."

"Dottie, can you have the ship's security check James' stateroom? That may give us some idea of his whereabouts."

Dottie nodded and signaled for the waiter. She asked him to have someone put her in contact with either the Captain or the First Mate.

The waiter placed a cup on the table in front of Ian, who looked at it stupidly.

"Ian, would you like some coffee? Have you eaten? It may help you feel better," Mic said.

"Perhaps some coffee," Ian said. "I had breakfast early this morning. James and I had planned to meet upstairs in the public dining area and take a last look at our presentation." He looked down at his feet and said in a soft, strained voice, "He never showed up."

"Did you present at the conference this morning?" Dottie asked, with her eyebrows raised. "Did you have access to James' notes and slides?"

Ian thanked the waiter for his coffee and said, "Yeah, I presented, but I wasn't able to present all of his statistical data."

"But why not? You seemed to be quite up on it yesterday," Dottie said, a quizzical look on her face.

"Mainly because I'm not a statistician. I don't know exactly how James analyzed the data. I knew I'd get dozens of questions relating to data analysis and I knew I wouldn't be able to answer them as well as James."

Ian paused as the waiter handed the phone to Dottie and said, "It's the Captain, Countess Borghase."

Dottie nodded and accepted the phone. "Captain, did the Coast Guard complete the rescue of the passenger on the island you mentioned?"

Michaela could hear the Captain's voice, but couldn't understand the words. She studied Dottie's face and realized the man wasn't the man overboard from last night.

Dottie clicked off the phone, handed it to the waiter, and said, "The man the Coast Guard rescued was not the man overboard from last night." She saw Ian Pennington's face fall. His glimmer of hope was gone and he buried his face into his hands.

Michaela touched his shoulder and said, "Ian, you seem sure that our man overboard is James O'Leary. Why are you so sure?"

Ian's face was pale and he was listless. "Because… Because he told me last night he received a note on his stateroom door late yesterday afternoon."

"A note? What kind of a note?" Dottie asked, a sound of fear in her voice.

Ian looked into Dottie's eyes and said, "A threat. It was a written threat. The note told James to back down on his speech or…"

"Or what?" Dottie pushed as she stared at him. "Or what? Ian, tell me. We can't help you if you don't tell us what you know."

Ian buried his head in his hands again. He opened his mouth to speak, but no words came out.

Michaela's eyes met Dottie's and could tell she'd become impatient. Mic shook her head slightly and spoke in a soft voice, "Let us help you, Ian. What else did the note say?"

Ian took a deep breath and said, "The note said for him to back down on his presentation or he'd be fish food by this morning."

The enormity of the threat staggered Michaela. She knew then someone had murdered Dr. O'Leary. He was, in her mind, the man overboard. "Dottie, we need to see the Captain and we need to search Dr. O'Leary's room, or at least have it cordoned off as a crime scene."

Dottie nodded and said, "I'm going to request the Captain's presence here in the dining room." She turned to Ian and asked, "Can you stay here for a few moments and talk with the Captain, Ian? It would be better for him to hear your concerns face-to-face."

Ian nodded, his face wan. Dottie rose from the table, went to the reception area of the dining room, and instructed the waiter to call the Captain.

Mic talked softly to Ian Pennington, "Ian, do you know that I'm a retired homicide detective? I don't know if I told you that at dinner last night. Also, Dottie and I have been known to solve a few crimes. We'll work on this for you if you'd like us to."

Ian nodded and Mic was pleased his face had a bit more color, "Yes, please help me. James is… was one of my best friends. I owe him this much. In some ways, I'll feel responsible if something has happened to him," he said, his speech broken.

Dottie returned to the table and said, "I overheard that. You? How are you responsible?"

"I… I pushed him to re-run the Quelpro data. I'd had two patients die from what I believe to be complications of Quelpro. I have two other patients ill with agranulocytosis…"

"What is agranulocytosis?" Dottie asked sharply. "I've heard of it, but I can't remember now."

Ian took a big breath and began to explain. "It's a blood disease, a hematologic disease, caused by Quelpro. At least, that's what I believe and what James' data proves. If agranulocytosis is untreated, the risk of dying is high. Death results from uncontrolled sepsis."

"Can these people be saved?" Michaela asked.

James nodded. "Yes. The condition can be reversed with treatment. Antibiotic and antifungal medications can cure the infection if the disease is properly recognized, diagnosed, and treated," Ian said as a little more color returned to his face. "Many of these people get infections that may appear superficial, involving mainly the oral mucosa, gums, skin, and sinuses. Some infections are worse and may be systemic and spread throughout the bloodstream. Those patients generally die from a massive blood infection.

Dottie nodded. "But, why do you think this is your fault? Why do you think you caused Dr. O'Leary's death?"

"Because I asked for the additional statistical testing," he blurted out as his voice broke. "Perhaps if I hadn't..." he said as he turned his head away from Dottie and Michaela and focused on his coffee cup.

"This is definitely not your fault, Ian, so don't go down that rickety road. Your work... You're doing your job as a physician, nothing else, just as James did his." Michaela paused for a moment and then continued, "I have to ask you this, and I'll be first of many to ask you this question. Of that I'm sure."

Ian picked up his coffee cup and said, "What's that?"

"Is there any chance that James O'Leary was suicidal? Is there any possibility he would take his own life?"

Ian's face flushed with anger and he shook his head vehemently and said, "Hell no, not a chance."

Mic watched as anger raged on Ian's face. "James O'Leary would never commit suicide. In addition to being an astute researcher and one of the best psychiatrists I've ever known, he was Catholic and loyal to the church to this day. The last thing he would ever do is throw himself over the railing of a cruise ship," he ended in a bitter voice.

Michaela nodded. "I understand, Ian, and I believe you. But, I had to ask," she said in an apologetic tone. "Did you see the note, the note that threatened him?"

Ian shook his head and in a cracked voice said, "No, no, I didn't see it. He just told me about it, Michaela. You don't understand." He waved his hands wildly in the air. "They killed him. Blake Pharmaceutical killed my friend. They knew his research findings would cost the company millions of dollars."

Michaela touched his hand and held it for a minute. "I know you believe that, Ian, but we have to collect the evidence. We've got to prove it. Build a case. Do you think the other physicians who agreed with Dr. O'Leary will talk with us?"

Ian nodded. "Of course, they will. They know Quelpro is a dirty drug. They've stopped prescribing it. I'm sure they'll come forward," he said with confidence.

"Do you think they'll come forward if indeed Dr. O'Leary is our man overboard?" Dottie asked. "Isn't it possible they'll think – like you – that they'll be new targets for Blake Pharmaceutical?"

Ian opened his mouth to speak and a whoosh came out. He closed it again and Mic could see the feelings and fear of uncertainty flicker across his face. He cleared his throat. "Well, I hope they will," he said, this time in an uncertain voice.

"Time will tell," Mic said. "Did James seem upset or frightened by the note?"

Ian shook his head. "No, not at all. He said it proved what we had always thought. That Blake knew… and knows… the drug is dirty… harmful and dangerous. But he also felt confident the Feds would recall it based on his data."

"Obviously," Dottie snorted. "Obviously, Blake Pharmaceutical was concerned." She shot a look at Mic who nodded slightly. Dottie knew Mic agreed with her.

"There are few people in this world that commanded the skill sets that James O'Leary possessed. I don't know of anyone else in the United States who could have put together such a scientific argument against Blake." He put his coffee cup down forcefully and coffee spilled and saturated the white tablecloth. "Those bastards killed my friend."

The waiter appeared and slipped Dottie a note. She said, "The Captain's just ordered a muster exercise. Everyone must check in with security in the next several hours." She looked over at Ian and said, "If your friend doesn't check in, Ian, his room will be designated as a crime scene and the FBI will be notified."

Ian nodded his head and stared into Dottie's vivid blue eyes. "I understand, Countess. But, James won't check in. His death…" he sighed and continued, "His death is about corporate greed and big money. Blake Pharmaceutical is sending a message to physicians and providers who challenge their medicines. It's about ethics and the practice of safe psychiatry."

Michaela's green eyes met Dottie's blue ones and she nodded. "Well, Countess, I think we have ourselves a case."

Chapter 17

Michaela stretched her legs, got up, and walked over to the water station on the far side of the dining room. For some reason, she was thirsty and couldn't seem to get enough water. She took a second look out at the beautiful Mediterranean Sea, the same sea that had most likely swallowed up a brilliant psychiatrist and researcher. Of course, that wasn't official yet, as other passengers hadn't checked in, but Mic was convinced that Dr. O'Leary was the man overboard. Mic filled two glasses of water and returned to the table.

"Thanks for the glass of water," Dottie said. "There must've been a lot of salt in that seafood salad we had for lunch. My mouth feels like dry cotton," she complained.

Michaela nodded. "Mine's dry too. Perhaps it was our lunch." She handed Dottie a crystal glass filled with ice water and said, "What time did Captain Wodensen tell you he'd be here? I think Senator Bostitch will be here in a couple of minutes."

Dottie shrugged her shoulders and said, "He said he'll be here when he can. There's no question in my mind that he's stressed," she said with a sigh. "I'm stressed and I don't have to command the ship," she confessed.

Mic gave her a sideways look and said, "I'm sure he is, Dottie. Who wouldn't be? He's has two possible murders aboard his ship and nobody has a clue who the killer is, plus the killer is running free."

"Yeah, that's the truth," Dottie agreed. "Unfortunately, the killer could be anywhere. This ship is huge, and you, I and the rest of the passengers only see about half of it."

"Half of it? What do you mean we see half of it?" Mic asked, with a puzzled look on her face.

"Well," Dottie began, "there's all sorts of equipment rooms and don't forget, there's almost nine hundred staff members that live below deck six. You probably never stopped to think about it, but the crew has their own little microcosm down there - they've got their cabins, their own bars, a fitness center, a movie theatre, and a couple of dining halls - all kinds of stuff. I can probably arrange for you to see it."

"Humph," Mic's green eyes were thoughtful as she ran her hand through her short, dark curls. "I guess you're right. I suppose there's essentially another cruise ship in the lower decks. That does put a whole new perspective on things." Mic turned her head and looked behind her. She could swear she had eyes on her back, but she didn't see anyone. Who could be watching her?

Dottie nodded, "Yeah, then there's the bowels of the ship - the engine room, the bilge, and storage. It's amazing. Imagine the food storage to feed three thousand people for ten days."

Michaela nodded her head. "Yeah, I hadn't considered that. This perp, or perps, could be anywhere. I'm just sorry we don't have a camera image of him. If we just knew an approximate size and weight, we could get going... or at least eliminate a few people." Mic tucked her head and said, "Dottie do you see anyone looking at me? I feel like I have a pair of eyes on my back."

Dottie looked ahead, her blue eyes flashed around the room. She shook her head and said, "No, why do you think so?"

Mic tossed her dark curls and rubbed chill bumps from her arms. "Don't know. It feels like someone is staring a hole in my back. It's creepy," she said with a shudder as she rubbed her arms again. "I've felt it before, like when we were in the Atrium last night after the man went overboard."

"I'll keep looking," Dottie assured her. "If someone is staring at you, I'll spot him." Dottie changed the subject, "Yeah, it would be helpful if we had an image. There could be one. I don't think they've gone through all the feeds yet. If there isn't an image, then whoever did this knew exactly how to hide in the shadows and approach Dr. O'Leary at the perfect time. I'm sure they've been watching him since we boarded."

"Yeah. No doubt. How else would the perp know he jogged between one and two in the morning?"

"James O'Leary was a pretty big guy," Michaela noted. "I'm wondering if there's more than one perp." She looked out the window at the balcony. "It'd take a pretty strong guy to hoist a man overboard all by himself."

Dottie's eyes looked beyond Mic and she smiled and waved. "Good afternoon, Captain. Has the muster drill been completed? Has everyone at sea been accounted for?"

The Captain, in full dress uniform, took a seat at the table. He shook his head and said, "No, I'm afraid not. These musters often take a full day because half the passengers sleep until three or four in the afternoon and don't hear the announcement bells."

Mic shook her head. "That's amazing. I can't believe people can't hear it. That whistle could wake the dead. It's hard to see how anyone could sleep through that."

The Captain grinned. Mic thought he was quite charming. "Well, believe it or not, they do," the Captain said in a matter-of-fact voice. "Right now, I've got cabin stewards checking their rooms so we should have a total and know who's missing in a few hours."

"Has… Has Dr. O'Leary been found? Did he check in on the muster?" Dottie asked in a hesitant voice.

The Captain shrugged his shoulders and said, "No, he hasn't. We've not heard from him."

Michaela's stomach contracted, and she changed the subject. "I'm not well-versed in maritime law," she admitted. "What happens when there's a crime at sea?"

The Captain pondered this question carefully, looked as though he didn't want to answer, and then responded. "We're obligated to follow up according to law in the country where the ship is registered. In this case, our ships are registered in Italy. Consequently, this crime will be reported to the Italian authorities. Also, since it's possible that Dr. O'Leary is the victim, it will be reported to the FBI."

"I thought it would be reported in the country that's the next port of call as well. Is that still the case, Captain?" Dottie inquired.

The Captain nodded. "Sometimes the local police from the upcoming port will become involved. For instance, if a passenger is attacked, hurt, or murdered and the next port is Athens, I, or my designee, may choose to report the crime to our registered agent or the local authorities in that country. Occasionally, there have been cases where the Athens police have arrested crewmembers or passengers they believe committed the crime, but usually, they choose not to be involved." He fiddled with his fork, played with his napkin, and continued. "If they do become involved, these types of investigations usually go nowhere." Mic thought Captain Wodensen seemed embarrassed or at least didn't want to discuss this subject.

"So, how does the FBI work in a situation like this?" Mic pressed the Captain. He'd averted his eyes and she knew he wasn't a willing participant in the conversation.

The Captain hesitated a moment, folded his hands and said, "If the cruise ship returns to a US port, the FBI will wait at the port and board the ship at the end of the cruise. In this case, The Regina Mediterranean ends her cruise in Rome. Generally, the FBI doesn't fly agents to foreign ports. In my opinion, they have a poor record in investigating cruise crimes that occur outside of their country, even if it involves a US citizen."

"He's absolutely correct," Senator Bostitch said as he entered the dining room. He smiled a greeting to all of them. "Historically, that's been a correct statement. But, things have changed. We've looked at this in Congress in recent years because of the number of families who've reported missing passengers or American citizens who'd reported a crime such as a mugging, rape, or whatever… in essence any kind of suspicious behavior. We found that crimes were rarely reported to us. Congress studied these issues in a series of hearings and in 2010, the President signed the Cruise Vessel Security and Safety Act that requires all crimes on cruise ships be reported. Now all cruise ships calling in US ports must report crimes to the FBI."

Michaela smiled at Senator Bostitch and said, "That was a timely entry. Of course, The Regina Mediterranean doesn't call in any US ports."

Senator Bostitch nodded and said, "That's true. However, Captain Wodensen and I have agreed we'll call the FBI if we determine that it is indeed Dr. James O'Leary who's missing and presumed overboard."

Mic nodded her head in agreement. "That would certainly be the prudent thing to do. Don't you agree,

Dottie?" She asked as she saw a flicker of anger pass over her friend's face.

Dottie reached for her purse, pulled out a tissue, and said in a defensive voice. "Not entirely. Cruise ships are about an escape from the world, an escape from bills, traffic, work, and crime. We sell a week of the perfect life, don't we, Captain Wodensen?" She asked as she carefully looked at him.

"Yes, Countess, this is our goal. We want to offer our passengers a perfect week - a wonderful memory," he said dutifully. "Often, it's the adventure of a lifetime. Unfortunately, many times crime does occur. There are rapes, muggings, or thefts, and the crimes may be caused by the passenger. Generally because of too much alcohol."

"But it's not always like that, Countess," Senator Bostitch said. "Unfortunately, in the past five years, the FBI has opened up more than three hundred cases of crimes committed at sea. At least twenty-eight people have gone missing and simply vanished. One was a young woman who disappeared from a cruise in route to Alaska. Do either of you remember the story?"

"I believe I do," Dottie said in a resigned voice. "This was one of the cases that was an impetus for Congress to develop the Maritime legislation. Isn't this the case where the young woman disappeared on her second day aboard and her belongings were put in a locker where they disappeared?"

The Senator nodded and continued, "Yeah, that's the story, although there's more to it. The young woman's father spent thousands and thousands of dollars on investigators and police to find out what happened to his daughter. To this day, we still don't know."

A chill moved up Michaela's spine. "That's a terrible story," she admitted. "It would be horrible if that happened to someone I loved. Was there any evidence at all?"

"Very little, if any," Dottie reported. "The young woman's cabin was cleaned and re-boarded the very same day. Any possibility of evidence was destroyed."

Captain Wodensen stood and said, "If you'll excuse me, I need to go check on the muster so we can be sure that Dr. O'Leary is indeed the person who went overboard." He paused for a second and looked at Senator Bostitch and Countess Borghase. "I assure you both that everything that can be done will be done, and is being done, to determine if a crime has indeed occurred. You'll have my utmost cooperation in settling this."

Dottie smiled and said, "I'm positive of that. Thank you, Captain."

"Thank you. I'll be off to my duties," he said with a stiff bow and then left.

"Well," Michaela said as she picked up her water glass. "He seems quite concerned. And maybe a bit defensive about this," she observed.

Dottie nodded. "He does, and he should be. I'm defensive about this as I have a substantial financial stake in the cruise line. We do not look favorably on any criminal activities aboard ship. The mindset is that the Captain should be in control of his vessel at all times." She shook her head and continued, "This won't be good for him. We need to solve this crime before we return to Rome."

"Let's do it, then," Mic said. "As soon as they determine the identity of the man overboard, and if it's Dr. O'Leary, can you manage to have the stateroom marked as a crime scene?"

Dottie nodded. "Not a problem. In fact, it's already done."

Mic smiled tightly and said, "Good." She turned to Senator Bostitch and asked, "What do you have for us, Senator? Have you been able to find the answers to the questions we asked you?" Mic turned her head to look behind. Her neck felt hot and flushed. She was positive someone was staring a hole in her back. She didn't see the young man gaping at her from behind a tall potted palm a short distance away.

Senator Bostitch's gray eyes were deep pools of concern. "Yeah, I have a couple of things to tell you. In fact, I've asked Dr. Pennington to join us for a bit. He's upset but has managed to speak to several of his colleagues about his concerns with Blake Pharmaceutical and, truthfully ladies, I'm concerned."

Chapter 18

Snake was tired of hanging out in the ship's bars looking for Vadim. He'd gotten the word on their new packages just a few minutes ago. The final victims and their timetable needed to speed up. The murders had to happen tomorrow or the next day. It would be too late when they arrived in Athens. He had to find Vadim.

He took his swizzle stick and stirred his drink of the day. It tasted like crap. It was some sort of coconut and pineapple concoction that kind of turned his stomach. He reached for his cell phone, put in his security passcode, and dialed Vadim. There was no answer. He cursed, picked up his drink, and decided to check out the public areas of the ship.

He walked into the Schooner Bar on deck eight and was sure a heavy-set man was Vadim. He walked up behind him, leaned over and examined the man closely. After a long inspection, Snake figured it wasn't Vadim and took a seat at a table on the aft side of the ship. He watched women and kids frolic in one of the ship's many public swimming pools. It was a beautiful day to be on a cruise ship. The Mediterranean Sea sparkled in the bright sunlight and the sound of a reggae band improved his spirits. He closed his eyes and considered a nap, but finished his drink before falling asleep.

He awakened when someone kicked his leg.

"Hey man, what's up?" Vadim stood at his table with sunglasses, wig and walking stick.

Snake shook his head and snarled, "You'd better not sneak up on me like that again, Vadim. Next time I might hurt you."

Vadim shook his head and laughed. "I'm scared shitless." He pulled his chair out and pretended to make polite conversation. "Are you enjoying your cruise?"

Snake took off his sunglasses and stared at his accomplice. Once again, he would have never recognized the Russian. Vadim face showed no scars or pockmarks. He looked entirely different than he normally did. He noted Vadim's knife glistening on the side of the walking cane.

"Stop staring, asshole," Vadim snarled at him.

Snake shook his head and said, "Nice wig. I'm not sure I would've recognized you if it wasn't for that ugly telltale nose that you've coated in white makeup."

Vadim gritted his teeth and blew smoke on him. "I don't care whether you recognize me or not, it's the others I'm worried about." He paused for a moment and then asked, "What's up? You have news?"

"Man, you gotta give me a way to contact you. We've got work to do and I don't know how to find you. Where the hell are you staying?" Vadim shrugged his shoulders. "I'm here and there, pretty much everywhere. I've spent most of this morning trying to find a place to hide, and a place to sleep if ship security turns up the heat. Plus, I've got a bad headache from last night," he admitted with a grin.

Snake had a visceral reaction. "You think they're looking for you?" He laughed and said sarcastically, "How could they not be?"

Vadim drew back his head and laughed. "Hell, yeah, they're looking for me, and they're looking for you, too. They got two murders on the ship so you know they're looking for somebody, right?"

Snake nodded, "I suppose so," he said as his eyes cut across the ship to a dark headed, petite woman with a huge dog on a leash. Recognition blew through him.

"Look over there, Vadim. You know that lady, the one with the big dog?" Snake's face was filled with hate.

Vadim glanced toward Michaela, shook his head and said, "Hell, no, why should I?" He watched anger spread over Snake's face. He paused a moment, "Apparently you do."

Snake continued to stare as he clenched his fists together and opened and closed his hands until the eyes of the snake tattoo seemed to spit fire.

Vadim looked at him and laughed, "Well, you know her. Looks like she must've pissed in your Cheerios," he said with a grin. "What happened? Did she kick your ass or something?" he asked with a smirk.

Snake's face was suffused with anger, "That bitch is a retired police detective and, yeah, she got in my way plenty. I'm gonna kill her - just as soon as I can," he snarled.

Vadim was impressed. "What the hell did she do to you? Did she beat you up? Outsmart you, you moron dumbass?" he said with a laugh.

Snake was furious. He gripped the side of the table and kicked over an empty chair. "Shut the hell up, Vadim. You don't know nothing. Nothing about her or me. Change the damned subject."

Vadim ignored Snake's hostility and continued to watch the woman. She took off her beach cover-up, slathered suntan lotion all over her body and put on a sun hat. There was something vaguely familiar about her. He just didn't know what it was.

"Who is she again? She looks vaguely familiar to me, too." he said.

Snake stared at Michaela. He watched her every move as his eyes glittered with hate. "She's a retired homicide detective from Richmond, Virginia. That's her dog, a retired police dog, and he's gettin' a bullet in his head as soon as I can manage it."

Vadim watched the woman a few more minutes and decided he didn't know her. He'd never been to Richmond, so he decided to tease Snake a little more. "Okay, dude. What did the woman do to you that's got your jocks all in a wad? Did she get the best of you?"

Snake ignored Vadim, but his anger escalated. He continued to watch Michaela. The dog lay in the shade near her lounge chair. "What the hell is that bitch doing on this cruise ship? That's just too coincidental," he thought. Snake's paranoia escalated. He knew he had to get it under control or he'd make some serious errors.

Vadim was bored. He decided his best tactic was to keep moving. He turned to Snake and kicked his chair. "Get over it, asshole. You can take care of her later. I'll even help you - but, first things first."

Snake nodded and his eyes left Michaela. Vadim was right. He'd tend to her later. This was the third time their lives had crossed so he was certain there would be another time, and he'd whack her then. He turned to Vadim, back on track. "Yeah, you're right. We've got some more work, just as I said, a couple more hits maybe. I got a message from our handler today."

Vadim's eyes lit up, as blue as the sea with the contact lenses that were part of his disguise. "Okay. Who, what, and when?" he asked non-committedly as his fingers drummed the table. He needed a drink. That'd take good care of his headache. He looked around for the waiter. "What the hell were you drinking with a damned umbrella in it, Snake Man? It looks like some pussy drink."

Snake's blood pressure raced and he gritted his teeth. He was in no mood for this, but he decided to let the insult go. "It's some sweet coconut thing. I had a free drink ticket I won at bingo this morning so I got me the drink of the day. It's as simple as that.

So, you got us more work? Vadim said softly as he cradled his hands around his cold glass. "What's the rate of pay?" he asked greedily as he pictured a home in the Caribbean and a bunch of half-naked women dancing around him.

Snake grinned, "Gotta double package, double pay for the next two. Our risk goes up since we're confined on this tub. We're gonna be rich," he said with an evil grin.

Vadim started to speak, but Snake cut him off as his hand sliced through the air. "Here comes the waiter," he said.

Snake ordered a beer for himself and a vodka on the rocks for Vadim. The waiter looked at him and smiled, "You not like?" he asked as he pointed to the glass?

Snake grinned and said, "it's okay. One is enough. Too sweet for me."

The waiter laughed and picked up his empty glass.

When the waiter was out of earshot, Vadim said "So, how big is this guy? Can one of us do it?"

Snake sat back in his chair and put his hands behind his head, "He's a good size, dude. I think he's probably close to six feet, probably weighs a hundred and eighty pounds or so. Got silver hair....He looks like a politician."

"What the hell does that mean?" Vadim asked. All the politicians in New Orleans looked different - all were smug, self-serving, crooked assholes.

Hell, I don't know," Snake said in an irritated voice. "He looks like the kind that would kiss a bunch of babies and kiss a bunch of ass to get what he wanted." he said. "He's tall and clean-cut." He reached into his pocket and pulled out his phone and pushed it toward the Russian. "Here, take a good look."

Vadim studied the face with a noncommittal look. "Okay, I got it," he said as he shoved the phone across the table to Snake.

"When do we strike?"

"I've got his stateroom number. He's traveling alone, a guest of Blake Pharmaceutical and I heard he's meeting them tonight for dinner. Apparently he's pissed about the guy overboard. My sources tell me he plans to confront them tonight.

"Well, in that case, I don't think he'll make it to dinner," Vadim said in a soft voice.

Snake nodded and grabbed his cold beer from the waiter who approached with their drinks. Vadim grabbed his vodka. He said to Snake, "Put this on your ship charge card. I don't want to use the safe cabin card. As far as the ship knows, it's empty."

Snake pulled his ship charge card from his pocket and asked the waiter for another beer.

When the waiter was out of earshot, Vadim said, "So you think one of us can do it?"

"Yeah, if we use the element of surprise." Snake said. "He's a normal-sized man, probably in his fifties. He's in pretty good shape, as you saw from his picture, but if we surprise him, one of us can do it."

"Do you have his stateroom number?"

"Yeah. He's up there with the rich people. On the ritzy floor. Blake Pharmaceutical is paying for his cruise."

Vadim cupped his drink with his hands and said, "I'll do it. Alone. I hate politicians and I'm itching for a good kill."

Snake stared at the Russian and said, "Okay. Don't screw it up. We've only got one chance."

Vadim looked at Snake and took a long drink of his vodka. He bent over until he was about an inch from Snake's face and said, "I never mess shit up. He won't make it to dinner tonight." Vadim finished his drink and slammed his glass on the table, got up and left.

Snake watched him depart. "That's one crazy son-of-a-bitch," he thought.

Chapter 19

Grady flattened his body against the side of the wall as Michaela and Dottie left the dining room and walked past him. It wasn't time for Michaela to see him, but that would happen soon. He'd set an extensive plan in place and nothing, no one could interfere with it. Michaela was his true love. She was his. She was his obsession, his prize, his fixation. She was his Juliet and he was her Romeo. Michaela was his Mary Lamb, his Ygritte, and his femme Nikitia. He was her Michael. Only, they would never be star-struck lovers. They would be lovers. The stars would align for them. Michaela would pledge herself to him in Athens. He'd clip her wings. He knew that. They would align soon. But there were things he must do first. Details that must be attended to.

He felt her chemistry as it pulled him toward her. She wanted him. The momentum of desire, the ache was severe. The sense of fate was astronomical and he could hardly contain himself he wanted her so badly. His body was charged with love. He wanted to race after her. But, he knew he must be patient. He panted until his heart rate settled. He had many things to do before he could be with his love. And, he must do them.

Their love union in Athens had taken years to plan. He would not ruin it now. Their meeting, their passion, and sojourn must come first. No one, or nothing, would get in their way. He gave her one last glimpse as he melted into the carved column of the dining room wall. As he stared at the ceiling, his mind conjured up thousands of images of Michaela, and how they'd spend the next few days.

Chapter 20

High Tea in the dining room was in full swing when Michaela and Dottie entered through the leaded glass double doors. There was a marvelous array of scones and desserts and more kinds of gourmet tea than Michaela knew existed. A beautiful young woman played the harp in the background.

"Oh, there's Senator Bostitch," Dottie observed. "Over there by the window, halfway back on the port side."

Michaela, Angel at her side on his leash, looked over just as Senator Bostitch waved at them. As the two ladies wandered his way, Michaela again appreciated what a handsome man the Senator was. She wondered if he had a wife back in Maryland. She smiled as he held her chair out for her.

"Good afternoon, Michaela and Countess Borghase," he said. "I must say, I haven't been to High Tea anywhere other than the Waldorf Astoria in New York, and this looks even better than that."

Dottie, who looked her usual perfect self, smiled at him, and said, "Senator, High Tea is my favorite part of the cruise. I'm delighted you could join us."

"Dottie, could I get you some Earl Grey, I'll pick us up a plate of goodies and then we'll start our conversation?" Michaela offered.

Dottie nodded and said, "That turquoise silk pants suit becomes you, Michaela." She gave her an admiring look and continued, "The jewelry is perfect as well. I suppose I should leave the turquoise necklace to you as well," she said with a flick of her hand.

"Thanks, Dottie," Mic smiled at her. "We both know you have excellent taste and yes, I do love the outfit." She turned to the Senator and asked, "Senator Bostitch, can I get you something? A scone or a pastry?"

Senator Bostitch looked as though he couldn't make up his mind, but finally said, "Yeah, I'd love some of those cream puffs. I'm going to the gym afterwards so I can work it off, the cream puff… and a lot of frustration," he added.

Mic looked down at Angel and said, "Stay, Angel. I'll bring you something good, I promise," Mic said as she ruffled the dog's fur.

Angel looked up at Dottie who nodded her head and said, "Oh, okay Angel. You win!" She opened her pearl handled pocketbook, took out a sealed plastic bag, opened it, and gave Angel a huge piece of duck jerky. Angel smiled up at her and licked her hand.

Dottie looked across the table at the Senator. "Angel's pretty spoiled, but I've got to say, he's saved our lives more times than I can count," she said as she gave the dog an affectionate smile.

The Senator watched Angel move to the side of the table and contently chew his jerky. "He's a big guy and I'm sure he could put the hurtin' on a lot of people. Is he a retired police dog?"

"That he is," Dottie said proudly. "He was Mic's partner and the first time he saved her life he took a bullet meant for her. The RPD retired him and he's lived with Mic ever since. She rarely, if ever, leaves him alone."

Senator Bostitch nodded and said, "Yeah. Those animals are amazing. I'm sure you know I'm active in the Canines for Warriors program. I think it's one of the best programs we have out there for our vets."

"I agree, Senator," Dottie said. "I totally agree. I'm a sponsor of the program in the US and a similar program we have in Italy."

Senator Bostitch nodded just as Mic appeared with a plate full of pastries. A waiter followed with two cups and a hot pot.

"That looks yummy," Dottie declared as she surveyed the petit fours, cream puffs, lemon triangles, and scones. "What did I miss?" Mic asked.

"Nothing really," Senator Bostitch said as he reached for a cream puff. "The Countess and I were discussing the Canines for Warriors program."

Mic nodded and smiled. "One of my favorite programs," she admitted. "Have you had a chance to talk with the higher ups at Blake Pharmaceutical?"

A frown flickered across the Senator's face and he said, "I have. I've spoken to several of their vice presidents in the last few hours. This evening, I'll be having dinner with executive staff and several of their Board of Director members, in addition to the pharmaceutical company's CEO."

"So, what did they say?" Dottie asked sharply. "Did they say anything about the disappearance/murder of Dr. James O'Leary?" Dottie gave the Senator a keen look and watched him closely.

"Yeah, they did. They said it was most unfortunate and agreed that Dr. O'Leary was one of the most learned and respected psychiatrists in the US. They think he'll be greatly missed." The Senator paused and said, "In fact, they plan to start an endowed chair in his name at the University of Maryland."

Dottie snorted. "I just bet they did," she said sarcastically. "That's why they killed him off."

"What do they have to say about the safety of Quelpro, the drug in question?" Mic asked. "Do they admit the drug has problems?"

Peter Bostitch shook his head and said, "It's their opinion, and this is official, that Quelpro is a safe and useful drug for the treatment of severe depression. They believe the few side effects of the drug are worth its efficacy. They have no intention of pulling the drug from the market."

Michaela wasn't surprised to hear this, but Dottie was angry. "Who the hell do they think they are? It sounded to me when we spoke to Ian Pennington, that Quelpro has significant issues with safety." She stared at Mic and the Senator, buttered a scone, and put it on her plate before continuing. "Why, Ian and James had both reported deaths of a couple of their patients who had taken Quelpro. They considered the mortality rate extraordinary. What other information do they need?"

Bostitch took a deep breath and said, "Countess, when a drug company recalls a pharmaceutical, it cost millions and millions of dollars. Certainly, Blake Pharmaceutical had motive to kill Dr. O'Leary. I've heard that to remove Quelpro from the market simply for further testing would cost them considerable money."

Dottie nodded at the Senator and asked, "What does it take to remove the drug from the market?"

"Work. It takes work and a lot of wheeling and dealing, to be honest," the Senator said in a soft voice. "It also requires strong, independent research data that is statistically sound and suggests the drug is unsafe. Of course," he said, "we lost the data, or at least the opportunity to present the data when Dr. Leary was unavailable."

"Surely that data can be reworked," Michaela objected. "There are other researchers who can provide a compelling argument that speaks to Quelpro's lack of safety."

Senator Bostitch nodded. "Indeed there are, and we'll find them," he assured her.

"I'd call that a bingo for them," Dottie said in an irritated voice. "I hate this big business where they don't give a rats ass about the individual person. If the drug's not safe, why not test it for six more months? It's not rocket science."

Senator Bostitch nodded patiently and said, "That's millions of dollars in costs for Blake Pharmaceutical, both in the cost to retest, the lost revenue currently being received, and the cost of putting the drug back through the FDA."

Mic chewed her scone thoughtfully as she considered the situation. "What's your opinion on this, Senator Bostitch? Do you think Quelpro should be recalled and checked for safety reasons?" she asked as she carefully looked at him.

Bostitch was quiet for a moment and then said, "I… I do believe it should be recalled for further testing. I also recommend it be taken off the market during that interim."

Michaela locked eyes with him and asked, "Is this what you discussed with the Blake Pharmaceutical management earlier today?"

He nodded and said, "Yes, it is."

"And…" Dottie snapped, her blue eyes blazing, "What did they say?"

Bostitch shrugged his shoulders. "They respectfully disagreed and said they weren't prepared to do that. They stand behind their research and believe the drug is safe and that it has helped millions of people."

"And you insisted. How did they take that?" Mic asked as she locked eyes with the Senator.

Bostitch grinned and shook his head. "Not well at all. I told them I planned to speak to the administrator of the Federal Drug Administration when I return from the cruise and that I plan to ask them to intervene. I also related to them I would personally act as an intermediary between Blake Pharmaceutical and the FDA – which should work in their favor, as I can speed up the process."

Mic ran her fingers through her dark curls and said, "That sounds like a great compromise to me. Isn't a lot of the expense because of the federal red tape and the time it takes to test these drugs? I think to have you as a congressional envoy, so to speak, would encourage them."

"I hope you're right," the Senator said with a baleful smile. "I honestly don't think I made friends with any of them today. But, ladies, that's my job as a physician and a United States Senator. I intend to do whatever is in my power to initiate a recall of Quelpro."

"Well, Senator, you've been a lot nicer than I'd be," Dottie said, her blue eyes glittering in the sunlight. "I think they should all go to jail for murder."

Senator Bostitch laughed. "I think that as well, Countess, but I'd like to be effective and cut through some of their red tape. I've long been critical of the way some pharmaceutical companies market," he admitted.

"How's that?" Mic asked. "I'm not sure I understand."

Senator Bostitch sighed deeply and said, "Oftentimes, the drug houses work hard to recruit or 'buy' physicians to sell their product. I know this because, as you know, I'm a physician."

"Buy? How in the world do pharmaceutical companies 'buy' medical doctors?" Dottie exclaimed. "What do you mean?"

Bostitch cleared his throat and continued, "Well, I've seen guys I went to medical school with make thousands and sometimes even millions of dollars touting the efficacy of a certain drug. Many of these physicians are on the pharmaceutical company's payroll and everywhere they go, they pump the drug – advocate the benefit of whatever drug they represent at meetings, at medical conferences and in their local medical group."

"That's horrible, and unethical," Dottie gasped. "It's like they're medical prostitutes." She paused and sighed. "It's even worse than that. They prostitute themselves, their education, and their patients. That's just wrong… particularly on a drug that most likely hasn't been independently tested," she said, her face flushed with anger.

Senator Bostitch nodded. "Yes, that's what it's like. And it's unfortunate. Lots of pharmaceutical companies set up endowed chairs in schools of medicine, which is the same as funding a faculty position. They set up these endowed chairs all over the United States as a conduit to get in and capture eminent physicians to market and advocate for their medicine. They also offer millions of dollars in research grants and incentives for physicians to test their products."

"That's more than lucrative for the docs, but it seems biased and certainly unethical." Dottie said as anger raced through her body. "I've always believed pharmaceutical research was independently done by independent researchers."

Senator Bostitch interrupted, "You're right. Often it is. These practices are not confined to the United States. This happens all over the world. I recently read a journal from the United Kingdom that said the Queen's former doctor called for an urgent public inquiry into drug firms' 'murky' practices. The Queen's physician warned that many medicines are less effective than originally believed. In fact, The Queen's doctor is part of a group of six eminent doctors who warn about the influence of pharmaceutical companies on drug prescribing. They claim that too often patients are given useless - and sometimes harmful - drugs that they often don't even need."

"Well," Dottie said as she shot Michaela a dirty look, "I've always believed that lots of pills are handed out that don't need to be." She paused and then continued with a sly smile. "I hardly ever take my pills."

Senator Bostitch frowned at Dottie and said, "That's not necessarily good, Countess. Many pills have great therapeutic results. You need to take them, or at least discuss it with your physician. It's never a good idea to stop taking your medicine cold turkey."

"Just as I've told her at least a hundred times," Michaela said as she gave Dottie a disdainful look.

"Take your medicine, Countess," the Senator urged. "Please take it."

Dottie nodded. "I'll think about it. Now, what were you saying about the National Health Service, the Queen's doctor?"

"Oh, yes, that's where we were before we digressed," Senator Bostitch said. "Anyway, the group believes drug companies currently develop medicines they can profit from, rather than those which are likely to be the most beneficial to patients. The same group has accused the National Health Service of not standing up to big pharmaceutical firms. So, you see ladies, it's not just in the United States. It's all over," Senator Bostitch warned. "It's corporate greed and it seems drugs have become more about making money than saving lives.

"This is a travesty… a nightmare," Dottie said loudly. "We have to do something about this, Michaela. This kind of crap affects everyone, and it's all over the world," Dottie continued with her blue eyes fixed on Mic.

Michaela nodded. "We will, Dottie. We'll find a way. I promise," Mic replied.

Bostitch nodded. "It's widespread. The drug companies give a couple of positions at X University in addition to two million dollars to study their drugs. Plus, they offer physicians a thousand dollars each time they mention the drug at a medical meeting. Don't you think it's possible that some of their research could be biased toward that particular drug?" he asked with a tight smile.

"Biased," Dottie said in a loud voice. "It's more than biased. It unethical. Most of all, it's just wrong."

Mic was concerned that Dottie had become too excited. "Calm down, Dottie. We're gonna handle this. With Senator Bostitch's help, we'll get to the bottom of all of the shenanigans." She turned to the Senator and said, "This is appalling, unacceptable, and totally unethical."

Bostitch nodded and said, "I agree That's specifically almost word for word, what I told the Blake Pharmaceutical people today."

Mic nodded as she carefully thought through the Senator's sticky situation. "What do you plan to say differently at dinner this evening?"

Senator Bostitch shrugged his shoulders and said, "Nothing really. I'll reiterate my position to their Board of Directors. I can be their best friend in a difficult situation or

I can tie Quelpro up forever in bureaucratic red tape. The choice is theirs."

Michaela took a bite of her pastry and paused, "If Quelpro, which is their most popular and most prescribed antidepressant, is recalled, how would that affect them?"

Senator Bostitch looked at her with approval. "It would significantly affect their bottom line and cast doubt on their research and development initiatives." He paused for a moment and added, "It would most likely affect any other drugs they have in the pipeline. Once the FDA has reason to look at a company, they can be quite tenacious," Senator Bostitch admitted.

"So what if it affects their bottom line," Dottie said angrily. "What about the patients who have died from taking this medication? Screw these people," she added as her blue eyes flashed angrily.

Michaela smiled. Sometimes she enjoyed Dottie when she was angry. "It seems to me that James O'Leary's research was extraordinarily detrimental to Quelpro's reputation. Ian led us to believe a number of psychiatrists were prepared to speak up this morning once the data was presented. Of course," she said sadly, "the data wasn't presented because Dr. O'Leary was no longer available to present it."

"That's true," Senator Bostitch said. "I was there at that meeting this morning and there were a lot of undertones about where James O'Leary was. A number of those psychiatrists were good friends, former students, and mentors. They'd have supported Dr. O'Leary."

"How did the meeting go?" Basically speaking," Mic asked as she reached for her tea.

Bostitch shrugged his shoulders. "Not well against Quelpro if that's what you mean. Ian presented his cases and concluded Quelpro was a strong factor in the mortality and morbidity of his patients. Mostly, everyone wondered where Dr. O'Leary was."

"Have you spoken up and expressed concern about the drug's safety?" Dottie asked Senator Bostitch.

Peter Bostitch nodded and said, "Yes, I have, but without James' evidence, they discounted my concerns. They always look for empirical evidence which Jamie had."

Dottie shook her head. "Okay, if I were working this crime in Richmond, Virginia, I'd say let's make a case and get concrete evidence," she said in a peevish voice.

Mic nodded, "Yeah, and I'm worried about the attack and murder of Dr. O'Leary. We need that evidence too. Of course, we have nobody who can validate a murder, at least not yet." She was quiet for a few moments as she considered the facts.

Senator Bostitch stood and said, "Thank you, ladies, for a delightful tea. I'll let you know how things go tonight at dinner."

Mic smiled and said, "Thank you for what you're doing, Peter. Be careful and stay safe," she warned.

Bostitch flashed his politician's smile and said, "I intend to. I'll see you later."

Chapter 21

Vadim sat at a small table in the rear of the Schooner Lounge, his thick hands clasped around his fourth tumbler of vodka. Who in the hell is that woman with the dog? I know I've seen her before. The fact that he couldn't identify her bothered him. Vadim never forgot a face. He continued to sip his drink as he watched the passengers come and go.

Tonight was a formal night aboard The Regina Mediterranean. Most passengers were in evening attire. Women sported long sequined dresses, statement jewelry, and elaborate stilettos, while the men looked GQ in suits and tuxedos. Again, loneliness engulfed Vadim. Anger and pain permeated his body as he imagined what it would be like to be aboard this cruise with his beautiful daughter and grandbaby. But oh no, hell no, he'd never share a cruise with the people he loved most in this world because they were dead. Dead at the hands of an incompetent female surgeon. He cursed to himself as anger wrenched through his heart. He signaled the waiter for another vodka, and continued to watch the crowd as they shuffled by. He saw a lovely young woman fall. He automatically rose to assist her, but several men beat him to it. He looked at her shoes and noticed they were probably over four inches tall. These women were crazy to wear shoes with those kinds of heels. But of course, his Ana had worn them as well… and she hadn't been crazy.

Several minutes later, Vadim checked his watch. He still had about thirty minutes before he had to show up at the Senator's stateroom. He'd assured Snake he could handle things alone. The truth was that he didn't want Snake getting in his way. He stared into his colorless drink, once again consumed by anger and sad memories. A feeling of rage overcame him. Vadim tried to shake the feeling, but he knew he'd never beat it. It was a feeling he'd encountered and learned to live with over and over for many years and he knew what would happen.

He signaled the waiter for his tab and charged his alcohol to Snake's stateroom. He smiled at the waiter, straightened his lapel pin, and walked slowly, with the use of a cane, out of the Schooner Bar to the main bank of elevators. He pushed the button for deck six. He exited the elevator mid-ship and took a right turn down a long corridor of staterooms. He stood in the shadow of the ship's laundry room and peered up and down the hall. Finally, after about ten minutes, he saw the tall, silver-haired Senator approach his stateroom door, reach in his pocket for his room key, and enter his room. Seconds later, the lock clicked into place.

Vadim scanned the hall and was pleased there was no one coming or going. He continued to hide in the space by the laundry room and waited another ten minutes. Then he moved near the Senator's door and pressed his ear to the wall. He heard the sound of running water.

Perfect. Just Perfect. This was gonna be a piece of cake. Vadim smiled to himself delighted with his good luck. He waited another minute as he anticipated his kill. He heard the shower shut off and waited another two minutes until he figured the Senator had toweled himself dry. No reason to deal with a slippery, wet body.

Several seconds later, Vadim picked the lock and slid quietly into the Senator's large stateroom. The bathroom door was half closed and he quickly moved to the other side of the door where he could watch the Senator's movements.

The bathroom was steamy from the Senator's shower. Vadim watched in the mirror as the Senator towel dried his hair. Vadim lunged through the bathroom door.

"What the…" Bostitch began, but he never finished his sentence. Those were his last words. His eyes were wide with shock as Vadim shot him an evil grin and showed him his brightly polished knife that flashed and shined in the bathroom light.

Minutes later, Vadim wiped the blood from his knife on a towel he dropped on the floor and left the room. He felt good. Really good. At least for a little while, he would no longer be angry at the world. Killing made him feel good. Completed. Sated. And that was that. Vadim was a new man and the good Senator Bostitch never knew what hit him.

Chapter 22

"Who told you this crap was supposed to make us feel better?" Dottie complained as she grimaced and swallowed her fruit juice concoction. "This stuff is vile. I'd prefer whiskey any day to this - or my sherry," she said as she offered Mic a pointed look.

Mic laughed and said, "Come on, Dottie, it's got all kinds of good stuff in it, pomegranates, kiwi, vitamins and minerals, an energy booster, and a few electrolytes." She cocked her head and continued, "What is it about you that you never want to do anything that's good for you or your body?"

Dottie glared at her. "What are you talking about? I do a lot that's good for my body. I go to the gym, walk three miles every day, and swim. I could flatten your ass any day. Besides, your health shakes are best described as hell shakes," she said and grimaced again as she took another sip.

Mic rolled her eyes, but didn't say anything. The two women sat in the shade under a canopy behind the pool, as far away from the band as they could get. "Just give yourself a break and do something for your digestive tract," Mic suggested. "All we've done for three days is eat."

Dottie tossed her head angrily, her silver white hair askew, and asked, "What makes you so sure this is good for us? If anything, I think it'll keep me on the toilet all night. It's some of the worst stuff you've ever given me," she moaned, "and honestly, you've given me some despicable concoctions in the name of good health over the years."

Michaela laughed again. "That's okay. Don't drink it. We'll switch to Irish whiskey after dinner. We aren't going out for dinner are we?" she asked with a hopeful look on her face.

"I never said that. I said we weren't dressing elaborately for dinner. It's formal night and everyone else is dressing up. I thought we'd go and eat at the Italian restaurant on deck nine," she said as she looked at Mic out of the corner of her eye.

Mic clamped her teeth. "I don't want to get dressed. I want to wear my pajamas and call room service. They've got a pretty good menu. Want to do that and work on the case?" she cajoled.

"Oh, Michaela. Why don't you want to go and eat Italian food?" Dottie asked heatedly as she waved her arms in the air. "The chef up there is excellent. You're aboard a ship, and when you're aboard, you eat like a savage, all the time! Everyone does. The chef was trained at the culinary school in Rome and his Italian sauces are world renowned." Dottie was practically begging Mic to go to dinner.

Mic shrugged her shoulders and said, "Why don't we just go up to the Lido deck? It's never too crowded there later in the evening."

Dottie's face fell in disappointment. "I hate eating up there. I feel like a mouse scurrying around in a food fight… everybody butts in line, and pushes in front of you… I hate that. I'd rather do room service," she said dismally.

For a moment, Mic felt guilty and said, "Okay, we'll eat at Angelo's. I've heard their food is good. Do we need reservations?"

Dottie gave Mic a sneaky look and said, "We already have them. For eight this evening," Dottie gloated as she pushed the remains of her health shake away. "I'm not drinking this." She examined her glass and held it up to the light. "Look at this stuff. It's turned into clumps of goo and it's probably gonna take a pick ax to get it out of the glass." She picked at the hardened fruit drink with her beautifully manicured fingernail. "This stuff is stuck like cement. Can you imagine what this looks like in your stomach?"

Mic shook her head and reached for the glass pitcher that held the health shake.

"Take that to your suite. You finish it. I'm gonna lay down for a while before I dress for dinner," she said in her tired, bossy voice. "Call me at 6:30 just in case I don't get up on my own. If I don't show up, it's because your health shake killed me," she moaned as her hand rubbed her stomach.

Mic stood, grabbed the shake, and said, "Okay, I'll call you at 6:30, pick you up at 7:45, and we'll walk up to Angelo's." She walked with Dottie to her room and watched her crawl into her king-size bed. "Get some rest, and Countess, if you'd drink your entire health shake, you'd be ready to walk the deck you'd be so energized," Mic scolded, a sly smile on her face.

Dottie frowned and said, "If I drank that entire hell shake, I'd be ready to walk the plank. You know better, Michaela. You're just like Cookie - she's always making me these damn health drinks at home and I pitch them in the garbage disposal the first chance I get."

Mic shook her head, "If you would listen to us, you'd probably feel a lot better," she said as she flashed a dour look at her.

Dottie sat straight up in bed. "If I listened to you and Cookie, I'd have died ten years ago and both of you know it. I'm eighty-two years old and I could probably beat either of you at just about anything," she said, a smirk on her face. "And, just how many times have I saved your life? Tell the truth."

Mic smiled and ignored her question. "Whatever you say, you tough old bird. I'm leaving. Get some rest I'll see you in a couple hours."

Dottie flipped over in bed, her back to Mic and said in a muffled voice, "Okay. Get out of here and let an old lady rest."

Mic shut the door of the Countess' suite and laughed. Dottie was right. At eighty-two years of age, she was amazing. She could bench press her weight and walk three miles without looking back. She swam miles in her pool every single day. She was in extraordinary shape for someone her age. But still, Mic worried about her. Dottie was her dear friend and like a grandmother to her. The Countess, Cookie, and Henry, Dottie's housekeeper and handyman, were the closest thing to family she had. Losing Dottie was going to be an awful thing. Why am I thinking such morbid thoughts? This day has been bad enough. She inserted her key into the slot and entered her stateroom. Everything appeared perfect. Angel followed her, but immediately alerted. He ran around the room, pawed at the floor, and circled the room repeatedly, pawing and sniffing everywhere. He whined to get into her closet.

"What's wrong, buddy?" Mic asked as she looked into his eyes. Angel on alert was a sight to see. His ears were back and his coat was thick. He bared his teeth and barked at the closet door.

Michaela opened her closet and stared into it. Her heart beat frantically, her stomach in a knot. Her clothes were ruined. Someone had taken a knife and ripped two of her evening gowns to shreds. Her heart burned in her chest and an overwhelming sense of dread permeated every pore of her body. She couldn't breathe. Who the hell has been in my stateroom and why have they destroyed my evening gowns?

Angel continued to circle the stateroom and sniff. Then he moved back and forth between the sliding glass door and the closet. "What is it, Angel? Did someone get in here through the patio?"

Angel barked and stood still. Michaela walked across the room and looked at the floor. She quickly spied a double-edged razor blade.

She looked down at Angel and said, "Well, I guess we found the weapon. She tested the lock on her door that led to the deck, walked across the room again, checked, and double locked her stateroom door.

Mic sat at her desk and patted Angel as she contemplated what to do. She waited for her pounding heart to settle down. As she sat there, she heard a soft tap on her door. She rose from the chair, looked out of the peek hole, and saw Sergio, her cabin steward.

She opened the door and smiled, "Sergio, how are you doing?"

Sergio, a handsome young man from Eastern Europe, smiled at her and said, "Miss Mic. I was going to ready your room for the evening, but I will come back when you go to dinner," he said with a broad smile. "Was your day good?"

Michaela gave him a bright smile and said, "Busy, how was your day?"

"The same," he said. "Do you need assistance with your room service order? I can take your order, and the Countess' order, down if you like."

Mic shook her head and said, "We've decided to eat at Anthony's upstairs," she said.

Sergio's handsome face lit up with pleasure. "Ah, Anthony's. That's very good," he said. "You will enjoy."

Mic nodded. "Sergio, have you been here all day?"

Sergio nodded. "Yes, Madame, since six this morning. I don't get off until ten o'clock this evening. Why, is something wrong?" he asked as a scowl appeared on his friendly face.

Michaela nodded. "Someone has been in my cabin. Have you seen anyone enter my stateroom?"

"No, but I have to clean the rooms around the corner so I could have missed something." A look of fear came on his face. "Did someone steal from you?" Sergio was visibly upset.

Mic knew that Sergio thought she'd accused him and that was far from what she was thinking. "Oh no, I haven't been robbed. But, someone entered my room and I certainly don't think it was you, Sergio. You can go for now. I'm going to call the ship's security. Thank you."

Sergio hesitated, "Is there anything else you need?"

Mic shook her head. "No, thank you but, by the way Sergio, the Countess is resting, so you don't need to go there right now."

Sergio nodded and moved down the hall. Mic knew she'd upset the young man.

Michaela opened her closet again and looked at her dresses hanging in shreds on their hangers. Tears jumped into her eyes. Whoever had done this was angry. Parts of the dresses had almost been reduced to strings. She felt hot tears rush into her eyes, but pushed them back. She pulled out her cell phone and took pictures of her dresses. Then she walked over and took a picture of the razor blade on the floor. She wished she could fingerprint the door. She returned to her desk, picked up the room phone, and dialed the number for security.

She paced the room waiting for security to appear, but they didn't. She decided to text pictures of her dresses and the razor blade to Slade. She knew he would probably catch the next plane and meet her in their next port of call. Michaela looked over at Angel who had curled up in his bed and was asleep. She lay across her bed. Ship security never showed up. Finally, she fell into a restless sleep.

Mic woke in a panic from a bad dream. She looked in her closet again and studied her shredded clothes. Her eyes wandered down to her shoes. Two shoes were missing. The same person who'd cut up the evening gowns had stolen two shoes. One shoe was a high heel that she used for dress, and the other was one of her favorite Nike tennis shoes. Michaela rubbed chill bumps from her arms and wished Slade were with her. Somehow, his presence always made bad things less bad and more tolerable.

Chapter 23

The ring of the phone next to her bed was shrill. Michaela jumped and grabbed it before it could pierce through the layers of her mind again. Her heart warmed at the voice on the other end, a half a world away.

"Mic, what the hell is going on? Are you okay?" She heard anger in Slade's voice.

Her voice quivered as she said, "Yeah, I'm fine. But I must admit, someone shredding my dresses into strings and stealing two of my shoes, has upset me. I have no idea who would've done that." Her heart raced as she relived the scene in her closet.

Slade was silent for a moment. "It's strange and it's also pretty sick. I'm sure someone on that ship wants to hurt you, Michaela," Slade said in a low voice as Mic's stomach raged and burned with stress. "Think back, who have you seen? Is there anyone you recognize?"

Mic picked at a loose thread on her bedspread. "No, not that I can think of. I'm in no way involved with the Blake Pharmaceutical stuff, but I think they probably know Dottie and I are concerned about it," she said in a tight voice. "But even so, that's no reason to come into my room, shred my clothing, and steal my shoes," she gulped. "That's something a crazy person would do!" Her eyes burned with unshed tears. "It's personal and very scary," she blurted.

Mic heard Slade sigh. "Unfortunately, I agree, Mic. It's someone who's angry with you. I want you to think back, replay the tapes in your head since you boarded, and call me if something comes up."

"I will, Slade. I promise," Mic said in a voice that wasn't her own. Then she realized how terribly frightened she was. Angel stood by her and looked into her face. He licked her hand. The dog could sense her anxiety.

"Okay. We'll work this out. We've been in scrapes worse than this," Slade assured her. "Tell the Countess that I'll meet you all at the next port. I'll arrange for a plane ticket. Where will you be when the boat stops again?

Mic chuckled as she pushed away her fear. "It's a ship, not a boat, Slade. We'll be in Athens in two days. At the port of Athens, which is Piraeus. It's only a short ride from the town to where the ship docks," she assured him.

Slate cursed softly and said, "A lot could happen in two days, Mic. I'm worried about you. Is there good security on board?"

"Now Slade," Mic said with all the confidence she could muster. "You know I'm a big girl and can take care of myself. Besides," she said with a short laugh, "I've got Angel here with me. He literally went crazy when we came into the room," she said as Angel looked up into her eyes. "He's standing here now."

"Yeah," Slade said impatiently. "I know Angel is about the best security anywhere but what about security on the ship?" He paused for a moment and repeated, "What about security on the ship?"

Michaela hesitated for a moment and said, "Well, they have security, but it's not exactly what you and I would consider security." She looked at her watch and said, "I called them two hours ago after I found my clothes ripped to shreds and my shoes stolen. They've yet to show up to check stuff out."

Slade cursed again, this time much louder. "Get Dottie to call the Captain. Get Dottie to call whoever the hell makes a difference on that damn ship." Mic could picture him balling up paper and throwing it at the wastebasket in his office.

"I will. I haven't told Dottie about my clothes or shoes yet. I'll go over there in a few minutes and tell her. We're on our way to dinner. Hopefully, she'll be able to get to the Captain."

"What the hell! Hopefully? Doesn't Dottie own the damn cruise line?" Slade asked angrily. "What kind of a tub are you floating in?"

Mic laughed again and attempted to relieve Slade's angst. "A very nice tub. You know the man overboard I texted you about? Anyway, there was also a murder in the casino the second night after we boarded. A passenger killed a blackjack dealer. So," she paused, "I'm telling you this because the Captain truly has been tied up."

Mic could visualize Slade pacing in front of the window in his office at the Richmond Police Department. For a second, she longed to be home, in Richmond, and not on the cruise of a lifetime.

"I don't give a damn how busy he is. He needs to hear from you and the Countess. Dottie should be able to pull all kinds of strings to get his attention," he said in an angry voice. Mic could visualize his blazing dark eyes and flushed face. She knew he'd be pushing back his hair that fell in his face.

"I'll tell her. She'll be devastated about my clothes and shoes. She'll get right on it. Besides," she paused, "I'll be fine, and it'll be great to see you, Slade, even though the situation isn't ideal," Mic whispered into the phone, as her heart accelerated in anticipation.

"I've missed you, Michaela," he said in a soft voice. "My life just isn't quite the same with you gone. Anyway, I want you to take every precaution. Please do whatever it takes," he urged.

Mic felt warm and fuzzy. "Well, you know, I really don't need clothes when I see you," she said softly and then was shocked she'd said it.

"What, what did you say, Mic?" Slade asked. "I didn't catch all of that."

Michaela laughed. She knew Slade had heard her. He just wanted her to say it again. "Nothing, I said I'd stay safe," she quipped.

"All right then," Slade said with a chuckle. "Is there anything else?"

Mic was silent for a moment. "No, but just so you know, Slade, security and safety on the high seas is very different from what we're used to. From what I've been told, crime is often ignored or goes unreported. There's really not much Dottie can do when there's no one to come," she lamented.

"Tell her anyway," he growled. "I'll be there as soon as I can. I don't want you and Dottie alone on this highly dangerous, cesspool of a luxury cruise ship," he said in a gruff voice. "Two murders isn't anything to dismiss, and some lunatic cutting up your clothes makes it worse."

"Really, Slade. The ship is excellent and so is the service. I think this cruise is just unusual, to say the least," Mic assured him, as she tried to lighten his mood.

"Unusual or not, I want you to go to the ship's Captain and get yourself a couple of firearms," he insisted. "I know you don't have one with you and I think you should and Dottie should carry one at all times. Plus, you need an extra for your cabin."

Michaela smiled to herself. She couldn't believe Slade thought she'd parted with her firearm. Her Glock was locked up in her safe, but she would carry it from now on and keep it on her night stand when she slept. Screw the tiny little evening bags. She was done with them.

"Don't worry, Slade. I've got my Glock and Dottie has her weapon as well. You know it would take an act of Congress for me to travel without a gun. Dottie got special permission for us to bring them on the ship."

Michaela could hear Slade's sigh of relief. "That's good to hear," he said in a relieved voice. "I still think you should go to the Captain and get each of you a second weapon. I'm sure they have a firearms cache on the ship in case of an emergency."

"Yeah, they do. Okay," Michaela agreed. "I'll do that and both of us will carry a weapon with us," she promised.

"Good," Slade sounded relieved.

"Also, Slade, if there's any surveillance equipment Big Dawg at RPD could recommend, will you bring it?" Michaela queried. "And some basic forensic gear. Anything you can slip on the plane. All I have here are baggies and gloves. I would love to collect a few fingerprints," she said wistfully.

"Okay, consider it done. I'll bring whatever the crime scene boys will give me, and whatever I can carry on the plane. If, I can't get everything I want, I'll contact the authorities in Athens. Of course, I have no way to negotiate this. Perhaps you could check with Dottie about that."

Michaela smiled to herself. She really cared about this man. "Ah, so admit you don't speak Greek?" She said with a smile in her voice. She hoped she wasn't going to be sorry.

She'd played this love game before with the handsome, Cajun detective, Slade McKane, and it had ended badly.

"Will do. I love you. Stay safe, keep in touch, and tell Dottie to make arrangements with the ship to let me aboard," Slade said in a low voice.

"Done," Mic said. "Gotta go. The Countess is beating down my door. I'll call you later," she promised as she hung up the phone.

Chapter 24

Mic opened her door to a furiously irate, beet-faced Dottie. "Who in the hell have you been talking to?" She growled. "We're gonna be late for dinner," she continued in a grouchy voice.

"I've been talking to Slade. Something's come up and I think we'll need his help…" she began.

"Oh, for heaven sakes, what's come up?" Dottie grumped. "Can't you stay away from him for six weeks?" she asked as she fixed her stormy eyes on Mic. Her fingernail clicked irritably on Michaela's door.

Mic shook her head. In truth, Dottie was a little… maybe a lot… jealous of Slade. "It's not that, Dottie," she pleaded. "Come over here. Someone's been in my room."

"In your room? Who's been in your room?" she asked as her blue eyes flashed with anger.

Michaela shrugged her shoulders, a concerned look on her face. "I don't know. Let me show you. It'll be a lot easier to show than to describe. Then, we'll go to dinner," she promised.

"Did you call ship security?" Dottie asked in a matter-of-fact voice as she eased her body into Michaela's stateroom easy chair.

Michaela nodded and rolled her eyes. "Yeah, I did, but they never showed up," she said, her voice a bit defensive. "Just sit down and stay there," Mic motioned toward the chair.

"Oh, all right," Dottie snapped as she crossed her long, elegantly clad legs. "It better be good cuz I'm starving to death."

Mic ignored her attitude and said, "When we came back from meeting with Senator Bostitch, Angel went nuts and sniffed all around the stateroom. He went crazy pawing and whining at my closet door. Then, after we looked in the closet, we found a razor blade on the floor. Look what I found," she said as she held her closet door wide open for Dottie to inspect.

"Oh my God, someone cut up your clothes!" Dottie said, her voice a tiny squeak, as she paled under her makeup. Her blazing blue eyes had turned into pools of dark anger. "Who in the world would come in here and slice up your clothes?" she asked in a tight, irritated voice. She paused a moment with wide-open eyes and then added, "That's a bit scary if you ask me."

Mic shrugged her shoulders. "I've no idea, but there's obviously someone on this ship who's pretty mad at me. The thing is, I've no idea who in the world it could be," she said ominously. "And, that's the part that really bothers me," she admitted in a low voice.

Dottie forgot about her hunger and sank deeper into the chair as she processed the destruction of Mic's clothing. "Oh my God, Michaela, This is most alarming! And you say you called security and they didn't show up?"

Mic nodded. "That's true. I called, but they never came."

"Pass me the damn phone. I'll take care of that right now," Dottie said in her Countess voice.

Several moments later, there was a sharp knock on Michaela's stateroom door. Mic answered it and saw two men, tough-looking guys with faces carved in stone. Both carried concealed pistols and sported body armor.

One of the men smiled briefly when he recognized Dottie. He stood up straighter, "How can we help you, Countess Borghase?" he asked in thickly accented English.

Dottie introduced Michaela, "Someone came into my granddaughter's room while we were out. Look, the man cut up her clothes. Look at this," Dottie ordered as she jerked Michaela's closet door open.

The two men gawked at Michaela's sliced up clothes. Finally, the security chief said, "When did you notice this, Madame?"

"On return to my room several hours ago," Mic said clearly. "I called security several times, but no one came," she said, her voice tight.

The second security officer gawked at her and said, "It looks as though someone aboard the ship doesn't like you, Madame. Perhaps a spurned lover from United States?" The man grinned and gave her an amused look.

Mic felt anger as the heat worked its way up her body. She was furious, shook her head, and clamped her mouth shut. She remained silent and decided not to honor the man's suggestion with a response.

Dottie stood, and even though she had shrunk a little in her old age, she was still remarkably straight and tall. Her blue eyes froze on the man. "What did you say?" she demanded as Mic saw her clench and unclench her fist.

Uh oh, gotta intervene. Michaela realized. She knew Dottie was about a nanosecond from punching the male chauvinist in the face. She jumped into the conversation. "No, absolutely not. I'm traveling with the Countess. We've met several people on board, but no one who wishes to harm me," she assured the man.

The officer gave her a thin, unconvincing smile. "Really? How can you be so sure?" he asked in an officious manner.

"I have offended no one on board," she said in a matter-of-fact voice, "and I want you to understand that." She paused for a second as the man's face hardened and a smirk appeared. She asked, "Is that clear?"

The man nodded. "I understand, Madame. However, you have most likely spurned someone's attention. Someone from one of the bars or anywhere else on board. Perhaps after a glass or two of champagne." He suggested and gloated with a sardonic smile.

Mic shook her head furiously. "I have not been in a bar after dark. There is no one."

The senior security official looked at his partner. "I'll file a report and will let the Captain know what has happened," he said as he looked at Michaela and Dottie.

"Could you take some pictures?" Mic asked. "As a part of the report." She hoped her voice hadn't sounded too sarcastic.

The man nodded, "Of course, Madame. It looks as though you were on your way to dinner. We'll take care of this once you're out of your stateroom."

Michaela shook her head. "No, no gather your evidence now. The Countess and I will watch you. It shouldn't take long and I'm sure we can delay our reservation, can't we Countess?" She asked as she turned to Dottie with a raised eyebrow, her eyes green and glistening with anger.

"Absolutely. They'll take us anytime," she assured Michaela. "But I'm going to call the Captain and have him come here as well. In my estimation, this is serious and worth the bother," she said directly to the security guard.

The security official nodded and said, "Please, do call the Captain. I know he's been tied up, but may be free now,"

Dottie called the front desk and requested the Captain's presence in Michaela's suite. "Sit down, Michaela. He'll be right up and I'm sure the men will wait. It won't be long," she said as she stared at the security officers.

Michaela smiled at Dottie and said, "Certainly, grandmother," and laughed. Dottie often referred to Michaela as her granddaughter in situations like this. It just seemed an easier way to explain their relationship.

"Of course. We'll stay here until the Captain arrives. I need an update from him anyway about a bunch of stuff."

"Of course, Grandmother," Mic teased again, her green eyes flashed with fun. "Whatever you say," she said happily.

Chapter 25

The man lay in his bed on lower deck four, just one deck up from the bilge. He fingered the strips of fabric. They were soft and beautiful… just like the woman who'd worn them. He imagined the fabric strips rubbing against her body and his spine tingled with excitement. And now they were his. His forever and no one would ever know, he thought as he ran his other hand through his dirty-blond hair.

The man raised the fabric strips to his nose and smelled them. He laid back, his head on his pillow, content as he inhaled in the scent of Michaela McPherson. He remembered the same scent from his recent visit to her stateroom. The same scent he remembered from the few times he'd entered her office at Biddy McPherson's, Mic's restaurant and bar in downtown Richmond. He continued to stroke the fabric as he reminisced about his former boss. He'd heard she was going abroad from one of the busboys at the restaurant and he'd decided to book passage on the same ship. He paid for his ticket with money his grandmother had left him. Of course, it wasn't nearly enough money. He'd taken care of the old bitch for two years. Two years of his life and all he got was her twenty-five thousand dollar life insurance policy. He became angry and pushed the memory from his mind. He wanted to be alone with Michaela but for now, the strips of fabric would have to do.

He remembered the night of the ice storm when he'd helped her to her car. It had been at least four winters ago. The two of them were the last to leave Biddy's where he was working as a busboy and dishwasher. He'd seen her slip on the ice and had come to her aid, as she lay sprawled on her back near her SUV. He'd helped her up and into her car. She'd been grateful, but that damn huge dog of hers had growled at him.

That was the night he'd told her that he loved her. Michaela had laughed at him and assured him she was much too old for a young guy like him. She'd been nice about it, but it had pissed him off. He was a man and just as big and handsome as that damn cop she sometimes dated, someone named Slade or something... No one at the restaurant understood their relationship. It was a joke among many of the wait staff. Slade and Michaela were on again, then off, and then on again. He hated the tall, Cajun cop. He was obnoxious and a smart aleck. Slade certainly wasn't good enough for Michaela. The only man good enough for Michaela was him. And she needed to understand that.

His thoughts returned to the three times they'd been together. He'd dreamed about them and relived them as he stroked the fabric from her dresses. He remembered the many times he'd peered into her windows watching her cook gourmet meals in her beautiful kitchen and entertain her guests. He always knew that one day he'd be seated at her large dining room table. He'd be cutting the prime rib – not that stupid Slade McKane. Just the memory of the Cajun cop boiled his blood. He clenched his fists and shook them at the ceiling. He was sure he saw McKane looking down at him. He closed his eyes tightly to blot out the memory. When he opened them, Slade was gone.

He continued to think about Michaela. Perhaps he'd tell her how much he loved her when he got her alone on the ship. Should he tell her while still aboard the ship or wait until they reached Athens? At any rate, he didn't want that old bat, the Countess Borghase, in his way. If he had to, he'd throw her shriveled, ancient ass overboard. Besides, wasn't

Michaela gonna inherit the old bitch's money when she croaked? That's what he'd always heard.

Anger boiled in him when he considered the Countess. She'd put him down and made him feel like nothing once, but that was one time too many. She'd get what was coming to her. He was so angry that he ripped one of the strands of fabric and then cursed. He got up, walked over to his safe, turned the knob, and retrieved another two scraps of fabric. He wondered if Michaela, the great homicide detective, had even discovered that he'd cut up her dresses earlier and taken some of the strands of her dresses with him. His eyes glanced down to the bottom of the closet where her two shoes were lined up perfectly. He bent down and retrieved the high heel. He picked it up reverently and walked over to his desk. He held the shoe carefully and gently caressed it as he dreamed of the vivacious dark-headed Michaela. The shoe was beautiful. It was a size six and a half. Little, dainty, and petite - like Michaela. He rubbed his fingers over the glittering rhinestones embedded in the heel of the shoe. He held it up in the light, but was disappointed that it didn't sparkle more. He knew he could shine it better. Yes, he'd make it so shiny it would blind Michaela when he returned it. He went into his bathroom, returned with a soapy rag, and continued to rub the shoe and shine the heel. Just think, when he returned her shoe to her, she'd feel just like Cinderella.

It had been a long time. And now it was going to happen. He'd lusted after Mic for almost ten years and finally, the wait was over. He'd have his wish and his love. Tomorrow evening, they'd be together, and then the next day, they'd tour Athens. Ah, Athens, the center of democracy and the home of Plato's Academy and Aristotle's Lyceum. Athens, the cradle of civilization. It was only right and just that their liaison would begin in Greece. A civilized relationship built on a love of democratic choice and love. His heart pounded in anticipation. They would kiss in the Pantheon and make love in the Temple of Zeus. Yes, a relationship built like a democracy. Perhaps, he'd return her shoes or… perhaps he wouldn't. And then after Athens, the world would belong to them.

He sat on his bed and continued to admire the shoe from afar. Then, he returned to his desk and picked up the shoe and fondled it as he would a lover. His fingers touched the indentions Michaela's toes had made into the soft leather. He sighed. It was the most erotic feeling he'd ever encountered. He almost passed out from the sensual feeling it gave him. He was breathless. For a second, he wished he'd taken both shoes, but he knew that would be excessive behavior. And, he wasn't excessive. He was as fair and democratic as any Greek god would be. He was determined, thoughtful, and patient. But his patience had run out. He had to have his love now. They'd be happy for the rest of their lives. Together. As one.

The man cradled and massaged the soft leather for another minute and then replaced it gently in his closet. Seconds later, he picked up Michaela's tennis shoe and deeply inhaled its scent. Some might consider the smell of the shoe a bit stinky and rubbery. To him it was perfect – down-to-earth, exciting, earthy, pure, and very definitive of Michaela McPherson at work. And that's where he knew Michaela – from their work. Oh, not just her restaurant downtown in Shockoe Bottom in Richmond, but also from the Richmond police department. He'd admired her from afar for years and years. His feelings for Mic were complex, volatile, and long-standing. A piece of him wanted revenge for the times he knew she'd deliberately avoided him. Those feelings scared him sometimes because he didn't really want to hurt Michaela. He knew he'd have to rein in his anger. But, he knew all of that would end when she learned to love him.

Within hours, he'd have what he'd wanted, hunted, and lusted after for years.

Chapter 26

Snake sat in his stateroom and flicked through the five channels on the ship's television. He cursed under his breath. Television at sea was useless. He hated it. There was nothing to see but some stupid Italian movie and the BBC. For some reason, the Turner movie channel didn't work in his stateroom.

He reached over and picked up his copy of The Wave, the ship's daily event schedule, and scanned it for the movie of the day. He checked his watch. It was almost six o'clock. He itched to know if Vadim had taken care of the Senator. Of course, he had no idea where the Russian was and that irritated the hell out of him.

He returned to the daily event paper and saw the movie was some stupid romantic comedy he'd never heard of, but he decided to go and watch it. He locked his room, caught the elevator, and pressed the button for deck six. This was his second trip to the ship's movie theater in three days. He stopped off for some free popcorn and entered the darkened theater. He looked around and saw the guy with the dirty-blond hair sitting on the far side of the theater. Snake thought he was the man he'd seen outside Michaela's stateroom earlier in the day. His heartbeat accelerated and he wondered who the guy was. As soon as other people milled into the theater, he got up and moved over into the same row as the light-haired stranger. Perhaps he'd strike up a conversation and learn a little bit about him. It angered him that a guy had been loitering around Mic and he was pretty sure this was the same dude.

Snake chomped on his popcorn and wondered why someone would loiter around Michaela and the Countess' staterooms. In a way, bizarre as it was, he felt protective of Michaela. Even though he planned to kill her, he wanted his prey left alone because indeed, Michaela McPherson was Snake's quarry and he intended to hunt her very, very soon. She'd already bested him once and he'd never let that happen again. But this guy, well, everything about him felt weird.

Snake kept one eye on the man during the movie and the other on the screen. The man seemed content and watched the movie to the end. The guy practically swooned at the ending and didn't seem to notice Snake at all. After the movie, Snake stretched in his seat and struck up a conversation with the guy.

"Did you like the movie?" he asked in his friendliest voice, which sounded strange to him. Snake was rarely cordial. In fact, Snake rarely spoke to anyone.

The guy shrugged his shoulders and said, "Yeah. It was okay. I've seen better movies. I did like the ending, though. I love happily ever-after flicks," he admitted with a wink and a sly, thin-lipped smile.

Snake studied the man carefully. He was shorter than Snake, and appeared in pretty good shape, like a guy who worked out in a gym. The man had a lazy eye, which seemed to be staring at him. "Where are you from?" he asked with a smile. "Have you been to Athens before?" Snake prodded in his attempt to make small talk. It was difficult for Snake. A monumental task.

The man's lazy eye was fixed on Snake as he said, "Nope, I haven't. But I like history and I've always wanted to go on a cruise like this."

Snake nodded. "You're from the US. What state do you live in?" he asked nonchalantly.

The man quickly glanced at him and said, "Yeah, I live in Virginia, just outside of Washington, DC. Where are you from?" he asked, his lazy eye still focused on Snake's face as the normal eye stared ahead.

"Hmm, that's a good question," Snake said with a rare smile, so rare that it hurt his face where his skin crinkled up. "I just kinda live around. Sometimes I stay up in New York, in Manhattan, but sometimes I stay in Virginia too. I have an RV parked in one of the campgrounds near Richmond," he said as he continued to engage the man in conversation.

The man nodded his head and said, "That's cool."

Snake continued to observe the guy. He was young, probably mid to late twenties. There was something weird about him in addition to the lazy eye. Snake got a bad vibe from him. "Buy you a coffee?" he asked cordially as they approached the coffee vendor.

"Buy me a coffee? The coffee's free, man. Where you been?" the guy asked with a look between slight smile and a sneer. "But, on second thought, yeah I'll take a caramel latte," he agreed as he pushed his dirty-blonde hair back with his hand.

Snake pointed toward a small table for two by the window. "Okay," he said. "Grab us a table and I'll bring the coffee over. I'd like to hear what you're gonna do in Athens. Maybe we can share a cab or something," he suggested.

The man nodded, "Yeah, okay. I'll get the table."

Chapter 27

Captain Wodensen entered the restaurant to have dessert with Michaela and Dottie. From a distance, he appeared worn and tired. His face was lined with fatigue. Mic's alarm bells rang in her mind when she saw his grim face. She knew something was wrong. Dottie knew something was up too. Dottie was stressed and Michaela looked at her with concern. The news was worse than they expected. It fact, it was horrible.

Dottie gulped and said, "The Senator is dead? How can he be dead? We just saw him at tea! Are you sure?" she asked in a shaky voice. Mic touched Dottie's arm. She was alarmed at her shortness of breath.

The Captain nodded and said, "I'm very sure, Madame. Very sure. I've just come from his stateroom."

"How did you find out Senator Bostitch was dead? Who do you think killed him?" Michaela asked, stunned by the news. Who in their right mind would murder a United States Senator… especially on a cruise ship?

The Captain shrugged his shoulders and repeated his story. "As I said, Ms. McPherson, his cabin steward found him. He knocked on the Senator's door to ready his room for the evening. There was no answer, so the steward followed ship policy and entered the cabin. He found the Senator hanging in his bathroom. He'd been stabbed."

"Stabbed, someone stabbed him? That's brutal and personal as well," Mic's head was spinning with possibilities. Her heartbeat skyrocketed. *What the hell was going on*? "We need to see the crime scene… see it immediately." She looked at Dottie who sat very straight in her chair but had clasped her hands tightly. She looked pale, but determined.

The Captain picked up his coffee cup, but said nothing.

"Captain Wodensen," Dottie said, "When we get into Piraeus, we need to meet with the Athens authorities, and you must call the FBI immediately. An American Senator, of all things, has been murdered on your... my ship. The FBI must be notified at once," Dottie insisted in a firm voice.

Mic nodded her head in agreement. "The Countess is correct. The FBI is a critical player in this case. The murder of a United States Senator is worse than serious." She paused for a moment and then continued, "Frankly, it's unbelievable."

Captain Wodensen nodded, but remained silent.

Mic replayed the events in her mind. "Do you think the killer is the same person that murdered the blackjack dealer in the casino?"

The Captain shrugged his shoulders. "It's too early to know. It's possible. Both men were killed with a knife, a blade." He looked at Dottie and spoke in measured tones, "We will notify the FBI. I'll notify them personally as soon as I leave your company." He paused as he re-considered Michaela's question. He turned to her and said, "And, I have no idea if the murderer is the same man. We've been looking for the man who killed our employee ever since it happened. We've gotten nowhere and have no leads."

Mic was surprised and she arched her eyebrows, "No leads? None at all?" She asked in a low voice.

The Captain shook his head. "We've searched the ship several times and looked in every nook and cranny where a man could hide."

"What about the witnesses in the casino? Surely they've been interviewed and must have seen something," Dottie snapped, her blue eyes blazing at the incompetency of the ship's security.

"There's nothing, Countess, nothing at all to report," he said wearily.

A flood of realization practically knocked Mic over. "Suppose he's not hiding. Suppose he's walking around just as we are…" she paused, "in broad daylight!"

The Captain was confused. "What do you mean? I don't understand," he said in an irritable voice. He was tired and had no time for word games.

The wheels turned in Michaela's mind. "It's conceivable he doesn't have to hide, that he's more invisible when he blends in with three thousand other people."

Dottie slammed her coffee cup on the saucer. "You're absolutely correct, Michaela. The guy's most likely wandering around like any other passenger." She turned to Captain Wodensen and asked, "Frederick, do you have anything at all?"

The Captain sighed heavily and said, "Perhaps, but it's not really a lead. Yesterday, my security detail trailed a man who met the physical description of the man who murdered the blackjack dealer. We followed him most of the day, but then lost him in the evening. We haven't been able to pick him up today," he said with a shake of his head.

Dottie nodded. "That's too bad. Perhaps they'll see him tomorrow," she said, a touch of sarcasm in her voice as she gave the Captain a wry look.

"Do you scan the camera feeds each day?" Mic inquired.

The Captain nodded. "Yes, we do. We scan them constantly. We're looking everywhere for him. My security chief thinks, like you, that he's most likely the guy who murdered the man in the casino, but all we have in common is the fact that they are knife wounds. No one saw anyone enter Senator Bostitch's room. There are no eye witnesses so we have no information about him," he said in a weary voice. "But what we do have on camera, at the elevator camera, is a grainy, poorly pixelated, image of a man who appears very muscular. The camera picked him up when he left the elevator. He had on a dark colored jacket or sweatshirt. Unfortunately, his face isn't part of the camera image."

"Is he anywhere on camera today?" Mic asked as a rush of excitement moved through her body.

The Captain shook his head. "No. We haven't seen him anywhere else. He kept his head down. He didn't want to be seen."

Mic nodded. "I understand. I'd like to see the crime scene and the camera images. Have you altered anything at all about the scene or the images?"

The Captain shook his head, crinkled his nose in disgust, and said, "No. It's untouched. In fact, we haven't even removed the Senator's body."

"I want to see the crime scene," Mic repeated.

The Captain steepled his fingers as he considered Mic's request. "I don't think that's a good idea, Michaela. The crime was heinous and the crime scene is horrific. In good conscious, I can't let you see it." His voice was grave and his tone was final.

Michaela took a deep breath and said, "Captain, I want to see the scene. I'm a retired homicide detective. I've seen crime scenes you probably couldn't even begin to imagine." She furrowed her brow and continued, "What one man can do to another is unthinkable and I assure you, the scene can't look any worse than others I've witnessed in the United States."

Captain Wodensen shook his head. His voice was firm. "No, I cannot allow it."

Michaela glanced at Dottie who was flushed with anger. "Countess, can you persuade the good Captain to let us see the crime scene?" she asked in an irritated tone. "We may be able to help solve these ghastly murders."

Dottie was silent as she considered the situation. As a major stockholder of the Mediterranean line, she could insist and usurp the Captain's authority. However, she knew there was a possibility he'd block her from other information and communications. Besides, she needed his help and his assurance that she and Michaela would remain safe. The attack on Michaela's personal belongings had been perverted and scary.

Mic tapped the table with her fingernails and repeated her question in an impatient voice. "Countess, can you intervene here? You and I both know we need to see the crime scene to help find the perp."

Angel, who'd been lying next to Mic's chair, stood at the sound of his mistress' angry voice. He looked up at the Captain and growled. Michaela patted his back and said, "It's okay, Angel. It's okay." Then she turned, glared at Dottie, and kicked her shin under the table. Dottie jumped and shot her an angry look, but she got the message.

"My granddaughter is correct, Captain Wodensen," Dottie began in a haughty voice. "Both of us have extensive experience in solving crimes. Once we finish our dinner, I want you to allow us into the crime scene. I also want you to provide us with two additional firearms to guarantee our personal safety."

The Captain was stunned. His face paled, his pupils dilated with disbelief, as anger flickered across his face. He opened his mouth to protest, but Dottie banged her fork against her plate and said, "I'm not asking for your permission, Captain, I'm telling you to give us access to the Senator's stateroom. And I'm ordering you to issue each of us a Glock. The attack on Michaela was fierce, troubling, and potentially lethal. And, your security hardly offers us any comfort. Do you understand me?" she asked in her Countess voice.

Angel growled again and Mic did nothing to quiet him. Several patrons turned and looked at them. The dog held the Captain's eyes with his own and bared his teeth.

The Captain was defeated. He compressed his lips, gritted his teeth, and said in a low voice, "I will allow you access to the Senator's room, but it's not our policy to issue weapons to passengers."

Dottie flushed. She was furious. Michaela saw the blush of pink crawl up her neck and stain her face. She was so angry her hands trembled and her eyes were inky black with rage.

Okay. Here we go. Mic braced herself for a Countess tantrum. They were never pleasant, but they were generally effective.

Dottie stood, glared down at Captain Wodensen, and said, her voice compressed with anger, "Let me remind you that I am not 'just a passenger.' I'm the primary owner of this ship and this cruise line. If you do not cooperate with me one hundred percent, you will no longer be in command of the ship."

The Captain's eyes glowed with anger as Dottie continued.

"I will make one phone call and you will be relieved of your command. First Mate Hensen will function as Captain until we reach Athens. At that point in time, you will be removed from the vessel and you will no longer be employed with the Mediterranean Cruise Line."

The Captain stood and bowed stiffly. "Countess Borghase, you'll have your weapons, and I will accompany you and Ms. McPherson to the Senator's stateroom along with my security chief. Once again, I want to warn you the scene is quite bad. In fact, it's appalling, but it is your choice to go. Meet me in forty-five minutes at the Senator's stateroom."

"What's his stateroom number?" Dottie asked in a low voice.

"His suite number is 652. The suite is on the same floor as you, down the same hall. I will be there in precisely forty-five minutes. That will give you time to finish your dessert and coffee," the Captain added as he bowed, turned away, and left the restaurant.

"Wow, Dottie," Mic said with a wide grin. "I guess you know that he's more than a little pissed at you." Mic laughed as she stared at the older woman.

Dottie nodded, "Yeah, he is that, but actually, he's just following the cruise line's policy. If we didn't have the background we have, and if you hadn't had your room disturbed, I probably wouldn't have insisted." She paused for a moment and smiled, "Besides, I like to pull rank every now and then."

Michaela nodded. "Yeah. That I do know. I understand the policy, but I think we can be helpful here. And besides, Slade insisted we get the extra weapons, even though we most likely won't need them.

"Well," Dottie demurred, "we'll have them now, and I hardly think we'll be attacked by pirates," she said as she took her last sip of wine. "Let's hurry; I want to change my clothes before we meet them at the Senator's suite."

Mic picked up her coffee cup. "Yeah, I just can't believe he's dead. We saw him just a few hours ago, and he was getting ready to tell Blake Pharmaceutical exactly how it was." She stopped for a moment as she remembered Senator Bostitch. Her dinner burned in her gut from stress and anger. "I liked him. He seemed ethical and honest and genuinely concerned about the Quelpro problem."

Dottie nodded and said in a gruff voice, "Yes, he was. That's precisely why he's dead. I'm sure Blake Pharmaceutical is behind his murder and Dr. O'Leary's disappearance," she professed, her ice blue eyes dark with anger.

Michaela nodded as a tight ball formed in her stomach. She knew Blake Pharmaceutical would murder to save their precious, but worthless antidepressant. How to prove it, well, that was a different story. But, she vowed she'd do it.

Chapter 28

Snake and the guy with dirty-blond hair finished their coffee and drifted over to the bar. Snake was convinced the man was after Michaela and he needed all the information he could get. The thought of someone getting to the police bitch before he could frosted his blood.

"So," Snake asked, "You gotta name, man?"

"Yeah, it's Grady," the man said as his wandering eye fixed on Snake's face. "Grady Jones," he said with a sly smile as he gazed at Snake's greasy, black hair. "You? You got a name?" he mimicked sarcastically.

"Yeah, they call me Snake," he said as he waved his tattooed hand at Grady. "Get it?" he asked as he glared at him.

"Got it," Grady said sarcastically. "Do I look like a moron or something to you? The stupid tattoo says it all," he said with a scowl.

Snake didn't reply as the waiter approached. He ordered a double martini with an olive. The coffee wasn't gonna cut it. He was uneasy, partly because the idiot across the table from him was hostile, and because he hadn't heard from Vadim.

"What do you want to drink?" Snake asked. "It's on my dime," he assured him as he pulled his ship charge card from his pocket.

"I want a Sex on the Beach," Grady said in a sullen voice. Snake could hear him grind his teeth as Grady fixed his normal eye on the drink menu.

Snake almost burst out in laughter, but managed to contain himself and said, "Dude, that's a great drink."

Grady was silent and stared at the table as he thumped the table with his leg.

"So, what do you do in Richmond?" Snake asked as he pretended to focus on his double martini. In truth, he watched the man's weird eye. It fascinated him.

Grady shrugged his shoulders. "Not much of anything. I'm between jobs so I don't really work," he said as he checked out a tall buxom blonde who sauntered by. The blonde turned her head and winked at the men.

"Man, she looks pretty hot." Snake observed as he saw the guy's eye follow the blonde out the bar as the other eye focused on him. "Wouldn't you like some of that stuff, dude?" he asked as he winked at Grady, a lewd expression on his face.

Grady shook his head emphatically, placed his hands on his head, and rubbed it.

"You got a headache, man?" Snake asked as he watched Grady massage his temple. This guy's a nut case.

The guy turned up his nose and said, "Nah. No headache. I don't like tall blondes. I like my women small and petite, with dark hair." He shook his head again, "That chick was too tall for me," he said with the salacious grin. "Why don't you go get her?"

Snake shook his head. "Nah, I ain't got no time for a shipboard romance. Besides, she looked too high maintenance for me. I like my women to be low maintenance," he said with a short laugh.

Grady stared at him as if he was from another planet. "Lots of people come on cruises just to find a shipboard romance," he said as his lazy eye rested on Snake's face.

Snake was silent as he picked up his martini.

"Who knows, it could turn into something permanent," the guy said, a dreamy look in his normal eye. "I have a woman on board," he admitted with a sly smile and a wink.

Snake felt anger sift through his bones. "You do. Who? Go get her so I can meet her," he insisted. "The drinks are on me," he said with a flourish of his hand. "I'd love to meet her."

Grady shook his head. His face was flushed with anger and his lazy eye burned with a strange light. "Can't. Not tonight. She ain't feeling good," he said as he gave Snake a suspicious look. "And, besides," he continued in a loud voice, "she's mine and I ain't sharing her with no damn body."

Snake didn't answer. He sat quietly and rubbed the stem of his martini glass. He knew people were staring at them. Guy's crazy, no question.

Grady moved his gaze to the window and stared out at the dark Mediterranean Sea.

Snake pushed the issue. "Man, so, you've found the perfect woman on the ship?" Snake waited patiently until the man looked at him. "Tell me about her," Snake encouraged. "Maybe she has a friend, or a sister, and we can have some fun in Athens."

The guy gave him a strange look and said, "I've had the woman of my dreams in my sight for almost ten years. I aim to get her soon," he said as he slammed his glass down. The heavy bottom of the glass banged against the glass table and the sound echoed through the bar.

A waiter appeared immediately. "You need something else, another drink?" he asked quietly as he shoved a bowl of peanuts at the two men.

Snake was pissed. The last thing he wanted was to bring attention to himself on the ship. Besides, the behavior of the waiter irritated him. Snake motioned with his glass and said, "Yeah, give me another one. Make it a double and him too," he said as he gestured at Grady, who was staring out the window again.

The waiter nodded and looked at Grady. "You, sir? Another drink?"

Grady shook his head and Snake said, "He'll have another. Put it on my ship charge card."

The man protested, his face red with anger. "I don't want another drink. I got stuff to do and it's getting late," he said as he stood.

"Oh, come on, buddy. I'm so lonely," Snake begged in his nicest voice. "You've got a girlfriend, or at least one in your head, and I don't have anyone," he said sadly. "Please dude, just one more drink," he cajoled.

Grady settled back in his seat and said, "Well, I don't really have her, at least not yet. But that's gonna change soon," he said as he settled back in his chair.

Snake smiled to himself. One more drink and I'll know everything on his stupid, cocky, feeble little mind. "How's it going to change?" Snake asked as the waiter set down fresh drinks in front of them.

Grady shook his head and sipped his drink. "Ain't tellin'. Ain't gonna jinx it," he said with a tight smile. "Ain't gonna jinx it, ain't gonna jinx it, ain't gonna jinx it," he repeated under his breath.

Snake nodded and picked up his martini. It was cold and good. A second later, he saw Vadim enter the bar, nod at him, and take a seat behind them. Vadim was dressed in formal wear, glasses, and he had a beard.

Damn, he's good at hiding. But, at least I can identify him easier, Snake thought as he turned his attention to Grady. "What were you saying?" he asked with a half-smile, half snarl, as he debated how to end their conversation.

"Nuthin', man. Nuthin'. I wasn't saying anything," Grady said.

"Gotta go," Snake said as he stood. "Enjoy your drink. See ya around the ship," he said as he nodded and left the table.

Chapter 29

Mic shuffled her feet outside of Senator Bostitch's room as her heart raced blood through her body. She could feel it pound through her arteries. She felt hot and flushed all over. What had happened to their long-awaited, peaceful Mediterranean cruise? So far, in only four short days, there had been two murders, one man overboard, and someone had broken into her suite, shredded her clothes, and stolen two of her shoes. Her gut constricted with uncertainty. She knew she was someone's target and The Regina Mediterranean was now a dangerous place for both of them.

Dottie stared at her as she leaned against the wall. "What do you think, Michaela? I can see the wheels turning in your mind from over here. Tell me," she insisted.

Mic shook her head and looking intently into Dottie's troubled blue eyes said, "I was wondering what happened to our luxurious, peaceful cruise. This ship is a floating cesspool of criminals. Nothing like this was supposed to happen."

"No kidding," Dottie scoffed. "I can't wait to see what kind of damage the Mediterranean Cruise Lines suffers when the news hits that a United States Senator was murdered aboard my ship! It'll be an international scandal of epic proportion." She paused as she imagined the news reports and the fun the news pundits and talking heads would have.

Mic shook her head and said, "It'll be okay, Dottie. So what if you lose a few million dollars? You have plenty to spare," she said with a smile. "We've gone through worse," she reminded her.

"Our reputation will be crap for several years and right now, I need to eat a pack of Tums," Dottie said as she rubbed her stomach. "The rich Italian red sauce has mixed with stress and it burns." She paused a minute and added, "Plus, I'm probably still sick from the crap shake you made me drink this afternoon," she moaned.

Mic immediately felt bad. She hadn't even considered her friend's position. She knew Dottie would lose millions, but Dottie had millions of dollars to lose. "I'm so sorry, Dottie. I hadn't even thought about your monetary loss." She looked at Dottie in her black running clothes and tennis shoes. She looked nowhere near her eighty-two years of age.

Dottie shook her head and laughed, "Oh hell, Mic, screw the money. I'm much more concerned about the pervert that broke into your room, cut up your clothes, and took your shoes. That's weird, chilling in fact."

Mic nodded. "Yeah. Me too. It's a wacked psycho if you ask me. Slade will meet us in Athens. I'll be glad to see him," she said with a sigh. "At least it'll be another gun on our side." Mic saw a shadow flicker across Dottie's face.

Dottie sniffed. She wasn't particularly happy about Slade McKane joining them on the cruise, but they did need someone. In truth, Dottie was more than a little jealous of Slade, but she knew Mic cared about him. Therefore, she'd decided to be nice. "Yeah, Slade will provide you some comfort and he'll keep you safe. In the meantime, you can sleep with me in my suite tonight and tomorrow night if you'd like," she offered.

Michaela shook her head. "Nah. Thanks, but no thanks. I'll be fine. You know I can take care of myself. Besides, I have Angel and he's the best watchdog in the world. He'll take care of me," she assured her. Mic knew she'd go crazy if she had to sleep in Dottie's room. She needed her alone time, especially when she needed to think.

"Where the hell is the Captain?" Dottie whined. "I'm tired of waiting for him," she said as she shifted her weight to the opposite side of her body. "Damn it."

Mic craned her neck and looked down the long corridor. "Here comes someone now. In fact, it's two men, the Captain being one of them," she said as dread welled up in her chest. She'd seen hundreds of crime scenes in her career as a homicide detective, but for some reason she feared this one.

The two men joined them in the hall and Captain Wodensen introduced Mic and Dottie to his security chief, a former Russian military officer who had little to say and an arrogant scowl on his face.

"Are you ready to go in?" he asked. "I'd like to warn you again that the scene is grisly."

Mic nodded at the Captain and Dottie and in a calm and even voice, instructed them to open the door.

The Captain opened the Senator's stateroom and the overwhelming smell made Michaela dizzy. Her breath was smothered by the metallic, sickly sweet scent of blood. She turned to Dottie who was equally affected. Dottie was pale and clung to the wall. Mic knew she was dizzy. "Dottie, why don't you wait down the hall for a moment until we can air this place out?"

Dottie nodded and moved a few feet down the hall. Mic knew the Captain wanted to close the door to confine the odor so other passengers wouldn't smell it. She turned to Captain Wodensen and asked, "Can you open the balcony door? The smell is overwhelming, stifling in fact."

The Captain nodded and the security chief opened the balcony door. The strong smell began to dissipate. Blood was everywhere. Someone had put a white towel down by the door to keep it from seeping out into the hall. The towel was drenched with blood.

Oh my God, this must be almost all the blood in the Senator's body, Mic thought to herself. For a moment she wasn't sure she wanted to walk through the blood. Of course, it would further destroy any evidence they might gather; but more than that, it was gross and would ruin her last pair of leisure shoes. I wish to hell we had some booties to wear. "Where's the body?" she asked in a voice that wasn't her own.

"It's… it's to the right… in the bathroom," the Captain said in a muffled voice. He'd covered his mouth and nose with a towel to block out the coppery, metallic stench of blood. Mic could see sweat glistening on his forehead.

Michaela's mind and nose finally accepted the smell and she very carefully eased her body inside the room, stepping as far away from the blood as she possibly could. Seconds later, she was standing in front of the open bathroom door.

The carpet was mushy with blood and sucked at the rubber soles of her shoes. She had to lift each shoe carefully with each step. She could feel the fluid gurgle under the suction of her shoes as she took several more steps. With Captain Wodensen beside her, she took a deep breath and stared directly at the body. What she saw took her breath away. She was dizzy and her ears buzzed with recognition. For a second, she thought she would faint. The Captain noticed her dismay and instructed her to take some deep breaths.

But Mic didn't want to breathe deeply. The smell of blood sickened her and her mouth tasted of metal. She steadied herself and raised her eyes until she looked straight at the body.

Senator Bostitch's body was hung upside down. The killer had affixed his legs to the shower rod. His body was pale white with a blue tint. Michaela looked down at the wound on his neck and said softly, her voice almost inaudible. "I know who killed this man. I'm sure I know who did this."

Captain Wodensen gave her a wild glance. He was taken aback. "You know the murderer, Ms. McPherson? Why would you know the murderer of the Senator?" Mic could feel the steely gray eyes of Captain Wodensen and the blatant angry stare of his security chief. She refused to look at them.

Michaela took a breath, sighed deeply, and said, "I'm positive this is the same man the New Orleans police have been tracking for years. She pulled out her iPhone and began taking pictures of the Senator's body. She wished she had access to basic forensic garments and equipment, but instead decided she'd throw her clothes away as soon as she got back into her stateroom. She leaned down and looked carefully at the knife wounds on Senator Bostitch's neck. Yes, the wounds were the same. The staging of the body was very similar to the man's body she'd seen in New Orleans just a few months ago. That man had been hung upside down from a telephone pole near the Mississippi River and his blood had pooled on the ground just as the Senator's blood had pooled on the bathroom tile and out onto the carpet. The stab marks appeared similar in length and depth. It was a signature murder.

Michaela's heart pumped and the adrenaline surge made her dizzy. She knew she was right. She continued flashing pictures as she wished for a pair of rubber gloves and bags to gather trace evidence. She also wished for a forensic kit, but she didn't have one and that was that.

"Michaela, Mic, what's going on in there? I want to come in," Dottie said in a tight voice outside the door. I want to see the Senator's body," she demanded.

Mic groaned inwardly. "You don't need to come in, Dottie. I've taken a million pictures. We can get them blown up by the ship's photographer. It's hot and it smells awful in here," Mic pleaded.

Captain Wodensen stepped out of the Senator's stateroom, and said, "Are you sure, Countess? I think even Ms. McPherson is startled and upset by this crime scene. I don't advise you to go in there."

"You won't advise me one way or the other, Captain," Dottie said in an angry voice. "I'll go in there if I damn well please."

Mic shook her head and hollered again, "Dottie, I've taken lots of pictures. You can come in here if you want to, but honestly, the smell is making me sick to my stomach. I'm gonna be out there in a couple of minutes, then we'll go upstairs to one of the meeting rooms, and we'll check the pictures out on the big screen."

"Well, I don't know…" Dottie said, torn in her decision, her pride not wanting to give in.

"Trust me on this, Dottie. I know who did this murder and he's aboard your ship. I need you awake, alive, and alert because I'm sure that about the time we get to Athens, The Regina Mediterranean will be crawling with cops from different nations."

"Well, if you say so," Dottie said shortly. "I'm fairly sure I can understand what happened based on the pictures."

"There's no question about what happened, Dottie." She flashed her green eyes at Captain Wodensen and said, "Captain, you have a serial killer on board your ship. I know this man. I've hunted and trapped him. He kills for fun and for pleasure. We're going to need all the help we can get when we get to Athens."

"A... An international serial killer?" Captain Wodensen asked with a look of shock on his face. The Russian security chief stared at Mic as though she was an alien. Then he had the audacity to roll his eyes. Mic wanted to slap him.

She flashed angry green eyes at the security chief as she left the Senator's stateroom and closed the door behind her. "Yeah, no question. Trust me; I know this man's work. It's the killer a New Orleans police commander and I chased and lost in NOLA. She looked around the scene and into the hallway and asked, "Can you put the Senator's body on ice? I know you can't leave the crime scene like this because I can already smell the odor of decomp, not to mention the stench of the blood."

Dottie nodded her head and said, "That's fine. We can't handle a lot of complaints about smells."

Captain Wodensen spoke softly to his security chief, who walked down the hall and called for the cleanup crew.

"I'd like to wait a while longer to remove the body," the Captain said. "The final show will be over in about twenty minutes and people will be returning to their staterooms. I don't think another hour or two will make a difference."

"It would be a good idea to go in there and cut the air conditioning down as low as you possibly can. The cooler we can keep the body, the less chance it will become a problem."

The Captain nodded, "We will do that. Is there anything else I can do for you ladies?"

Dottie looked at Michaela who shook her head and said, "I don't think so, Captain. I'd just advise to heed my warning and keep your men on alert. If Michaela says this guy is bad, I can assure you that he is."

Mic nodded and said, "Honestly, Captain. The New Orleans police have looked for this man for years. He's responsible for dozens of deaths in the Big Easy and probably more than that all over the world. I tracked him with Commander Jack Françoise of the New Orleans police department. They believe he's killed many more people than they know about. He's decidedly a psychopath and kills for pleasure. Because he likes it," she added with a tight grin.

The Captain looked uncertain, "How do you know this, Ms. McPherson? Why would this man from the United States be on my ship? We are a long way from the United States and New Orleans. Why would he be on a cruise ship in the middle of the Mediterranean Sea?"

Michaela shrugged her shoulders. "I've no idea for sure, Captain. But he's on the run. He's an international criminal. He's Russian. Perhaps he has some business in Athens to take care of. Perhaps he's a hitman for a criminal organization. We've no idea. But," she added as she looked the Captain directly in the eyes, "I'm positive it's him."

The Captain shook his head, "But how can you be so sure?"

Mic sighed. "I just said this but let me repeat. Because I've studied this man, Captain. I've seen a body that he's killed. I've seen crime scene photos of dozens of his victims. He always turns them upside down to let the blood run out. Some call him St. Germaine. Others call him The Vampire.

If you know the St. Germaine legend, you know that St. Germaine was a French Viscount who left France shortly after the French Revolution and turned up in New Orleans. It was widely rumored that he was a vampire. Ever since then, crimes occur where the victim is slashed in the neck and positioned similar to Senator Bostitch. The bodies are hung upside down until all the blood drains out. Exsanguinated. Law enforcement believe the crimes are related."

Captain Wodensen stood erect and quietly said, "I do not believe in fairytales or folklore nor do I believe in vampires, Madame. I will inform my security team that we have a potential serial killer on board and to stay alert.

Mic nodded, shrugged her shoulders, and said, "One more thing. St. Germaine is a master of disguise. I'm sure he killed your blackjack dealer, and has been parading around the ship incognito ever since."

The Captain nodded stiffly. "I'd like this conversation to stay between you, me, Countess Borghase, and my security chief," he said quietly. "Agreed?"

"That's fine with me, Captain. But you must be sure your security people know about him as well and that he is very dangerous."

The Captain nodded and said, "Of course. I will tell them."

Michaela turned to Dottie and said, "I'm going back to my stateroom to call Commander Françoise in New Orleans and Slade. I know Jack would like to know where St. Germaine is."

Dottie nodded and turned to the Captain, "Thank you. I appreciate your patience and willingness to let Michaela and me know about the Senator's death. Let us know if anything else develops."

The Captain followed her and said, "Yes, yes, I have to move this body. Unfortunately, I already have one body in the morgue and we only have a couple more stretchers. So, if we recover Dr. O'Leary's body, I'll be short on morgue space."

Dottie looked into Captain Wodensen's eyes and asked, "Are you positive the person who went overboard is Dr. O'Leary?"

The Captain nodded. "Well, Countess Borghase, I'm as positive as I can be without a body sitting in front of me." The Captain shook his head and continued, "He's the only person on the ship that didn't muster in security during the roll call. I've had my men search everywhere for him and I'm sure he's no longer on board the ship."

Mic saw Dottie's face begin to crumble. Mic flew to her and put her arm around her dear friend. "Dottie, you know we thought it was Dr. O'Leary from the very beginning. He's just confirmed what we've always thought."

Dottie covered her eyes and her shoulders shook. "I'm just so sad about it. From all accounts, he was a brilliant young physician and had lots to offer the world. It makes me sick that someone would destroy a man like this," she said with a stifled sob as she stubbornly wiped a tear from her eye.

Mic was choked up, but mainly worried about Dottie. She managed to say, "Yeah, I know. I guess I'll talk with Ian and Alana as well. I think they know it's Dr. O'Leary, but actually hearing that he most likely is indeed dead is much more upsetting than I would've anticipated."

Dottie nodded, "I suppose you're right, Michaela. I guess we can wait until tomorrow to tell Ian. It's getting late. It's after eleven o'clock now."

"What time is it in the US, in New Orleans?" Michaela asked Dottie. "Well, let me see, they're an hour behind us in Virginia so it's between six and seven in the morning."

"That's perfect. I've got to make some phone calls. Mic turned to Captain Wodensen and said, "Captain, you have your men soak up the blood, but not wash down the cabin, at least not until we reach Athens. I know the crime scene will basically be destroyed, but perhaps if they only put towels and plastic over the blood that will contain the stench and cause less disruption to the crime scene."

The Captain shook his head, "I don't think I can do that, Ms. McPherson. This is a cruise ship. People don't expect murder. I can't in good conscience not clean this room."

Mic shook her head. She was tired, aggravated, and had a lot to do. "Honestly, Captain, can you try? We could find trace evidence, possibly a lot of evidence that would help us find where this man is staying on the ship."

Captain Wodensen looked at Dottie and said, "Madame, all I can do to meet Ms. McPherson's request is to mop up the blood and secure the cabin. However, if the first passenger complains of a smell or stench or anything on this floor, that cabin will be wiped down with bleach not once or twice or three times, but the entire cabin will be washed with bleach at least five times."

Captain Wodensen watched the ladies return to their staterooms and shook his head. This had become the cruise from hell.

Chapter 30

Grady watched Michaela and her old lady friend as they stood in the hall, and talked with the cruise officials. He wondered what had happened to cause so much commotion. He was pissed because he'd wanted to go back into Michaela's room to leave her a gift he had bought her in the ship's gift shop. He removed the small beautifully wrapped package and stared at it. Maybe he'd just lay it on her pillow tonight while she was sleeping. He smiled to himself as a thrill seized his body and an idea raced through his mind.

Yeah, that's exactly what he'd do. He'd sneak in there later and watch her sleep for a while. He rubbed his hands together in anticipation. She was his dream, his goddess, the woman in his dreams. His Juliet! He knew she wanted him… lusted for him. He deserved to be in her room at night… Every night. Of course, he'd have to do something with the damn dog. Electricity raced through his body. He was on fire.

Grady smiled to himself as he planned the night in his mind. He reached into his pocket for the beautiful strip of fabric that was his and his alone. It was ecstasy to touch it, to stroke it. It was like touching Michaela's flesh.

"Dude, are you listening to me," an impatient voice asked. "Where the hell's your head?" Snake asked as he gave him a strange look.

Grady stood and said, "I gotta go. Got stuff to do…" Snake stared at him as he finished his drink quickly.

"Wait man, are we going into Athens?" he asked the retreating back.

Grady didn't answer. He had other stuff to think about and it exhilarated him.

It wouldn't be long now. He and Michaela would be together. They would be together and the two of them would become one in love.

Chapter 31

Michaela and Dottie sat at the table in Michaela's stateroom as she dialed Jack Françoise's home phone number in New Orleans. The phone rang three times before a female voice answered. Mic recognized the voice right away. It was Jack's wife, Monique Desmonde, an eminent psychiatrist who managed the psychiatric department at Crescent City Medical.

"Hello, Monique. I'm sorry to call so early but I was looking for Jack. This is Michaela McPherson from Richmond by way of the Mediterranean Sea."

Mic could imagine Monique as she pinned up her beautiful long hair and applied her makeup getting ready for work. Monique was tall, elegant, and charming. She was also one of the most respected psychiatrists in the world. Mic wanted to speak with her about her experience with Quelpro but that would have to wait.

"I knew exactly who it was, Mic," Monique said happily. "I recognized your phone number. Aren't you supposed to be in Rome or somewhere exotic with Dottie?" She asked with a laugh that sounded totally different from how she looked. Monique's laugh was deep, hearty and untamed.

Michaela smiled and said, "Yes. I am. We had a wonderful three weeks in Rome visiting Dottie's family. Now, we're on a luxury cruise ship, The Regina Mediterranean, which is the flagship of Dottie's cruise line."

"Oh my, how lucky, I'm envious," Monique said in a happy voice. "Is it as great as you thought it would be?"

Michaela laughed, took a deep breath and said, "Well, Monique, it could be wonderful. Unfortunately, it's been quite brutal. There have been two murders on board ship and one man overboard, which may be a murder as well."

Monique gasped. "Oh my God! What in the world is going on? You're on the ship from hell."

"We are indeed. This evening someone murdered Senator Peter Bostitch, the senior senator from the state of Maryland."

"Oh, my God, I know Peter Bostitch. He's a physician. I've known him for years." She stopped for a moment and said, "I can't believe he's dead, he was doing great stuff in Congress with health reform, particularly for psychiatric patients." Mic knew Monique was stunned.

"Wow, Monique. I'm so sorry. I didn't know you knew Peter." Mic paused for a moment and continued. "So much has happened. There's a pharmacy convention on board sponsored by Blake Pharmaceutical. There's a bunch of psychiatrists here touting the hell out of their drug, an antidepressant, Quelpro. Do you know about it?"

Monique's voice became cool and distant. "Yeah, I know about it and I wouldn't prescribe it to my worst enemy. It's got side effects that are life threatening, and the company is marketing it as if it's the key to curing every depressed patient in the world. I'm not sure it does anything good."

Mic flashed Dottie a smile and said, "By the way, Monique, I have you on speakerphone. Countess Borghase is here listening. Anyway, I want to talk with you about the Quelpro thing later, but I need to get to Jack because I just saw a body, the body of Senator Bostitch, and I swear I think St. Germaine killed him."

"St. Germaine? You think St. Germaine is on the same cruise ship with you and Dottie?" Monique's voice displayed her fear. "You guys need to get off that ship first chance you get. That man is a psychopath and Mic, if he recognizes you… he'll come for you, you know that, don't you?" Monique's voice was quiet and worried. "Promise me you'll leave at the next port."

Michaela took in a quick breath and said, "Honestly, I hadn't thought about that Monique, but you're probably right. But, I do have another creep who is stalking me. He's been in my stateroom and messed with my clothes and shoes. Slade McKane is leaving Richmond tomorrow and will meet us in Athens when the boat docks in Piraeus. So, I should be fine," she finished in a breathless voice.

Monique was quiet for a moment as she considered Mic's stalker. "What exactly did this guy do in your room, Mic? Can you tell me?"

Michaela took a deep breath. "Sure, I don't mind. Sometime today, he managed to get into my stateroom and ripped two of my evening dresses into shreds," she said her voice broken and quiet. "Plus, he stole two shoes. Not two pairs of shoes. He stole two shoes. One was a tennis shoe and the other an evening shoe. That's it."

Monique processed this information and her heart began to thud. "I don't like the sound of this, honestly I don't," she said as she put on her psychiatrist hat. "Is there anyone from Richmond who followed you onto the ship? Anyone in Richmond who is enamored with you and has been stalking you at any point in time?"

"No one I can think of. No one at all," she said in a soft voice. "And, you can bet I've thought about it." Mic fought for control. The anxiety and fear over her own safety was overwhelming.

"Countess, have you seen anyone following or staring at Mic? Anyone hanging around her?" Monique asked.

"Nope, no I haven't, Monique. But Mic and I do different things during the day. I play bridge, have lunch in the dining room, and go to High Tea and Michaela usually goes to the gym, the pool, and the spa, so I really wouldn't know," she said with a note of fear in her voice.

"Well, I'm just gonna say it because I know Jack would say the same thing. You ladies need to stay together; at least until Slade arrives, and I'll bet you Jack's gonna get to Athens as soon as he can too. He's been dying to find out where St. Germaine is and he's cursed every single day since you guys lost him back when you were here, Michaela."

"I've thought about it a lot, Monique. I can't be a hundred percent positive, but I'm pretty damn sure it's his signature on Senator Bostick's neck. Can you locate Jack and get him to call me?"

"That I can. He left early today. He has a meeting up in Baton Rouge later today that he's going to attend if you can believe that. Maybe he hasn't left his office yet, so when we hang up, I'll try him there and on his cell phone. If I don't get him, I'll have Jason Aldrich locate him. We'll have him call you stat, I promise, Mic."

Mic sighed with relief. "Thanks so much, Monique. I appreciate your insights on my dress ripper/shoe stealer guy. If he haunts me or comes in my room again, I'll call you back. In the meantime, let Jack know I need to talk with him."

"Done, Mic. I want you and Dottie to promise me to stay safe. Will you do that?" Monique insisted, her voice serious.

Dottie responded. "Monique, we'll be fine. We both have our weapons and we have Angel, and as you know, Angel is the toughest police dog in history and he'll take care of us."

Monique laughed loudly. Mic loved her laugh. It was surprising to get such a loud boisterous laugh from such an elegant, refined woman. "Well," she said, "if Angel's there, I won't worry at all!"

Angel's tail thumped on the floor. Michaela smiled and said, "He heard your voice and he's wagging his tail, Monique. Angel sends you his love," Mic assured her.

"Perfect. I'll get Jack to call. It should be in a few minutes," she promised.

When the conversation ended, Dottie looked at Mic and said, "This is getting exciting, Michaela. We may catch ourselves a couple of murderers and a stalker in the next few days."

"Well, I've got to go to bed. If we have to do all that, I need to be alert," Mic said with a smile. Angel and I are leaving, but I want you to call me for anything, anything you hear or if you need something, promise?" she asked as she stared down at the octogenarian.

"Yeah, yeah, sure, you know I will," Dottie said hotly. "But, rest assured, I'll be fine. No one wants to rip up my clothes," she said with a snort as Mic's cell phone rang.

Chapter 32

"Michaela, Mic, are you there? I can't hear you," Jack Françoise barked into the phone. "What the hell is wrong with your damn phone?"

Mic smiled to herself. Jack was irritated, excited, and on edge. She could see him pacing in front of his office window in the Big Easy. With a head of salt and pepper hair, the man was a mountain of energy and impatience.

"Jack, I can hear you just fine. I'm several oceans away from you though, you know?" she chuckled. She could picture NOPD Commander Jack Françoise in his office at One Police Plaza in New Orleans. Mic knew him well. She'd spent a week with him in the spring when they'd identified and hunted the St. Germaine serial killer. Mic imagined the sunlight shining on his hair as he quickly moved his massive body around his office. The burly policeman was a go-getter and Michaela had incredible respect for him. But, by far the best thing about Jack Françoise was that he was still a street cop at heart. He was a cop's cop and his men loved him.

"Did you catch him yet? Did you catch that miserable son-of-a-bitch?" he hollered into the phone. "Monique said you're sure St. Germaine is on the same ship with you and the Countess." Mic could hear the excitement and feel the tension in Jack's voice. She knew he was about to jump out of his skin.

"No," she sighed. "I haven't caught him and I haven't seen him either. Several days ago, someone killed a blackjack dealer in the ship's casino. Of course, it's been kept pretty hush-hush and the passengers don't know."

"Yeah, yeah, but what about St. Germaine?" Jack said, once again impatient, his voice full of excitement and anxiety.

"Let me tell you the entire story, Commander," Mic said in a firm voice. "Then, it'll make more sense to you when I'm done. Is that okay?"

Jack felt guilty for rushing her. "Yeah. Sure, sure, give it to me from the top."

Mic took a deep breath and began. "There are a lot of physicians, primarily psychiatrists, on board this cruise ship. Blake Pharmaceutical offered this cruise as a reward and/or incentive for psychiatrists who had prescribed their newest antidepressant, Quelpro."

"Yeah, and..." Jack said in a tight voice. "That's why medicine's cost so much…that kind of stuff pisses me off," he said loudly.

"Dottie met a young physician and his wife from Washington, DC. We had dinner with them and Senator Peter Bostitch from Maryland. We learned a large number of psychiatrists aboard the ship have concerns about this antidepressant. Dr. Pennington and Senator Bostitch are two of them," Mic continued.

"Yeah, Monique knows Bostitch. She's upset," Jack interrupted. "I think they went to school together or something."

"Yeah, I know. Another physician, Dr. James O'Leary, a psychiatrist and researcher who represented a significant group of concerned psychiatrists, was to present data with the hopes of having Quelpro recalled by the FDA and retested for safety and efficacy. That night, a man fell, or was thrown, overboard and Dr. O'Leary hasn't been seen since."

Mic paused and added, "The Captain believes Dr. O'Leary was the man overboard."

"Humph." Jack was thoughtful. "Don't know. That's not like St. Germaine. He doesn't kill like that… but I guess he could change his MO," he said in a disappointed voice.

Mic shook her head and laughed, "I'm not finished yet. Don't interrupt me."

"Okay, I won't. Sorry, Mic," Jack apologized in a contrite voice. "You know how much I wanna get this guy."

"Yeah! Exactly. I know that. And I want to get him too." She paused for a minute, laughed, and then asked, "Can I continue, Commander?"

"Yeah, please do. I promise I'll shut up, or at least I'll try harder," Jack promised.

"Dr. O'Leary didn't show up for his lecture yesterday morning, the lecture that would hopefully persuade Blake Pharmaceutical with sound, empirical evidence and force them to recall their drug. Now, it's believed that Dr. O'Leary is the man that was thrown overboard as I said earlier."

"Yeah, that one. Damn," Jack said angrily. Mic could practically hear Jack think.

"Dottie and I talked… rather we had tea with Senator Bostitch yesterday afternoon. He was supposed to have dinner with the Blake Pharmaceutical executive team last night and tell them that he was going to the FDA and have Quelpro, the antidepressant, recalled."

"Yeah, and…"

Mic paused for a moment, "So, to summarize, we've got a dead blackjack dealer, a doctor we know was threatening to Blake Pharmaceutical and most likely thrown overboard before he could present incriminating evidence against

Blake Pharmaceutical, and a dead Senator. Are you with me?"

"Yeah, Yeah. I got it. Go on," Jack said in a gruff voice. "Then what happened?"

"Senator Bostitch never made it to dinner with the Blake Pharmaceutical executives. Last night, Captain Wodensen told Dottie and me the Senator was dead. Murdered, or rather, butchered in his stateroom."

"What? What the hell! Are you telling me that some son of a bitch killed a United States Senator on the ship in the middle of the Mediterranean Sea?" Jack's voice was so loud Mic laid her phone on the table.

"Yeah, that's exactly what I'm saying. Dottie insisted the Captain allow us to view the body. He resisted, but Dottie pulled rank."

Jack laughed shortly. "Yeah, I'm sure. Doesn't she pretty much own the cruise line?"

"She owns a large percentage of it. Anyway, the crime scene was bad. One of the worst I've seen," Mic admitted.

"Describe it," Jack ordered.

Mic took a deep breath as the heinous scene flashed before her eyes. "Senator Bostitch was hanging upside down in his bathroom. His feet were tied to the shower rod, his body rested on the side of the tub and his head was on the floor. His throat had been slit and he had exsanguinated."

Jack was silent for a moment. He cursed and said, "That sounds just like St. Germaine. Did you get any pictures?"

"Yeah. I'm texting them to you now." Mic said as she texted the graphic pictures to Jack in New Orleans. "Are they coming through?"

"Hang on. Let me look at them," he said impatiently. "Damn, they're taking forever. So damn slow," he growled.

Mic patted Angel and scratched his ears as she waited for Jack to view the three pictures she'd texted of Senator Bostitch's body. Her stomach was in knots as she waited for him to reply.

"Damn, Michaela. It sure as hell looks like St. Germaine to me!" Jack said in an excited voice. "So, you think the pharmaceutical bastards murdered the doctor and the Senator to keep their damn medicine from being taken off the market?"

Michaela sighed. "Yeah, I do. That's my theory and exactly what I think, along with several physicians aboard the ship." She paused and continued, "But, I gotta tell you, a lot of them have quieted down since they learned of James O'Leary's disappearance. When they learn the Senator has been murdered, that may stop everyone from speaking out."

Jack cursed and tapped his pencil against his yellow pad. "Yeah, well damn. No surprise there. I'm sure of that. Who knows the Senator's dead?" he asked.

Mic quickly replied. "The Captain, his security team, his cabin steward, Dottie, and me. I think that's everyone. Dottie told the Captain to call the FBI. I guess he'll wait until nine a.m. in the United States."

"I'll call our FBI contact here in New Orleans. No one in the entire FBI knows St. Germaine any better than Travis Stoner does. When do you get into port?"

"We're in Athens in two days. We dock at nine in the morning."

Mic heard Jack's sharp intake of breath. "I'll be there with Special-Agent-in-Charge Stoner of the FBI. I'll call the

Washington Bureau or have the Governor call them. Senator Bostitch's family must be notified. I'll also have the FBI and an Athens law enforcement official take control of the bodies of the blackjack dealer and the Senator. Can you think of anything else I need to do, Michaela?"

Michaela thought for a few seconds and said, "See if you can negotiate some crime scene investigators to come aboard the ship to gather evidence. The Captain plans to remove the Senator's body ASAP because of the smell. They also want to clean the stateroom for the same reason."

Jack was quiet for a moment. "Well, he'll probably have to do that, but ask him to leave as much of the crime scene intact as he possibly can. Have him ice both bodies."

"Will do. There's a morgue onboard. The blackjack dealer is already in there."

"I hope so. Most likely, St. Germaine killed him too," Jack said as he cursed under his breath.

"Yeah. Probably so," Mic sighed. "From what I heard, it happened so quickly that no one saw anything… or at least that's the Captain's official story. Whoever slit the man's throat, pushed the body to the floor and then quickly shoved it under the blackjack table. Then the perp walked out, free and unencumbered."

Mic could hear the wheels turning and Jack's mind.

"What an SOB," Jack said with a low whistle. "The guy's got balls. Nobody can deny that!"

"Yeah, then he disappeared into thin air. No one in the casino or the ship's staff can offer up any kind of description at all," Mic said with a sigh, "except for the casino cashier and she can't remember him. There's a poor image caught on camera that's not helpful at all."

"Can't, or won't?" Jack asked sarcastically. Mic heard the familiar squeak of his chair as he lowered his body into it. Thousands of miles away in the Big Easy. Technology is pretty incredible. For just a moment, Mic longed for a Muffeletta from the Central Market. Her stomach growled as the room service menu flashed through her mind.

"No idea, but I'd guess can't since I think most of the staff would be honest. They are desperately poor and need their jobs," she acknowledged.

Jack mulled Mic's statement over in his mind. "Yeah, you're probably right. That quick and easy murder sounds like St. Germaine," Jack said. "He's dangerous, fast, and deadly." He paused. "Anything else?"

"Yeah. There's one more thing, Jack. Slade McKane is coming to Athens too. Why don't you and Travis Stoner meet up with him and the three of you can board the ship before they allow people off. Perhaps you can view the ship's security camera footage and look at the passenger manifest to see if you can spot him."

"Hell, yeah! If St. Germaine makes it off that ship he's never gonna get back on. He'll get lost in Athens and we'll lose him again."

"Exactly," Michaela said. "Here's Slade's cell number. Coordinate with him and I'll see you in a couple of days."

A thought crossed Jack's mind and he said, "Why is Slade coming? Of course, I'm glad, because he's one of the best police officers I've ever worked with and it'll be great to see him."

"Oh," Michaela said, "That's another whole story. I'll save that for another day," she said.

That seemed to satisfy Jack. "Okay, Mic. I'll text you my arrival info, contact the FBI, and let them deal with the

White House and the Senator's family. I'll also talk with Slade. See you at nine in the morning, two days from today."

"Sounds good, Commander. If anything else comes up, I'll let you know. Bye."

Michaela heard Jack click off the line and turned to Dottie. "He'll be here in two days. Jack, Slade, and the FBI will board the ship before anyone is allowed to disembark. Do you think that'll be a problem for Captain Wodensen?"

"Not in the least," Dottie said with a smile. "But, I'm tired and I'm headed for bed." She paused at the door, turned around and said, "Are you sure you don't want to stay in my suite tonight?"

Mic laughed and said, "I'm positive. "I've got Angel and two weapons. I'll be fine," she assured her.

Dottie shot her a dirty look and scowled, "I hope you're right. I've saved your butt more than twice," she said in her haughty, Countess voice.

Mic threw a pillow at her and said, "Good night, Countess!"

Chapter 33

Grady lay in his bed in his tiny cabin and thought about his conversation with the greasy-haired man with the snake tattoo on his hand. He didn't like the guy. There was something about him that made him angry. The guy was pushy. Nosy. He was fishing for something. He'd been okay at the movie theater, but then, when they had gone over to the bar for a few drinks, the guy had gotten downright intrusive.

Grady sat on the side of his bed and pondered his conversation with Snake. It seemed like Snake wanted to know everything about his girlfriend. It was almost as if the guy knew Michaela and that made him angrier than hell. I'll kill the son of a bitch if he gets near my Michaela, he promised himself. He rose from his bed and paced his stateroom from the bed to the door, from the door to the bed, and back until he was dizzy. Then he sat in his desk chair and studied his image in the mirror. He preened in front of the mirror. It was true, he looked pretty good. Of course, his hair was a little wild and he looked a little ragged around the edges, but in truth, he was good looking. At least that's what women had told him in the past. And, he was buff. He'd spent hours in the gym until he'd honed his body into a perfect machine.

Grady returned to his bed, but he couldn't calm down. That was the thing about liquor. It calmed most people down, but agitated him. That was probably because he shouldn't drink with his medications. He checked his watch and it was after eleven. It was time for him to get to work and brew a few potions. His heart beat rapidly as he excitedly gathered his 'medicine.' Amazing what a man would do to rescue the woman he loved, Grady thought as he smiled to himself. He cursed as he drooled on an assortment of pills and liquids. He was as excited as he'd ever been.

He went over to his desk, gathered the strands of fabric from the drawer, and rubbed them once again between his fingers. The feeling was amazing; it was magical how the dress scraps calmed him and fed his soul. He knew Michaela would love and honor him for the rest of her life. He returned to the closet and caressed her shoes. The touch and smell of the soft leather comforted him. But there wasn't time for that any longer. This time tomorrow, he'd be holding Michaela as they planned the rest of their lives. He wouldn't have to rely on scraps of fabric and shoes.

A sharp knock on his door startled him for a moment. He laid the treasured scraps of torn fabric back into his desk drawer and answered his stateroom door. It was room service. Grady smiled at the waiter, tipped him with a ten-dollar bill, and accepted the tray. The tray had warm apple cobbler and a pot of Sleepy Time tea. It smelled delicious. She'd love it. He retrieved a package of beef strips wrapped in foil and placed them on the tray. He'd make something really 'special' for the dog. He hated the massive beast.

Grady quickly went into his bathroom and removed a package of hair color from his backpack. He quickly combed the color through his hair until it was quite dark, at least ten shades darker than its normal sandy-blond color. He reached for a pair of oversized eyeglasses, placed them on his nose, and smiled at himself in the mirror. Yeah, he looked good. Two steps later, he was in his closet where he put on a pair of dark pants and a white shirt. He looked just like a room service waiter. Once again, he preened in the mirror, surprised and pleased that he didn't recognize himself. He grinned, picked up the tray, and sprinkled his 'magic' potions in the apple cobbler and tea, and on beef strips. He picked up the gift he'd purchased Michaela and headed toward the elevator. This was going to be the first long, lustful night, a night he'd dreamed of for eight years.

Chapter 34

Michaela and Dottie met Ian and Alana Pennington for lunch in a private dining room. This meal lacked the excitement and gaiety that had made their first meeting exciting and exceptional just a few days ago. Ian seemed sad and defeated. He appeared to have aged ten years in only three days. Alana was pale and wan.

"Had you two planned to do something special in Rhodes tomorrow?" Dottie asked Alana.

Alana smiled and said, "Yes, we had. I'm so sorry the ship isn't stopping there, but I'm excited we're going there after Athens. Rhodes is one of my most favorite places on the Mediterranean. I spent time there when I lived in Malta. I visited Rhodes several times. It is quite beautiful with lovely beaches," she said happily.

"Will you take a tour or head off on your own when you go?" Michaela asked.

Alana smiled again and said, "We plan to meet friends. I have friends, old friends from my time in the Mediterranean. I'm anxious to see them," she said quietly. She turned to her husband and as she gently touched his hand asked, "You're excited too, aren't you Ian?

Mic studied Ian Pennington. He was a shadow of the handsome, loquacious man she'd met earlier in the week.

Ian reached for his wife's hand, touched it, and said warmly, "Of course, I am, my dear. Why wouldn't I be?" he asked as he gave her a strange look. "The extra day will give us time to explore and plan another climb on Mt. Attavyros," he teased. "Of course, now we may be too old make it to the top," he said, as he grinned at his wife.

"We can definitely reach the top… and have time for Afandou Beach. We're still young, and we can make it," she assured him with a smile.

"How have the other physicians on board reacted to the rumor that the man overboard was Dr. O'Leary?" Dottie asked Ian.

Ian was surprised at the question and shrugged his shoulders. "They're shocked, saddened. We all are. And, if the rumor is true – the rumor that Senator Bostitch is dead, well, that's tragic," he said as he raised his eyebrows and looked directly into Dottie's eyes.

"And the conference, how is the conference proceeding?" Mic asked as she deftly changed the subject.

Ian pushed a piece of filet mignon around on his plate. "It's going fine. Blake Pharmaceutical is working hard to recruit physicians to prescribe their drugs, not just Quelpro. It's as though James O'Leary's death, and possibly Senator Bostitch's death are in vain," he said sadly.

"Do you think the psychiatrists will rally again and try to have Quelpro recalled?" Dottie asked as she searched Ian's eyes for hope.

Ian shook his head. "I've no idea. The doctors I'm friends with are just going through the motions. Everyone knows the drug is bad, but you must admit the death of two notable people is quite intimidating, not to mention frightening, Countess Borghase. I imagine it will be quite some time before anyone takes action against this drug, or any drug produced by Blake," he said honestly.

Dottie shook her head angrily and growled, "All this is bullshit, and it's just not right."

Mic flashed a dirty look at her. "Really, Countess, such language at dinner?" she added with a smile. "It's bad; it's so bad that I don't know how to give it a name."

"As I said, it's bull," Dottie retorted, her face flushed with anger.

Michaela nodded and said, "Ian, you can be sure that when we return to the US, Dottie and I will look at all of this. We have powerful political friends who are hard hitters and a network of law enforcement officials, both at the state and federal levels. You can be sure, Ian, that Dr. O'Leary did not die in vain," Mic assured him.

"And, I'll second that," Dottie said. "Michaela and I will work when we return to Richmond. I'll need you to supply us with all of Dr. O'Leary's research that you have access to. We'll have it reviewed and analyzed so that we can proceed as quickly as possible."

Ian's eyes brightened and he looked alive again, "That would be wonderful. So, you really will help us?" he asked, his handsome face alert and eager.

Michaela nodded and said, "Of course, we will. But, I think it's best you keep it to yourself until we're back in the United States. I think it's best for all of us here, at least at this point, to let Blake Pharmaceutical think they've won."

Dottie snorted, made an ugly face, and her eyes flashed anger, "They may think they've won, but actually, this is just the first inning."

Ian smiled and reached for Alana's hand. He squeezed it and winked at her. "I told you, things would somehow work out."

Alana smiled happily, but then a frown crossed her face, "Countess Borghase, can you tell us if Senator Bostitch is truly dead? There are rumors that suggest that he was murdered. And, no one has seen him at all today."

Ian nodded. "Alana is correct. He didn't appear at any of the conference meetings today. Nor did he come to the breakfast or any coffee breaks." Ian paused and continued, "He always attends breakfast,"

Mic shook her head and said, "Where do you think those rumors originated?" she asked with a frown.

Ian shook his head. "I've no idea where they came from, but they are rampant. A psychiatrist I don't know asked one of the Blake representatives if the Senator was still on the cruise."

"And, what did the Blake representative say?" Dottie asked curiously.

"He said he'd heard the Senator had been recalled to Washington and was no longer on the ship," Ian said as he locked eyes with Dottie.

Mic stared at Dottie. "So, that's the party line, I guess," Dottie said sarcastically.

"Is Senator Bostitch dead?" Alana asked in a soft voice as her eyes plead for the truth.

Mic nodded and said, "This is for your ears only, and it's not to be shared, correct Countess?"

Dottie nodded and simply said, "Someone killed the Senator before dinner last night."

Alana's face paled and she looked at her husband. "I want off this ship tomorrow. I want to return home before they come after you, Ian," she said in a stubborn, determined voice.

Ian remained silent and looked at his wife. It was clear they read each other's minds. Ian knew he was probably Blake's next major enemy.

Mic gave Dottie a slight nod. They'd discussed his potential danger earlier. "I think your fear is well-founded, Alana. I do think Ian is on their list, but there is no way they would attempt another murder on the ship.

"How... how do you know?" Alana asked in an uncertain voice.

"I can't be certain, but statistically and operationally, it would be unwise for them," Mic said with more reassurance than she felt.

"I can arrange for you to disembark in Athens, Ian," Dottie said. "As a matter-of-fact, the Mediterranean Cruise Line will pay your return airfare to the United States and any expenses you incur along the way. For instance, if you wanted to stay in Rhodes for a few days, and then visit Athens, Mykonos, or any Greek Isle, we will foot the bill. It would be a gift from the cruise line," she said graciously.

Alana's eyes lit up, "Oh, Ian, we can spend an extra day with Maya in Rhodes and then take the couple of nights on Mykonos," she said excitedly.

Ian squeezed his wife's hand and said, "Countess Borghase, Dottie, this is a truly generous gift you've offered us. From the bottom of my heart, I thank you," he said as he got up and kissed Dottie's cheek. Alana rose from her seat and kissed Dottie's other cheek and said, "Thank you, Countess. I love your ship and meeting you and Michaela has been a real treat. But honestly, I'll be happy to get off."

Dottie nodded, laughed, and said, "I'm pretty ready to get off too, and I own the damn thing. I'm delighted you've accepted our gift. Believe it or not, most folks really love my cruise line!"

Mic looked across the table and gave Dottie a warm smile. For a crotchety, snotty, rich old lady, the old girl had a heart of gold. And, she looked magnificent in a rose-colored dress and her pearls. Dottie looked lovely and she was ageless.

"Well, that settles that," Dottie said in a matter-of-fact voice. "I'll alert the front desk to make your plane reservations to wherever you want to go until you return to the United States. Now, let's have dessert," she said as she waved for their waiter.

Mic and Dottie ordered tiramisu while Ian and Alana shared chocolate cheesecake, with raspberry sauce. It was delicious.

"There is one more thing I'd like to ask you guys," Michaela said. "I need a little help."

"Sure," Ian said between bites of cheesecake. "Anything."

"Some friends of mine will be coming aboard in Athens to help search for the murderer. In truth, that's why we changed the ship's itinerary. We didn't want anyone to escape the ship tomorrow in Rhodes. There will also be a representative, a Special-Agent-in Charge-from the FBI, and other law enforcement officials to meet us."

Alana's mouth opened part way as she stared at Mic. "Is there any clue as to who the murderers are or who the murderer is?" she asked as a look of fear crossed her face.

"Yeah, we have an idea who it might be," Mic admitted. "We hope to arrest him, or them, in Athens. Later, maybe a day or so later, we plan to have the FBI and other police and law enforcement officials, meet with the Blake

Pharmaceutical officers at dinner in the Captain's private dining room or another place," Mic informed them.

Ian nodded and listened carefully as he held Alana's hand and stroked it tenderly.

"The plan is tentative but I'll issue them the ship's invitation, just as you were issued a few days ago," Dottie said with a conspiratorial wink. I'm sure they'll accept and they'll be held captive by yours truly and international law enforcement. I can assure you they'll be asked some hard questions, very hard questions," Dottie repeated with a look somewhere between a smile and a smirk.

"I've got a few questions I'd like to ask them," Ian said with a snarl as he put his fork down." Alana grabbed his arm and squeezed it. "No," she hissed, "we're leaving in Athens. We won't be on board the ship."

Michaela laughed and turned to Ian, "You've certainly got a wife who loves you and wants you out of danger. However, I'd like for you to come up with a few questions that you think would be helpful to help law enforcement look for information about the usefulness and safety of Quelpro."

Ian nodded. "I'm happy to. I'll give you the list soon, certainly before we disembark," he promised.

"We're specifically looking for motive to implicate the pharmaceutical firm for murder," Dottie said in a tight voice. "So anything you can come up with will be helpful… anything," she repeated.

"I'm your guy. I'll have it to you tomorrow," he promised with a smile.

"Now, I'm going to get us a bottle of champagne to begin your new vacation," Dottie said as she clicked her finger for service.

Mic rolled her eyes at Dottie and saw only happiness on the faces of Ian Pennington and his lovely wife.

After a glass of bubbly, Mic stood and said, "I have a date with the pool and then the spa. You all enjoy your champagne and I'll catch up with all three of you later."

Alana and Ian hugged Michaela while Dottie rolled her eyes and said, "How can anyone give up excellent bubbly to sit in the sun and sweat? It makes no sense at all."

Ian raised his glass in tribute to Dottie and said, "I'll drink to that, Countess."

Michaela left the room, the sound of laughter in her ears.

Chapter 35

Michaela slept late the next morning, and awakened with a pounding headache. It was a little after eight. In twenty-four hours, she'd see Slade. Her spirits picked up in anticipation. She lay in bed for a few minutes because she felt too tired to get up. As she lay there, she recalled the numerous dreams she'd had last night. She'd dreamed a stranger, a man, was in her room. A man who was familiar and yet, she couldn't place him. He'd loomed over her most of the night and, at one point, had gone to her closet, taken out her ruined clothing, and laid it on her bed. She felt chill bumps pop out on her arms and trembled at the memory. The dream was so real and the stranger, the man in the dream was familiar. She shuddered and as her head continued to pound. She'd looked into the man's eyes and they'd been filled with lust. His voice had sounded like a robot. He'd mumbled words to her most of the night and jerked her toward him each time she tried to turn away. He'd told her he loved her and that they would soon be together forever.

Did the man kiss her in the dream? Michaela touched her hand to her cheek, but it felt completely normal. It'd just been a nightmare… just a nightmare that wouldn't go away. The dreams had lasted the entire night, even when she flipped and flopped in her bed. At one point, she'd felt like a prisoner in her own body. She'd wanted to run, to escape, but she'd been powerless. She'd felt paralyzed. Finally, she fell asleep.

Mic sat on the side of the bed. A piercing pain shot through her head and raged through her body. She was dizzy and shaky. She covered her face with her hands and tried to focus. Her vision was cloudy and she couldn't see well. Again, her mind returned to the dreams and the memory of the night unnerved her. She finally rose and trotted over to the sliding glass doors. Her legs didn't seem to want to move. They felt heavy and useless. She opened the curtains and looked out onto the glittering Mediterranean Sea. She could see land in the distance. Athens, perhaps? Sure, it was the Greek coast. She hadn't been to Athens since she'd graduated from college. She remembered the little breakfast Bistro she and Dottie planned to visit and smiled to herself. She was excited to visit the ruins that made the city so famous. Mic's headache beat steadily, and she felt a little woozy, so she took a seat in her chair. Then she noticed Angel.

Angel lay in his kennel with one eye open, gazing at her sleepily. For a moment, she was concerned. Angel always awoke earlier than she did. Generally, her beloved dog was up early and usually was staring at her when she finally opened her eyes.

Mic sat on the floor and rubbed his ears. "What's up, buddy? Are you a sleepyhead today? It's our last day on the ship before Slade gets here to help us catch the bad guys," she said with a yawn as she reached for a glass of water and two headache pills.

Angel looked up at her, but didn't move. Fear permeated Michaela's heart. Was something wrong with Angel? She'd never known him to lie around like this, not even when he'd gotten shot, or when his leg had been repaired a few months ago from a knife wound. The powerful dog had always stood, even when she was afraid he would bleed to death. Mic was breathless with anxiety as she assessed Angel. Her headache forgotten.

"Do you need some water?" She asked as she went into the bathroom with his water bowl. She could feel Angel's eyes follow her as she walked across her stateroom. She rinsed his bowl and filled it with fresh water. She laid the bowl at his feet and he leaned over and drank greedily. Michaela watched him carefully. "You're a thirsty boy, aren't you?"

Angel stopped drinking for a moment, looked at her, and then finished all the water in his bowl. A second later, dread surged through her and she was afraid his renal failure had returned. Angel had been critically ill with acute renal failure a few months ago, but had recovered nicely. Mic felt panic as she considered how ill he could be and her vet was thousands of miles away.

Mic lay on the floor with her dog and stroked his massive body. He licked away the tears that had fallen onto her cheeks and her face. She was so scared. Her bones were numb from terror. Finally, she said, "Let's get up and go, buddy. Let's get up, go out on the balcony, and enjoy the morning breeze. That'll wake you up," she said with assurance. "Come on, get up, and come with me."

Michaela watched in dismay as Angel attempted to stand. He couldn't. More hot tears jumped into her eyes and streamed down her face. Had he had a stroke? What was wrong? Something was seriously wrong with him. He couldn't walk! Fear encapsulated her heart and she was sick with fear.

Mic kneeled next to him as Angel struggled to his feet. He finally stood, but his hind legs trembled with weakness. She encouraged him and he took several steps toward the door and then collapsed. Mic sat on the floor with him and rubbed his ears. "That's okay. You must be tired. I'll let you rest a couple of minutes while I get you some more water. Then we'll try again."

Angel gave his tail a feeble wag as Mic picked up his bowl.

"The door is only another few feet. I think the outside air will make you feel better," Mic said reassuringly as she ruffled the fur on Angel's back and massaged his front and hind paws. Angel looked at her sadly. He had a bewildered look in his eyes and seemed a little confused.

She lay next to Angel on the floor and he looked at her, a strange look in his eyes. It seemed as though he wasn't all there, but he wanted to be and he struggled to be alert. She offered him water and the dog drank greedily. Michaela watched him as she ticked off things that could be wrong with him. She wondered if it would do any good to call the ship's physician.

"You just lay here, buddy. I'm gonna go take a quick shower and get dressed. Dottie is gonna knock on our door in a little while and we'll need to go to breakfast," she said as the words choked her. She wondered if Angel would be able to leave her stateroom. Hot tears burned her eyes but she wouldn't shed them. She didn't want to upset her dog. She couldn't imagine life without him. Nor could she imagine taking him to a vet in a country where she couldn't even speak the language.

Mic rose, opened the balcony door, and allowed the breeze to flow in on Angel. When she returned from her shower, Angel looked a bit more alert and struggled to stand.

"Maybe you're just tired," Mic said as she watched her dog rise on four legs. "Tell you what," she said as she took his leash. "Let's see if we can get on the balcony and you can lie out there for a while. Then we'll try to walk a little bit on the Promenade. That way, you can get your strength back."

She watched as her massive dog, the love of her life, and her dearest friend walked slowly and painfully onto the small balcony and look out at the sea. Mic followed him and put his water bowl in front of him. "Here's a couple of duck jerky treats to hold you over until we get your breakfast," she said, slightly reassured that Angel walked a short distance.

Mic walked through her suite and noticed the half-eaten apple cobbler and empty pot of tea on her dresser. Fat lot of good the Sleepy Time tea had done her. She'd hardly slept. She picked up the tray and set it in the hall outside her stateroom. She knew Sergio would take it for her.

Her headache had slowed to a dull roar. She combed her short dark hair and dressed in a dark green running suit. She walked over into her closet and removed her only pair of tennis shoes.

Mic grimaced when she saw the blood on them, Senator Bostitch's blood. She quickly took them into the bathroom, ran hot water over the rubber soles, and doused them with shampoo. Finally, the soles of her shoes almost sparkled. She dried them as best she could with her hairdryer and put them on. She checked her watch. It was almost ten. She wondered where Dottie was.

She called for Angel and the dog slowly walked toward her. Mic leaned down for a doggy kiss, which Angel quickly offered. She attached his leash to his harness and closed the stateroom door quietly. Mic didn't want to disturb Dottie. The last few days had been exhausting for them and at eighty-two years of age, Mic couldn't imagine how Dottie felt.

Michaela and Angel walked slowly, side-by-side to the elevator. Mic didn't see the man ogling her from behind the wall near the laundry, nor did she see Snake loitering near the elevator. Grady saw both of them.

Chapter 36

Michaela shoved her eggs around on her plate as she gazed out the window at the Mediterranean Sea. She and Angel had taken a painful walk around a quarter of the Promenade deck before Angel's eyes had begged her to let him rest and he'd lain down. She checked her watch and decided to call Dottie. Her headache was now a dull thud on the top of her head.

She jumped when someone tapped her on the shoulder. It was Dottie.

"You're a bit jumpy today, aren't you?" Dottie asked pleasantly. Dottie was dressed for lunch in a love pants set. She looked at Michaela carefully and continued, "Plus, you look tired."

Mic's eyes filled with tears as she motioned for Dottie to sit down.

"Oh, Dottie." she wailed. "Something's wrong with Angel. This morning, he could barely walk. He couldn't even get up or stand."

"What?" Dottie asked sharply. She jumped out of her seat and walked around to where Angel lay on the floor next to Mic. She reached into her pocket and pulled out a treat. Angel accepted the treat, looked at Dottie with grateful eyes, and then laid his head back on his front paws and closed his eyes.

"See what I mean? Any other time he would have gotten up and licked your hand when you gave him the treat," Mic said. "I just don't understand it."

Dottie was troubled and her face was grim. "Is he any better at all? Is he drinking water?" she asked in a tremulous voice.

Mic nodded. "Yeah, he drank a lot of water. In fact, he's had at least twice as much as he generally does. And, he's eating as well. He ate his kibble this morning." Mic looked down at Angel and scratched his ears.

Dottie pulled out the chair next to Michaela, sat down, and faced the dog. There was no question that Dottie loved Angel. Just six months or so ago, the brave dog had saved her life. Angel loved Dottie, too. "What should we do?"

Mic shrugged her shoulders. "I don't know for sure. I think I'll call his vet in a couple of hours and see what he thinks. I'm worried that it could be his kidneys," she said with tears in her eyes.

"Now, now, now," Dottie blustered. "Don't make things any worse than they are. He's been great up until this morning, right?" She asked as she pushed her silver hair back into a tortoise shell comb and brushed imaginary crumbs from her silk blouse.

Mic nodded her head. "Yeah, earlier it seemed like he was a little confused, like he really wasn't in there. But now, he's a lot more alert and seems to be with it. He's just so tired," she said as Angel licked her hand for reassurance.

A million thoughts invaded Dottie's mind as she looked at the massive, retired canine. "He walked down here, didn't he?" She asked as she watched Angel lick Michaela's hand.

Mic nodded. "Yeah, we took a short walk on the Promenade deck. We got about a quarter of the way around the ship and Angel collapsed. He was too tired to go any farther. I let him rest for about a half an hour and then we walked up here."

Dottie considered what Mic had said. "Well, it sounds like he's better than he was when he first got up, right?" She was searching for positive things to say. It killed her when Mic was upset.

Michaela nodded slowly. "Yeah, he is. I guess he's considerably better," she said as hope surged through her bones. She paused and remembered, "When he woke up, he couldn't even stand up," she added as fear raced through her heart at the memory.

Dottie motioned to the waiter for some yogurt and hot tea. "Okay, here's the deal. I'll ask the Captain if there's a veterinarian on board and if so, we'll see if he'll agree to see Angel. How does that sound?" she asked as she gave Mic a wide smile.

Relief flooded Michaela's face and she said, "Oh, Dottie. You're the biggest pain in my butt, but honestly, I don't know what I'd do without you," She gratefully kissed the older woman's cheek.

Dottie smiled broadly, "I don't know what you'd do without me either," she quipped as she flashed a triumphant smile at Mic. She paused and inspected Angel. He did look sick. "Give him a bone, one of those dental bones he loves, and let's see if he can chew it," she suggested.

Michaela, who always had a treat or two with her, offered the bone to Angel and he chewed it slowly, but certainly not with the excited anticipation that usually followed his favorite treat.

Dottie reached for her phone and called the Captain's quarters. She asked the duty officer to have the Captain check the passenger manifest for a veterinarian. She ate a spoonful of yogurt and asked, "Did you sleep last night or did you stay awake and look for the bogeyman?"

Mic shook her head. "I didn't sleep well. I had crazy dreams, like there was a man in my room. He was talking to me and saying things to me. In fact, it seemed so real that I can't believe there wasn't someone in there."

"Well, was he good-looking?" she questioned as she raised her eyebrow, offered Mic a conspiratorial grin, and reached for a scone.

Mic tried to reconstruct her dream, but parts of it were blurry and disorganized. "I don't think I ever saw his face," she said honestly. "It was just weird. It felt like I was a prisoner in my own body and couldn't move." She paused a minute and said, "I felt paralyzed in my own body."

Dottie arched her perfectly groomed eyebrows and adjusted the tortoise-shell comb in her hair. "What did you eat before you went to bed? Did you order any food or binge on chocolate?" Dottie asked as she studied Mic carefully. She was concerned over her distress. "That'll give you some bad dreams," Dottie grimaced. "I know from experience. Firsthand experience."

Michaela's eyes opened wide as she remembered, "Listen to this. Late last night, it was after eleven o'clock, room service delivered a tray to me. I didn't order it," she said as the implications permeated her body and her mind processed what had happened.

Dottie's eyes glittered blue and they held Michaela's green ones. "What was on the tray? Did you eat it?" she asked as her nervous fingers folded and unfolded her linen napkin.

Michaela's face was white. "Yes, I did. It was pot of chamomile tea and apple cobbler. I drank all of the tea and ate some of the cobbler," she said as realization dawned on her.

Dottie stared at her and clamped her teeth together. "Where's the tray? Is it still in your room?"

Mic shook her head frantically as her anxiety spiraled out of control. "There were dog treats on the tray. I thought the tray was from you – that you sent Angel some filet of beef treats." Mic's heart hammered in her chest and her teeth chattered so hard she could barely speak.

Dottie reached for her hand, held it in hers and said, "Focus, Mic. Focus. You're okay and Angel is feeling better. Where's the tray now?"

"It's on the floor outside my room. Someone tried to poison my dog, dammit. Someone tried to poison Angel!" She said wildly as she looked around the dining room for someone to blame.

Dottie took Michaela's arm and held it tightly until she was calmer. "Keep your voice down," she said softly. "Stay quiet and we'll check everything out."

Michaela could stand tough with any perp, murderer, predator, or creep at any time. But, for someone to hurt her dog infuriated her. She was so angry and distressed she could barely breathe.

Dottie watched Michaela carefully as her breathing slowed. She waved the waiter over for a big bowl of water for Angel. "We're gonna let him drink all he wants so he can get whatever poison that's in him out," she said in a determined voice. "Here comes Captain Wodensen."

Captain Wodensen looked rested. He smiled at Michaela and Dottie. "Good morning, Countess and Ms. McPherson.

What can I do for you?" he asked pleasantly as he nodded at them.

"Someone was in my stateroom last night and they hurt my dog. He's sick," Mic blurted. "Someone delivered room service to me and it had several dog treats placed on a small dish. Now, my dog is sick. I need a veterinarian and… I need help," she said angrily. Michaela had passed the point of fear and entered the zone of anger.

A look of concern passed over the Captain's face, as he looked down at Angel, asleep at his feet. In the five days they'd been in the Mediterranean, he'd never seen the dog asleep. The dog always had his eyes trained on his mistress. He watched her every move and listened to her every word.

The Captain nodded slowly. "We have a veterinarian on board. She'll meet us in the sickbay. Can your dog walk?" He asked gently.

"I… I think so," Mic choked as she stood.

Captain Wodensen watched as the powerful German Shepard attempted to stand. The dog fell several times, but finally stood and they all slowly walked toward the elevators.

"Captain," Dottie said, "get the cabin steward to retrieve that tray and hold it in the kitchen. If the dog and Michaela were poisoned, then we have another crime on our hands and we'll need the evidence."

The Captain nodded and said, "Consider it done, Countess," Captain Wodensen pulled out his cell phone and sent a text to his First Mate as the three of them and Angel walked slowly to the sick bay.

Once again the Captain reminded himself that he was on the cruise from hell.

Chapter 37

The female veterinarian who examined Angel was tall, dark, and lovely. Angel seemed comfortable with her and that's all Mic cared about.

"What, what do you think?" Mic asked, as she watched Angel tremulously walked the width of the ship's sick bay. "What do you think is wrong with him?" Her eyes were full of pain and fear.

The vet looked at Mic and said, "I'm not sure yet. Has he had any problems with seizures or walking or standing before today?"

Michaela shook her head aggressively. "No, no. Not at all. In fact, he was in perfect health until he got a stab wound earlier this year. It was during that emergency visit that they discovered he was in acute renal failure," she said as her heartbeat increased rapidly at the memory. "But, he recovered completely from that," she said as she breathed a sigh of relief. "He sees his vet at home every couple of months for blood work and so far, he's been fine."

Mic watched as Dr. Yvette Neary continued to examine Angel carefully.

"Has he eaten and drank today?"

Mic nodded. "Yeah. In fact, he's drinking three times more than he usually does," she said as she hoped that was a good thing.

Dottie, who'd been quiet during the examination spoke up and said, "Okay, what do you think, doctor?" In her strong, authoritative voice, she added, "This dog means the world to both of us."

"I'm not sure yet, Countess." Dr. Neary said as she turned to Michela. "I'd like to get some blood work and give him some subcutaneous fluids under his skin. That way, he can eliminate the substance more quickly, if it is indeed a substance," she said. "Does that meet with your approval?"

Mic nodded, "Absolutely. But, how will we get his blood analyzed?"

"We won't be able to until we get to Athens. The Captain has a veterinarian in Athens that he's contacted. The veterinarian will see Angel tomorrow and analyze his blood work."

"So, what do you think happened to him?" Mic asked in a tight voice as her anxiety escalated. "Will he be all right?"

Dr. Neary nodded and said, "Yes, I think your dog will recover. He'll need a complete work up in Athens, but my preliminary diagnosis suggests he's eaten something he shouldn't have or has suffered a mild neurological complication, possibly meningitis."

"Meningitis?" Dottie interrupted loudly. "How would Angel contact meningitis on a cruise ship? How can it be meningitis?" She asked in a frightened voice.

"It's entirely possible he could have contracted meningitis, but I think it's more likely that..." The vet broke off her sentence and looked at Michaela.

Michaela knew it was bad and felt shivers run up her back, "More likely that what?"

"If I were a betting person," Dr. Neary said, "I'd bet someone deliberately poisoned your dog, ma'am."

Even though Mic had suspected this, she was devastated by the news and slipped into a chair. "Why? What can you do, how can you help him?"

Dr. Neary gave her a kind look and said, "I'll give him fluids, and take his blood. He doesn't seem in acute distress now. I'd suggest you exercise him off and on today and let him rest for long intervals in between. Hopefully, by this evening, he'll be back to normal."

Mic was so relieved she jumped up and hugged the young Australian woman. Even Dottie cracked a smile for the woman.

"Dr. Neary. Would you and your family like to join Michaela and me for High Tea? I understand it's the best High Tea on the High Seas," Dottie said with a smile. Her amazing blue eyes focused on the vet.

"I'd love to, Countess Borghase," Yvette Neary agreed.

"We'll see you then," Mic smiled.

Chapter 38

"Slade, oh Slade, I'm so glad to talk to you. Where are you?" Michaela asked with relief as she snatched her phone from its charger. The pall of depression that had crippled her for most of the day disappeared at the sound of his voice.

"Fricking Heathrow. Jack's with me. We met up with each other in Charlotte," Slade said in his deep voice that not only calmed Michaela, but also made her breathless as she imagined how he looked. He'd probably dressed in jeans and gym shoes for the trip. "Damn, I'd forgotten how much I hated Heathrow."

Mic laughed into the phone. She knew Slade hated to stand in lines and Heathrow always had a long line of tired, grumpy travelers. She figured it was even worse with all the terrorist activity around the globe. "Well, at least you've only got one more plane to catch… provided you get through security at Heathrow," she teased.

"I hope so," he grumbled. "Any news there?"

Mic was silent for a moment and then said, "Well, there are no new murders… at least that we know about, but…

"What? What?" he asked in a sharp voice. "What's happened?" Slade knew something was wrong by the slight tremor in Michaela's voice.

"Someone tried to poison Angel… and me," she said in a small voice that didn't sound like her. Her eyes darted to Angel who lay attentive at her feet.

"Poison. What the hell, poison?" Slade was enraged. "How did they ever get close enough to Angel for that to happen?" he hollered. Slade was blind to the stares of people around him. He didn't care if anyone heard him. Jack stared at him with a troubled look on his face and touched Slade's shoulder with his hand.

Michaela gulped and said, "These folks are smart, clever in fact. Last night, I received a room service tray that I didn't order. It was a pot of chamomile tea, apple cobbler, and two beef dog treats for Angel."

"And..." Slade demanded in an angry voice. She could see him in the crowd at Heathrow, tall, dark, and handsome, his chiseled face in a scowl as anger radiated off his body. She knew he'd kick his suitcase and curse under his breath. Slade didn't like to feel helpless. It infuriated him.

She began again with more reassurance in her voice. "Anyway, I thought Dottie had sent the tray. I drank the tea and ate some of the cobbler. Angel devoured the beef treats in less than two seconds," she said as she choked down a sob. Mic knew she was about to lose it again, so she took a deep breath.

"What, what, talk to me, Mic. Then what happened?" he asked in a patient voice. Michaela could imagine his tense, facial muscles.

She stifled a sob and said, "Angel couldn't move this morning. He couldn't walk. He was like... well it was like he was paralyzed."

"Paralyzed. What the hell!"

Mic heard panic in Slade's voice. He loved Angel as much as she did. "He's better now," she added, "but he's still slow."

"But he can walk?" Slade asked in an uncertain tone.

"Yeah. For short distances. He's eating and drinking, though, which is good," Mic said softly as she rubbed Angel's neck.

"How do you know it was poison? Is there permanent damage? What about his kidneys? Is this gonna mess with his kidneys?" Slade asked. Mic heard the fear in his voice.

"There's a vet on board. She's from Australia. She gave Angel fluids and took blood. She diagnosed him as poisoned, but thinks he'll be okay. But... but..." Mic couldn't finish.

"But what? What else, Michaela?" Slade demanded.

"There's a chance it will mess up his kidneys again," she said as she broke down into tears. She paused for a moment and gathered her thoughts. "She said only time will tell..."

Slade interrupted. "He'll be okay, Mic. You know how tough Angel is. I promise he will be," Slade said in a low, soothing voice. He hoped he'd convinced her because he sure hadn't convinced himself.

"I... hope... so," Mic said as the tears flowed. "I know he's getting old and he was already sick this year," she wept. She looked down and saw Angel's soft eyes watching her. She reached down to touch his head and he licked her hand.

"He'll be fine, we'll get him back to the US and back to our police vet, and he'll have him fit as a fiddle in no time. Now, what about you? How are you doing?"

Mic took a deep breath and said, "I had a terrible night. Had bad dreams, like someone was looking down at me and talking to me. Just sayin' stuff... you know," she said as her voice faltered. She needed another moment to compose herself.

"No, I don't know," Slade said in a tight voice. "What kind of stuff?" Once again, Mic could feel the anger jump through the wireless connection.

"Oh, just sexually suggestive junk, mostly that he loved me... that's all. I felt like I was trapped in my body...

couldn't move." Mic felt as if she would suffocate as she told her story. "I was detached from my body. I guess that's the best way to put it."

"And then what?" Slade asked, his voice tight with rage. Michaela could image him clenching and unclenching his fist as the muscles in his face jumped in anger.

"Nothing really. That's about it. I have no idea how long it lasted, but it was as if I was above my body looking down. This morning, when I woke up, I was dizzy with a bad headache."

"How are you now?" He asked softly. "We've gotta keep you, Angel, and Dottie safe for another twenty-four hours."

"I know. I'm okay, but I feel helpless and that's a feeling I never have, Slade. I feel like I can't protect myself, much less Angel and Dottie."

Slade groaned inwardly. "You can, Mic. I promise you that you can… only for a few more hours."

"I will. I can do anything for twenty-four hours even if I have to sit up in my bed all night with a loaded gun," she said with false assurance. She paused and then added, "I think I'll sleep with Dottie tonight. No one has bothered her, but these perps are devious."

"Good idea," Slade said. 'I'd prefer the two of you were together with Angel. Is there anything on Senator Bostitch's killer?"

"Not that I know of, Slade, but the Captain is tight-lipped. Truth be said, I'm sure he can't wait for us to get off the ship. I think he believes Dottie and I have caused all of this crap," she said with a small smile.

"Well, I can't wait to get you off there, all three of you!" Slade said with a low growl. "How do you feel now?"

"Just tired. I'm worried about Angel although he seems better. He certainly isn't up to par though. The ship's doctor believes I was given a date rape drug in the tea, most likely Rohypnol, a roofie," she said, disdain in her voice.

Slade was furious, so incensed he thought he'd pass out. Whoever gave Michaela a date rape drug was as good as dead. He glanced over at Jack, who'd been staring at him during the entire conversation clenching and unclenching his fist. Jack's eyes glittered with anger and his face was menacing. Slade knew Jack would be beside him all the way. Neither man could wait to kill whoever was after the two things he loved most in the world. Michaela and Angel were his life… and of course, the Countess, even though she still intimidated him.

"A date rape drug?" he roared. "The doctor thinks the perp gave you a date rape drug?" Slade was shocked, but when he considered someone had been in Mic's stateroom, carved up her clothes, and stolen her shoes, he considered it a real possibility.

Michaela sighed. "Yeah, it sounds like that. Those things are ten times more powerful than Valium and lots of times, people forget what happened to them."

Slade was silent, but the silence was deadly.

Michaela could imagine what was running through Slade's mind because it was the same thing that had been running through her mind. "I remember all of it. Perhaps my dose wasn't that high. Let's not worry about me, but focus on Angel and getting the bad guys," she suggested in a strong voice.

Slade sighed and took a deep breath. "We will. Jack and I are gonna grab a beer and some food, meet up with Travis Stoner, catch our flight, and we'll see you at nine o'clock in the morning. We'll see you earlier if the ship pulls into port sooner."

Mic's heart did a flip-flop as her body warmed with the thought of seeing Slade, "I can't wait, Slade. Angel and I will be here," she assured him as she imagined the sensual gleam in his eyes.

"Love you, Mic. Please stay alive until I get there," he said softly.

"I will, Slade. Stay safe," Mic assured him.

Mic put down her phone and looked at Angel. "Hey, you wanna go for a walk?"

Angel stood, unstable at first and then off they went.

Chapter 39

The sun had just come up when Mic opened her balcony shades. She walked outside and sniffed the fresh air. She could see land in the distance and knew they were close to Athens. She checked her watch. It was a little after six in the morning. She called for Angel who got up, a bit shakily, from his bed and walked toward her.

Angel stood beside Mic and stared at the sea. Mic sat in her deck chair and looked deeply into her beloved dog's eyes. She was delighted there were no signs of confusion. Angel's eyes were clear. Thank God, he's better, she thought as a shiver ran through her body. She refused to dwell on yesterday because she knew today was going to be a big day. Hopefully we'll catch St. Germaine!

"We're gonna see Slade today," she said as she rubbed his fur and softly patted his head. He laid his head in her lap, studied her face, and whimpered.

"You must feel better today - of course, anything has to be better than yesterday," she said with relief, as she scratched his ears. Angel lavished in her love as the sun shone brightly on his back.

Angel looked up at her, gave her a doggy smile and Mic's heart raced with excitement. The two of them continued to watch the water and feel the movement of the ship for about an hour. Then her cell phone rang.

Mic ran into her suite and grabbed her phone. It was Slade.

"Are you here?" she asked breathlessly as she imagined him in the distance. She hoped the answer was yes.

"I am. I'm having coffee with Jack and Travis Stoner, who heads up the FBI's New Orleans office," he said, a note of humor in his voice. Suddenly, Jack Françoise was on Slade's phone.

"Mic, what you doing? Are we gonna catch St. Germaine today?" Jack barked into the phone.

Mic smiled to herself and said, "Hell yes, Jack. I'm dying to catch him. Have you guys worked out a plan?"

"Yeah, we're doing that right now. And eating us a little bit of breakfast. It's a hell of a long way over here from New Orleans," he complained. "You know how I hate airplanes," he said.

Michaela heard Slade and Stoner laugh in the background. She could imagine the fun they made of the burly New Orleans police commander. It was a known fact that Jack hated to leave the Big Easy.

"Stand up for yourself, Jack," Michaela urged. "Don't let them get the best of you," she encouraged with a laugh.

"It'll be a cold day in hell before that Irish Cajun bastard cop gets anything over on me," Jack laughed. "Here he is now," Jack said as he handed the phone back to Slade.

"Has anything else happened there?" Slade asked Mic. "Anybody in your room or snooping around?" He asked casually, but Michaela heard the anger in his voice.

"Nope, nothing to report except that Angel's a lot better today. He's more like himself," she said as she looked at her dog and saw the rapt expression on his face. He knew Slade was on the phone. Mic reached out and petted him.

"How was sleeping with Dottie?" Slade asked, a hint of laughter in his voice.

Mic groaned. "Honestly, I just couldn't do it. I tried, but I left in the wee hours of the morning," she confessed.

"Not surprised to hear that. Just glad you're okay," Slade said in a low voice. "I will say one thing though, Angel is a survivor."

"Yep, he surely is," Mic said as she leaned over and ruffled the fur on Angel's neck. She paused for a moment and then continued, "I honestly tried to sleep in Dottie's room last night, but she drove me stark raving mad so I came back over here."

Slade laughed. Mic loved it when Slade was happy. Oftentimes he adopted the dark, sometimes morose, personality of his black Irish ancestors. When he did laugh, it was memorable.

"What's the plan?" she asked.

"So far, I think Stoner and Jack plan to be in the area where passengers disembark. We've been told by Greek authorities that the crew disembarks in a different area. So, we'll be there as well."

"Sounds good, but what will Dottie do? You know she's gonna demand a part," Michaela said. She listened as Slade repeated the message to Jack and Stoner.

Jack laughed and said, "I'll take the old girl. She's a tough cookie," Mic heard him say to Travis Stoner. "You're in for a treat, Stoner. This lady is eighty-two years old and she can probably out shoot and out think any of us on any day."

Michaela heard more laughter, but couldn't hear what Stoner mumbled. She'd never met the man, but knew that both Slade and Jack had great respect for him. She was anxious to meet him.

"Have you liaised with the Greek authorities? Are they going to be available to help us?" she asked.

"Yeah, they'll come on board as soon as the ship docks and immediately go to Senator Bostitch's cabin and pick up any forensic information or evidence there is. Jack and Stoner will go with them. They're more acquainted with St. Germaine's work than I am," Slade reported. "The ship will not allow passengers to disembark until we are finished in Senator Bostitch's room. Also, Greek law enforcement will be at the pier and will have officers with all of us as we check passports and passengers." Slade paused and said, "Oh, and we'll have the Counter-Terrorist Unit of the Hellenic Police as well. That's the Greek version of a US SWAT team. Pretty much anything we want."

"Sounds good to me. Will you text me just before you board? I'll meet you at the Senator's stateroom. It's just down the hall from mine," Mic said.

"Will do," Slade promised. "I'll see you soon, sweetie. Can't wait."

"Neither can I," Mic said softly. "Wait a minute, Slade. Angel hears something. He's alerted."

A second later, Angel's head jerked. He pawed at the door and then lunged toward it. He scratched at the carpet near the door. "Let me go, Slade," Mic said in an anxious voice. "There must be someone in the hall Angel doesn't like," she said quickly. "He's on full alert." Angel's face had contorted into a snarl and his teeth were bared. His fur was standing on end. He was ready to attack. His growl was ferocious.

"Take your Glock, Mic. I'd prefer you just stay in your stateroom, but I know you won't," Slade said as he wished he were on the ship with her.

"I've got this, Slade. I'm just gonna take a peek out there. I'll see you in a little while," she said as she clicked off her phone.

Mic quickly walked over to her closet and pulled her gun out of the safe. She threw on a sweatshirt and yoga pants. She put her gun hand in the pocket. "Let's go, Angel. Let's see who tore up my clothes, stole my shoes, and tried to poison us," she said angrily as she slowly opened her door. She didn't see the letter near the closet where Angel's paw had pushed it. Nor did she see the small gift in the corner.

Chapter 40

Grady Jones slipped his love letter and gift under the door. He cursed when Angel lunged against the door. Why hadn't the damn dog died yesterday! He'd put enough ketamine in the treats to kill an elephant. Damn that dog. He had to go. Grady cursed to himself and swiftly ran to the elevator. Thankfully, it was still on Mic's floor. Grady jumped in and pushed the button. The elevator door had closed partway when Angel came for him. A second later, Angel knocked Grady to the floor. Angel stood on his chest and held him securely to the floor. Angel snarled at him, every tooth bared as he stared into the eyes of the terrified man.

Mic, pistol in hand, ran over and looked down at his face. She was shocked when she realized who he was. "Oh, my God, Grady Jones. What in the hell are you doing on the ship?" she asked sharply as confusion seeped through her mind and she tried to figure out why he was there. "What the hell are you doing here, especially outside my stateroom?"

This guy was a former busboy from Biddy McPherson's her Irish restaurant in Richmond, the favorite watering hole of the Richmond police force. Mic studied Grady's face. He had changed a lot in the few years since Michaela had seen him. He was bigger, buff, and in great physical shape. She recalled him as young and thin. His normally sandy-blond hair was dyed brown.

Grady stared up at her. His eyes narrowed and his lips parted in half. "Yeah. It's me. The guy who loves you and the busboy you fired years ago." Grady's anger seethed through clenched teeth. "Get this damn dog off me," he demanded.

Mic remembered that Grady had had a serious crush on her years ago when she'd let him go from the restaurant after it became awkward. She'd given him a good reference to work in a similar pub in Charlottesville. She hadn't heard from him since. And now he was on a cruise ship in the Mediterranean staring up at her while Angel held him captive on the floor in the elevator.

Grady was angry and defiant, "Get this frickin' dog off me," he hissed through gritted teeth.

Mic stared at Grady as anger seeped through her as she realized Grady had poisoned Angel. Red anger flooded her mind and she could hardly think. Fortunately, she recovered quickly, "So you were in my room the other night, you disgusting pervert." she said as fury propelled her to action.

Angel's weight crushed Grady's chest. The dog snarled and growled at him non- stop. One word from Mic and Angel would tear into the man's carotid arteries and Grady would be history.

"Get the damn dog off me. NOW," he screamed. "He can't be with us. He isn't part of our relationship. You'll have to shoot him," Grady ordered as his lazy eye wandered up to look at Angel and his other eye held Mic's angry green eyes.

Mic was shocked. "What? There is no relationship. We have no relationship, Grady. We never have." She held her gun on Grady, dug her phone out of her pocket, and called Dottie who answered in a sleepy voice.

"Michaela, is everything all right?"

Mic laughed shortly and said, "Get your security people here. I know who broke into my room, cut up my clothes, and stole my shoes. I have him, or rather Angel has him, captive in the elevator," Michaela informed her.

"Done," Dottie said shortly, and several minutes later, she appeared at the elevator dressed in an elegant royal blue bathrobe. Her jaw dropped as she looked at the man on the elevator floor and recognized him.

"What the hell? Michaela, isn't this the creepy teenager that had a crush on you for years?" she asked as she stared down at an openly defiant Grady Jones.

"You're such a bitch, a nosy, interfering old bat," Grady hissed at her. "I hate you, you old-lady bitch," he yelled.

Angel snarled and looked at Mic for direction. Then the massive canine turned back to Grady.

"Well," Dottie sniffed as she examined him closely, "at least you look a little better than you used to. Your hair is nasty, but your acne's gone and you have a couple of muscles."

Mic laughed, astonished at Dottie's assessment. "He's no different, just the same old Grady Jones… a little older and the same someone who wants what he can't have," Mic said as she ridiculed the young man.

Grady glared at her with murderous eyes. "You'll be punished for that, Michaela," he promised.

"Punished?" Mic said as she arched her eyebrows, with her angry green eyes fixed on him. "I hardly think I'll be punished. And he's the one who poisoned Angel," she told Dottie as she held Angel's harness and kept her gun trained on Grady's head.

"You little pock-faced bastard." Dottie choked. "Let Angel take him out," Dottie suggested. "He tried to kill him and he gave you drugs," she snapped and then added as she smiled, "That's poetic justice."

Mic was furious as she searched Grady Jones' eyes. "What in the hell do you think you're doing, Grady?"

Grady looked up at her, his eyes bold and empty with a strange mixture of cold and fire behind them. "I'm getting you, Michaela. I'm making you mine… just like it should be."

That's when she realized he was insane.

Grady gave her a small, sly smile, his eyes cold, and his tone icy. "I'm taking you, Michaela. You know we're meant to be together, but somehow I never could make you understand that."

"Not in this lifetime," Mic promised.

"Get the damn dog off me," Grady insisted. "You've got a gun pointed at me."

Michaela stared at him. Part of her felt sorry for him, the other part hated him. "At ease, Angel," she said. Angel jumped off Grady's chest. "Go to Dottie," she commanded. Angel walked over beside Dottie, but his eyes never left Mic.

"Grady, you're in a lot of trouble for this. You'll be arrested and held prisoner on the ship," Mic said as she looked down at him.

Grady laughed at her as he sat up on the elevator floor. He was much larger and more powerful than Michaela remembered. She took a step back from him. A second later, Grady karate-chopped Mic's lower leg, and knocked her to the floor. Her gun hit the elevator wall and bounced from her hand. Grady's snatched the gun and pinned her down to the floor. He trained her gun on her face and slapped her hard.

It happened so quickly. Mic was stunned and saw stars from the blow to her head. Her lower leg screamed pain and for a moment, she wondered if he'd broken her shin bone with the blow.

Angel growled and pulled against his harness, but Dottie held him firmly. She fished her gun out of her blue bathrobe and pointed it at Grady.

"Let me go and we'll let it go. We won't press charges," Mic pleaded, her green eyes dark with concern and pain. "Dottie will work it so the ship's police don't arrest you, right Dottie?" Mic asked.

Grady laughed shortly. "No way will I ever let you go, Michaela. We're meant to be together. I've tried to show you that over the years, but you've scorned me. Now, you must accept it. This is our time," he said, a small smile on his face. "Starting now, we'll be together for eternity." His face was flushed, and there was a strange light in his eyes.

"Let her go, dumb, stupid teenager," Dottie said between clenched teeth as she held her gun on him. "Now, you little pervert," she threatened, "or I'm blowing your fricking brains all over the elevator." Her voice was steely, very much unlike her own.

Grady laughed and looked at her. "Screw you, you old bat. You shoot me, I'll shoot her, and then you'll be all alone… you and the dog," he said with a laugh. "The old bat and her big dog," he mimicked as his lazy eye fixed on Mic and the other on Dottie. "No, on second thought, I'll kill the dog and then you'll be ALL alone," he said with a maniacal laugh.

"No, Dottie. No," Mic pleaded. "I've got this," she promised. She gave her a ferocious look. "Put your gun away," Mic said as she turned back to Grady. "You're not taking me anywhere. Let me go, dammit," she said as she struggled against Grady's superior strength. She had no idea the man was that strong.

Grady smacked her in the face again. "Stop struggling or I'll hit you harder. Don't fight me or I'll shoot you, the old girl, and the dog if I need to," he said forcefully as he wagged the gun at her and then stuck it on the side of her neck.

"You'll never shoot me, Grady. We both know that," Mic scoffed as she rolled her eyes, and pivoted her body to get away from him.

Grady nodded his head and pushed the gun further into her neck. "Yeah, I will. Trust me. If I can't have you, no one else will either," he assured her. He paused for a moment and watched anger flash across Michaela's face. "Now, you're gonna get up slowly, very slowly and we're gonna push this button, take the elevator down, and get off. Then we'll hide somewhere and wait until it's time to get off the ship," he sneered at her as he reached for the elevator button.

Mic laughed at him. "Not on your life, Grady. Why the hell would I go anywhere with you? You tried to kill my dog and you gave me drugs. You were in my room the other night," she glared, her emerald eyes burned with disgust.

Grady smiled as he remembered their tantalizing night and said, "Yeah, I was. But you were unable to do a damn thing about it. Yeah, like you can't do anything now," he teased as he gazed at her with cold eyes.

Dottie was livid with anger. "You're a little chicken bastard, Grady. You'll never get away with this," she told him.

Grady kept his eyes on Mic's face and said, "Tell the old bitch to shut up. If she doesn't, I'll kill you first," he said as he stared into her eyes. "Tell the old girl to put her gun away or I'll kill you," he promised in a soft voice.

Mic knew he was serious. "Dottie, take Angel and go. We'll be okay. Please, I mean it."

Dottie started to argue and Grady slapped Mic in the side of her head. "If you don't leave, old lady, I'm gonna smack your friend until you can't recognize her," he threatened.

"Okay, we're gone," Dottie said. "Don't hit her again. The dog and I are leaving."

Grady watched Dottie and Angel disappear. He held Mic tightly, the gun burrowed into her neck. "Push the button, bitch," he said as he pushed her toward the elevator buttons.

Mic gaped at him and struggled against his strength, but it was useless. He was rock solid and outweighed her by fifty pounds.

Grady smirked at her efforts. "If you don't cooperate, I'll give you more drugs, and then you'll do exactly what I say," he said with a dangerous look on his face. He paused for a moment and then added, "And, this time, I won't be nearly as kind as the other night." A strange light shone through his eyes and Mic's blood chilled.

She shuddered on the inside and stood quietly in the elevator as it descended into the bowels of the ship. She considered her situation. She knew she'd be able to get away from him at some point, but first she needed to retrieve her gun.

The elevator stopped and Grady pushed her body forward. He snarled at her. "Now get off the damn elevator and keep your mouth shut," he said as he jerked her arm and pulled her off the elevator and into a dark hall.

"Where... where are we?" Mic asked as she looked around. She knew her location was aft, but the area and the lower deck were totally unfamiliar. It was dark and dismal and no one was around.

Grady saw the confusion on Michaela's face and smiled a thin evil smile. He was in control of her for the first time in his life. "We're as far down in this boat as we can go," he said in a rough voice. "The engines are down here and there are a few cabins that are rarely used."

Mic nodded as she tried to remember the ship's diagram she'd seen in her stateroom. She was cooperative as Grady hustled her past blocks of maintenance areas and equipment. No staff or employees were around. Michaela wondered if they were between shifts, but she truly had no idea. She was lost in the bowels of the ship.

"We'll get off the ship in a little while. In the meantime, you'll do exactly what I say. Is that clear?" he demanded and gloated with a happy grin as he opened the door of a small cabin.

He gestured her toward the bed.

Mic gritted her teeth, moved forward, obediently sat at the end of the bed, and stared at him. Her heart beat steadily as she looked around and plotted her getaway.

Grady shook his head and frowned. "I can see from your face you're scheming to leave, but rest assured you'll be dead before you get to the door. I'll throw your body in the bilge or the propeller. No one will ever know what happened to you," he said with a sly smile.

Mic saw the crazy look in his eyes. "You'll never get away with this you piece of slime. Never." She said angrily through clenched teeth. She hated to feel helpless.

Grady moved closer to her and his eyes held hers. "Yeah, I will, and that's what scares you, isn't it?" His eyes raked over her body. "Now, isn't it convenient you have on loose clothes," he said with a lewd smile.

Michaela's muscles flexed as he came for her, gun in hand.

"Now, lay down," he said as he struck her once again on the side of her face.

Michaela obeyed him and lay down on the bed, her ear ringing in pain.

Chapter 41

Slade had finished breakfast when his cell phone pinged. He recognized the Countess Borghase's phone number on his digital display and his heart sank. Something was wrong. He frowned as he answered his phone.

"Countess, what's happened?" he asked in a terse voice.

"Michaela's been taken, just a few minutes ago," Dottie said breathlessly. Slade heard the fear in her voice.

"Taken? What the hell do you mean, taken?" The color drained out of Slade's face as he slammed his fist on the table and overturned two coffee cups. He was furious. Jack and Stoner watched him with concern as uncertainty consumed them.

"Who the hell took her? How did they get her?" Slade growled as he spat the words from his mouth.

Dottie sighed, "Do you remember the busboy from the restaurant that always had a crush on Michaela? It's him! His name is Grady Jones. The busboy from Biddy's. She fired him a few years ago."

Slade's fingers clenched the cell phone, his fingertips bloodless. He didn't remember a star-struck kid in love with Mic. Of course, it didn't surprise him. "No, no. I don't know any busboy that wanted Mic," he said angrily. "Who the hell are you talking about?"

Dottie's voice seeped with anger. How dare Slade McKane speak to her with such disrespect? He was supposed to understand. She decided to let it pass, took a deep breath, and continued, "When I got to the elevator, Mic had a gun on the man, and Angel was on his chest. Mic called Angel off and the man grabbed her ankle and lower leg and pulled it out from under her. Then he karate-chopped her shin and she fell down on top of him. The gun flew out of her hand and he got it." Dottie hesitated for a moment to think.

"What, what, then what happened?" Slade asked in a tight voice.

"He slapped her. The guy slapped her hard," Dottie said as she grimaced at the memory. "The blow stunned her, because he got the best of her. The next thing I saw, he was on top of her with her gun pointed at her face."

"Then what?" Slade asked in a harsh voice.

"Then nothing. They left in the elevator. He took her and now she's gone… they're gone," she corrected herself.

"This guy took Michaela?" Slade seethed. "I can't believe some guy came in, hit her, and wrestled her to the floor," he said angrily. "I've never known Mic to lose her gun."

Dottie was pissed. She'd had enough from the arrogant Cajun cop. But this was about Mic, so Dottie let go of her anger and as patiently as she could possibly be said, "I'm telling you, Slade, the guy karate-chopped her leg, pulled her down to the floor, and slapped her hard. When she fell, she lost her gun. That's it. That's how it happened. I saw it." Dottie gritted her teeth as her heart raced blood through her body.

Slade was quiet as he played the scene out in his mind.

"Say something," Dottie hollered into the phone.

"I'm thinking, Dottie. Give me a minute," Slade barked.

"I think she was stunned for a moment," Dottie said angrily. "You couldn't have done any better than Michaela did. That I'm sure of," she added as the reality of her story sank in.

Slade covered his face with his hands and said, "I'm sorry, Dottie. Have they searched for her?"

Dottie's temper flared. "Hell, yeah, they're looking, but I shouldn't have to tell you that we're almost in Athens and there are few officers and security available to search. Besides, the ship is huge and we haven't found St. Germaine yet, and we've been looking for him for days," she reminded him in a hostile voice.

Slade hesitated and said, "Tell me again who took her. What does he look like? I'll put you on speaker phone. Commander Françoise and Travis Stoner with the FBI are with me."

Jack Françoise grabbed the phone. "Countess, it's Jack. In your opinion, is this man dangerous?"

Dottie's eyes rolled nonstop. What is wrong with these people? "Yeah, he's dangerous. He broke into Mic's stateroom, cut up her clothes, and took her shoes two nights ago. He also poisoned, perhaps I should say, tried to kill Angel, and drugged Mic for an entire night." She paused for a moment before continuing. "Yeah, I'd say the motherfucker's dangerous. Wouldn't you?" Dottie was shocked by her own language, but let it slide.

Jack cursed under his breath and Stoner locked eyes with Slade.

"Countess Borghase, we'll be on the ship the second it docks."

"I'll be waiting with the ship's security," she assured them and hung up. She shook her head. What a trio of morons. Slade and Jack had done nothing to ease her anxiety. She looked down at Angel and said, "It's up to us, old boy. I guess we'll have to get her back ourselves."

Angel looked at her and Dottie was sure he nodded his head in agreement. She rubbed his ears and said, "Yep, we'll get her." Dottie stroked Angel's neck and said, "We'll get all of those bastards," she said as Angel watched her carefully.

Chapter 42

Dottie stood by helplessly as Jack eyeballed every passenger that disembarked The Regina Mediterranean in Athens. As she watched hordes of people leave the ship, she remembered the pair of tickets she'd found in the hall near the elevator after Grady Jones had abducted Michaela. They were tickets to the Athena Temple.

Dottie paced anxiously between Commander Françoise, Slade McKane, and Travis Stoner. She felt anxious and useless. She decided to leave. "Commander Françoise, I'm no help here. I'm going to take Angel into Athens. There's a small café Mic and I had planned to visit. It's near the Temple of Athena Nike. I'm gonna go there, just in case she's managed to get away from him."

Jack stole a look at the Countess Borghase. He didn't know her well, but had heard plenty 'Dottie' stories over the years. He thought she was awesome in many ways. She looked like Monique would look in another forty years. Several years ago, he'd gone duck hunting with her in Virginia and the old girl hadn't missed a single shot. She had his respect.

Jack nodded as he noted how tired and frustrated the Countess was. "Let me send a Greek police officer with you," he offered. "It's a foreign country and he'll be able to help you if you run into any problems."

Dottie shook her head and laughed. "No, Jack. No policeman. I'm practically Greek myself. I speak the language and I know my way around Athens, trust me. Besides, you, Slade, and the FBI man need to catch St. Germaine and all the police officers should stay and assist you. Right now, my focus is on Michaela and I assure you, it's Angel's concern as well."

Jack nodded and patted the massive dog. "Give me your cell number and let's sync our phones. You say you're taking Angel?" He asked as he admired the German shepherd. The dog was more than impressive. For a second, he wondered if the elderly woman could handle him.

"Yeah," Dottie said with a wide grin. "I'm kind of Angel's second mother. He and I have saved Michaela's butt a couple of other times. If she's out there, we'll get her, I promise you," Dottie said with assurance.

Commander Françoise nodded. He believed her. "Go for it. But, let Angel sniff those dresses and shoes in Michaela's closet before you leave. That way, it'll be fresh for him," Jack suggested.

Dottie grinned and said, "I will, but I know the scent of that atrocious man is all that's on Angel's mind. If that son-of-a-bitch is within ten miles, I'll guaran-damn-tee-you we'll get him," Dottie said with a malicious grin.

Jack grinned and said, "Have at it, Countess. Call me if you need help. I've got a car right over there," he said as he pointed to a cruiser in a no parking zone.

"Oh… so that's your car," Dottie commented in her uppity Countess voice. "That's why they couldn't get my limo parked there. I had the ship order a limo for Angel and me and because of your vehicle, I couldn't have my spot," she said in a grumpy voice as she shot him a dirty look.

Jack got the message. "I'll have one of the men pull it up. They'll pull your limo right there," he said as he motioned for one of the officers to move his car into the fire zone.

"You do that, Commander. I'm going to take Angel to Mic's stateroom, let him sniff those clothes, and then disembark the ship. See you later. Get that nasty murderer, will you?" She directed.

Jack laughed shortly. "I intend to. You just get Mic. We'll take care of the other monster. As soon as we get him, I'll text you," he assured her.

"Deal. Tootle loo, Commander," Dottie said with an aristocratic wave of two of her fingers.

Jack shook his head as he watched her depart, her back straight and head erect, every silver hair in place with the huge dog at her side. The old girl and the dog will probably find Mic," he said to himself. And that would be a great thing.

Chapter 43

In an effort to disembark the ship unnoticed, Grady had Mic put on a long dark wig, a pair of jeans, and a camo jacket, clothes she'd never pick for herself, and then he managed to immerse them into a large group of brightly dressed folks from all over the world. As they moved with the group, Mic saw Slade studying every face that left the ship. She tried to gesture to him, but Grady placed his arm around her like a vice and stuck the Glock into her left hip.

"I'll shoot you in a heartbeat, my love," he whispered sweetly. "It wouldn't be a bad thing if we departed this earth like Romeo and Juliet… Two star-struck lovers who could never, ever be together," he threatened in a low voice.

"I'll never be your lover," Mic spat at him as her green eyes froze on his face. "You're scum, a pervert, and a criminal! I'll die before you touch me," she hissed. "Anyone who tries to kill their lover's dog doesn't love them," she said as she kicked his shin as hard as she could.

Grady cursed under his breath and gripped her tightly around her neck. "I'll kill that bastard dog just as soon as I can… and you'll watch me," he promised with a threatening look.

Mic was as furious and helpless as she'd ever felt. She was impotent. She'd never in her life considered Grady Jones a formidable enemy, but now, here he was and he could kill her in an instant. She struggled for control of her situation and decided to back down and wait for her best opportunity.

Several minutes later, the couple was off the dock and surrounded by a horde of gaily-dressed passengers and crewmembers looking for transportation into Athens for a day of sightseeing.

Mic wiggled out of Grady's grip in an attempt to flee, but a millisecond later, he kicked her in the back of her legs. She fell on the concrete and cursed as pain spread through her knee up into her hip.

He looked down at her and said, "Oh no, my lovely, you've fallen again." He reached down for her and jerked her up just as a cab pulled in front of them. Grady pushed her to the cab and hissed, "If you ever, ever do that again, bitch, I'll shoot you. I'll shoot you in your face," he threatened.

Mic was docile as Grady pushed her into the back seat of the cab. Her knee was bloody and bruised. Her hip was throbbing. Grady held a gun against her neck angled toward her cranium.

"Where you go?" The cab driver asked in broken English as he focused on his breakfast pastry. He paid no attention to the couple in his cab. Mic doubted he'd even looked at them.

"The Temple of Athena Nike," Grady said. "We can't wait to see it, can we, my dear?" He turned and kissed Michaela long and hard on her lips.

Mic turned her face away and swallowed constantly to keep the nausea at bay. Grady was turning out to be more formidable than she had anticipated. He was strong and powerful but most of all, he had her gun.

Grady glared at her. "You'll love the Temple of Athena Nike, the patron saint of Athens. When we get there, you'll pledge your life to me and I'll 'clip your wings,' so to speak," Grady said with an evil grin. "You'll never leave me, and you'll be mine forever," he said in a dreamy voice.

"In a pig's eye I will. I'll never pledge anything to you, you crazy lunatic," Mic said as she spat at him.

Chapter 44

Dottie motioned for her limo driver to pull over near the Temple of Athena Nike located on the southwest corner of the Acropolis. Her driver let her out at the small Greek bistro that she and Mic had planned to visit. The bistro was famous for its pastries and coffee. Dottie let Angel out of the limo and the two of them crossed the street and took a seat outside at a small table with a green umbrella. Dottie had a perfect view of the temple. She ordered coffee and a pastry and pulled some treats out of her purse for the 'ever watchful' Angel.

The dog quickly consumed his duck jerky, but his eyes never left the Temple of Athena Nike. Dottie scratched his head and said, "I don't know why, Angel, but I think this might be the place where Grady brings Mic. She reached into her handbag and pulled out the two tour tickets she'd found near the elevator on the ship. Dottie offered the tickets for Angel to sniff and he pawed the ground. Dottie knew she had a hit. Angel recognized the scent. Dottie's heartbeat picked up in anticipation. They were gonna get the bastard. She could feel it!

Angel stared at her briefly but quickly looked back to the temple. The Temple of Athena Nike was closed during the early morning hours. There was no one around at this hour and the ticket office was empty. In fact, the entire Acropolis was closed. Dottie sipped her coffee slowly and pretended to read a newspaper, but her eyes were constantly searching the classical structures located on the southwest corner of the Acropolis. The Temple of Athena Nike had a prominent position on a steep bastion at the corner of the Acropolis to the right of the entrance, the Propylaea. She knew Grady and Mic would have to approach the temple from the south because of the rocky wall behind it and uncertain, difficult to ambulate terrain. The wall had been built by the Mycenaeans in an effort to protect the natural citadel of the Acropolis and served as protection for the city.

The temple was smaller than the other structures. It stood as a shrine to Athena Nike, the patron goddess of Athens whose winged statues appeared all over Athens. The temple had been built around 421 BC, and served as a symbol of Athens' superior military and political strength. The temple was surrounded by a guardrail, or parapet, that protected Athenians and other visitors from falling off of the Acropolis.

Dottie knew where Grady would bring Michaela and continued to watch carefully because she knew the approach had to occur from that area. She looked up, smiled at the young waitress, and accepted a refill of her coffee.

"The coffee is delicious, my dear. It's a beautiful day, isn't it?" Dottie asked in her most gracious voice. The young woman smiled and nodded her head.

"When does the temple open for tourists?"

The young woman replied in Greek. "It opens at eleven o'clock, in just about one hour," she told Dottie with a smile after she'd checked her watch.

A moment later, Angel stood and raised his massive head. He growled. The young waitress jumped, but Dottie quickly reassured her she was safe.

Angel continued to stand, a low growl coming from his throat as he stared at the Temple of Athena Nike. Dottie turned her head and searched the area. In the distance, she saw two people, a man, and a woman. It looked like the man was forcing the woman to walk and she did, quite painfully.

He had an arm around her shoulders and most likely a gun to her neck.

Dottie took off her sunglasses for a better view as Angel continued to growl incessantly. She peered at the couple as they approached the Acropolis from the southwest side of the temple. It was Michaela. She recognized her walk, even with her limp. She grimaced as she saw Grady slap Mic in the face. Angel strained on his leash, but Dottie held him tightly. "We'll go in a minute, Angel. Let's see where he plans to take her in the temple."

Angel lifted his head, gave Dottie a clear look, and then looked back at his mistress as she struggled to stay upright in the ruins. It was obvious her leg was injured.

Dottie watched as the couple disappeared around the first few ionic columns in the temple.

"Let's go," she ordered Angel.

The pair crossed the street and stayed in the shadows of the temple and other classical structures. They hurried around the statues and columns, Dottie cursing frequently at the unstable terrain. Each time they spotted Mic and Grady, they hid behind a column. Dottie watched Grady carefully as she tried to determine where they would stop. They continued to follow the couple through the temple and around the columns until they saw Grady force Mic against the famous wingless statue of the goddess Athena. His hand was at her neck as he screamed at her to 'obey' him. Dottie could hear his scream in spite of the wind. Mic refused him. Each time she refused, he hit her again.

Angel strained against his leash. "Come, Angel. We must get closer before we attack," Dottie cautioned the dog. The pair moved closer to the statue until Dottie could see Mic. Her face was a mess. Dottie's heart filled with hate. She'd get the filthy bastard.

Dottie and Angel moved until they were within forty feet of the couple. Dottie removed Angel's leash and the dog ran swiftly, bounded through the air, and landed on Grady's back. Angel quickly brought him to the ground, his mouth inches from Grady's carotid artery. The gun bounced from Grady's hand when he hit the marble floor of the temple. Dottie moved closer, her Glock in her hand as she trained the weapon on the man's head. Angel snarled and made the most vicious sounds Dottie had ever heard. It frightened her and for a second she wondered if Angel was out of control. Angel was one second from ripping the man's arteries out.

Dottie looked at Mic who hadn't moved, but gawked at them. She heard strange guttural sounds come from Michaela's mouth as her hand pointed to the ropes around her body. Grady had tied Michaela to the statue. She couldn't move.

Mic made another loud noise. Her green eyes were filled with fear as she pointed to Grady's arm as he reached for the gun on the ground. He was less than an inch from it. A horrific scream came from Mic as Dottie drew her Glock and delivered a perfect head shot to Grady Jones' forehead. The man slumped and fell back on the marble floor. Angel remained on the man's back.

Dottie ran to Mic and untied her from the Athena statue. Mic slipped to the limestone and marble at the bottom of the statue of the goddess and hugged her dog. Angel licked her face anxiously removing blood, rocks, and dirt. Then she reached for Dottie who hugged her and looked anxiously at her.

"Are you okay?" Dottie asked as she scanned Michaela's face for permanent damage. "Can you talk? Your face is so swollen."

Mic tried to smile as tears poured down her face. "A little…" she mumbled and then pointed to her jaw and looked at Grady's body, her eyes wide with approval.

Dottie nodded as she glanced over at the corpse and complimented herself on the bullet in Grady's head. Damn if she hadn't made the perfect shot. She'd tease Mic about it later, but now she needed to get her some help.

Mic read Dottie's mind and gave her a thumbs up. Again, she tried to smile, but couldn't. Dottie nodded, gave her a thumbs up in return, and then looked up at the beautiful wingless, sculpted statue of Athena Nike. Most statues of Athena had wings, but in her temple, her house of worship, her wings were gone. Athenians had wanted to keep their patron goddess at home and had removed her wings. For an instant, Dottie wondered if Grady Jones had planned to 'clip' Michaela's wings at the statue as a symbolic gesture to make her subservient to him. Yes, that was it. That was exactly why he'd brought Michaela to the Temple of Athena Nike. A second later, Dottie pulled out her phone to call an ambulance.

"We're going to the hospital, Michaela," she said firmly as she stared down at Michaela who was still sitting at the feet of the statue.

Mic started to wave her hands and tried to talk.

Dottie shook her head, "You're going, your face is a mess, your leg is messed up, and I think your jaw may be broken. They'll be here in a minute," Dottie assured her as Michaela continued to stroke her dog.

Mic sat against the feet of the statue and nodded. Dottie was right. Her face did hurt like hell. She was quiet as she waited for the ambulance.

Chapter 45

Slade was frustrated and sick of the sun in his eyes. Screw the Mediterranean. He'd much rather be on the Mississippi in New Orleans, in a flat boat on the bayou, or in his adopted city of Richmond. His face was set in an angry scowl. Nothing had happened. No passenger met the description of St. Germaine. He'd watched passengers and crew disembark for almost two hours and hadn't seen anyone that met the description of St. Germaine and he certainly hadn't seen Mic. He cursed under his breath.

"I'm taking a break," he said as he shoved the pictures of St. Germaine and Michaela toward the Greek SWAT Commander. The Commander's team was in the black SUV about a hundred feet away.

The guy nodded and Slade headed toward Stoner, who was watching the computer monitor as close-up shots of passengers were displayed and compared with their ship identification.

"We got nothing," Stoner said as he shook his head. "I haven't seen anything or anyone at all who resembles St. Germaine." He frowned, "Zilch… not a thing, no one who even resembles him."

Slade shook his head. "Well, maybe the bastard isn't getting off. He may still be aboard. Passengers can disembark whenever they want," Slade said.

Stoner nodded. "Yeah, but these are the pictures of the people who haven't left the ship and none of them look like St. Germaine," he said in a disappointed voice. "My guess is he got by us in one of his disguises," Stoner decided with a shake of his head.

"Has Jack looked at these?" Slade asked. "He could tell better than us, don't you think?"

"Maybe, but I don't think so. He's only seen St. Germaine a couple of times and we have the same mugshots of him. The best picture is on his New Orleans vendor's permit," Stoner said as he pointed at the picture. "You know he was an organ grinder with the monkey and calliope, right? He hung out in the Quarter near the river."

Slade nodded. "Yeah, the man was a fixture for years." Slade pointed and said, "Why don't we move over there? Then we can see passengers approaching to leave the ship from the elevator and the stairway."

Stoner grunted and hollered for Jack. The three men stood by the stairs.

"We got a great big zero," Jack said, a frown on his face. His body language suggested his disappointment. "There's no other way they can get off the ship, is there?" He asked Slade and Stoner.

Slade shook his head. "Not that they're telling us or that I know of," he said, a sullen look on his face as he watched a man with dark, greasy hair, walk down the steps toward him. The man was familiar. Slade studied him for a couple of seconds and felt his gut constrict in recognition. Slade's eyes immediately shot to the man's hand where he saw the snake tattoo vivid and colorful in the morning sun.

Snake scanned Slade's face. Recognition popped in his eyes and he turned around and ran back up the steps three steps at a time.

"Son of a bitch," Slade said as he took off after him. He hollered at Jack and Stoner. "There's the guy that tried to kill Michaela at her house earlier this year. It's the perp who stabbed Angel. What the hell is he doing on this damn ship?" A second later, the three men as well as two Greek cops were in pursuit of Snake.

Chapter 46

Snake knew he'd been spotted. He cursed under his breath as his tall frame clung to the outside wall of the ship and saw a squad of Greek cops headed his way. He pressed his body against the side of the boat and stayed in the shadows. His arm muscles burned as he strained to hold on to the thick rope.

He looked for a way to escape. Unfortunately, the crowds had thinned out in the pier area. There was no way for him to escape into a crowd under the cover of other people. He continued to press his back against the side of the ship, but he was in a precarious position. If the ship slipped away from the massive piling, Snake's legs would be split in two. One leg was secured on a concrete block on the pier and the other dangled by in a foothold outside the ship.

Snake felt fear for the first time in a long while. He cut his eyes to the back of the ship and wildly searched for something to hang onto. He wanted to pull his body back on board and hide until the ship left Athens. That offered his best chance for escape.

But, that wasn't gonna happen. He knew he'd have to hit the water. Seconds before he fell into the deep, brackish Mediterranean Sea, he looked to the rear of the ship where crew had unloaded cargo. He saw three stretchers and assumed one was the Senator and the other was the dead casino dealer. He guessed the third one was a patient who must have died onboard. He thought his eyes had tricked him when the body on the third stretcher moved. He watched mesmerized as a hand poked through the heavy plastic and searched for the zipper at the top of a bag. Then the corpse wheedled his way to the bottom of the stretcher.

Fascinated, Snake watched as a short powerful man unzipped his body bag, jump off the stretcher, pause a second to straighten his clothes, and look around. That lucky son of a bitch Snake thought to himself as he recognized Vadim. That bastard got off the ship on a morgue stretcher. What a lucky son of a bitch. Snake smiled and shook his head in awe.

A second before Snake fell into the sea, he saw St. Germaine look back at him. Vadim smiled his wicked grin, and gave him a short salute.

Twenty minutes later, after treading water in the sea, Snake found himself about a mile and a half down the Greek coast near a fishing village. He crawled out of the sea, kept his body crouched low to the ground, and moved in crab-fashion up the embankment until he got lost in a small community market of umbrellas and vendors. He reached in his pants pocket, pulled out his wet money, and asked a clothing vendor for directions to a hotel.

The merchant smiled and pointed up the hill. Snake pulled off his shirt and pointed to his jeans. The man went behind his counter, pulled out a new set of jeans and a big denim shirt. Seconds later, Snake emerged from behind the tent completely dry and clean. He nodded goodbye and walked up the hill to the hotel. Twenty minutes later, Snake lay in a hotel room fresh from the shower with clean clothes and a beer. A few minutes later, he was cursing at the Greek television set. Finally, Snake threw the television remote out of the window and laughed aloud as he thought about Vadim escaping the ship on a morgue stretcher. It was a good thing there were three morgue stretchers. After all, Vadim had filled up the first two with bodies.

Snake continued to laugh as he remembered Vadim's goodbye salute. He wondered if he'd get a chance to work with the old boy again. Truth was, he kinda liked him. The old guy was a survivor, no question.

Chapter 47

Slade searched frantically and desperately for Snake Man, as Snake was known to the Richmond police. A dozen Greek officers assisted him, but they came up with nothing. The man had just vanished. Poof. Gone into thin air. Slade cursed under his breath.

"He has to be around here somewhere," Slade said angrily to anyone who would listen. "No one disappears like he did," he insisted, but his words fell on deaf ears.

The Greek officer shrugged his shoulders and said, "I have no idea. My men will continue to search for him. We believe he must have dropped into the water. We have no record of him leaving the ship."

"Find him," Slade snarled as his text alarm sounded. He jerked it out of his pocket and saw a picture of a happy, but very battered Michaela. Her eye was blackened and it looked as though her face had been pistol-whipped.

"Slade. Slade, Dottie and Angel saved me," Mic said painfully. "I'm safe and I'm going to the hospital," she said as her green eyes sought his and her dark hair clung to the side of her face.

Dottie interrupted and said, "Stop talking, Mic. Your jaw looks bad." Dottie grabbed the phone, "I think her jaw is broken, Slade."

Slade's heart warmed with joy. Michaela was going to be all right. "Thank goodness they saved you, Mic," he said in a soft voice. "That's the only news that's been good the entire day. What about your stalker, Grady, or whatever the hell his name is?"

Mic's green eyes widened, even the blackened one and she said, "Dead. Dottie shot him in the head. He won't take me again," she said, her speech garbled.

Slade was impressed. "The old girl got him with a headshot?" He said as his heart swelled with pride for the aging Countess. "Way to go, Countess!

"Bastard got what he deserved," Dottie said as she shushed Mic again. "I aimed for the head."

Slade laughed. "I hear you, Countess, and I believe you," he said honestly.

"Damn good thing," Dottie hissed. "Nobody can get anything done around here except for Angel and me," she said in a biting voice. "Who have you and Jack caught?"

Slade cleared his throat, "No one, absolutely no one," he admitted, "but it's not for lack of trying."

"No one? No one, Slade? What about St. Germaine?" Mic asked in a disappointed voice.

"Stop talking, Michaela," Dottie insisted. "You're gonna be worse."

"Zilch. No sign of him," Slade admitted. "We've looked and looked. But, Angel… how is Angel?"

Michaela leaned over to pat her dog who lay on the floor next to her feet in the ambulance. "Angel's fine. Angel put Grady… put him on the ground and took a few bites of his wrist. Grady managed to get his gun arm out from under his body, but it was too late. Dottie had the drop on him," she said with a small gasp as she remembered the entire incident.

Slade's body was flooded with relief. "Mic stop talking. I can hardly understand you. Please, just get back here where I can keep my eye on you. We've had too many near misses lately."

"What do you have? Anything? You said no St. Germaine?" Dottie asked with anxiety in her voice.

Slade's voice was disappointed. "No. Nothing on St Germaine. I assume he got away or he's still on the ship," Slade said. "We watched every face that got on or off the ship, food service workers, staff, ship crew, and passengers and no one got off the ship that looked like Vadim."

Mic was quiet and she pondered Slade's words. She struggled to speak. "Where could he be? He has to be somewhere, Slade. He couldn't have escaped all of those law enforcement people plus you, Jack, and Stoner who know him so well," she said, an incredible edge to her voice.

Slade was quiet for a second. "Well, the way I see it, he did. Perhaps he worked up some masterful disguise, made himself ten feet tall, had plastic surgery, but I'm here to tell you, that Vadim didn't get off the ship today. Mark my words."

Mic lay back against the pillows. She knew that voice and she knew she needed to back off. "Got it. I'll be back soon. Dottie wants me to go by and see a friend of hers who is a plastic surgeon. She thinks my jaw is broken," she said with a giggle.

"She's had a lot of pain medicine, Slade," Dottie said. "I think she's gonna fall asleep."

Slade was quiet for a second. "Do what Dottie says. You're getting harder and harder to understand and your words are slurred," he informed her. "I think you're coming down from an adrenaline rush," he continued, with a smile in his voice.

"See, I told you so," Dottie said in the background. "How come you listen to him before you listen to me?" She asked in an irritated voice.

Mic shrugged her shoulders, nodded to Dottie, and signaled she planned to hang up. "Is there anything else, Slade?"

Slade hesitated and said, "Yeah, there is. Guess who else was on the ship?"

"I can't imagine. Who, who else could be on that ship?"

"Snake. Snake Man from earlier this year. Tattoo boy," Slade said angrily between compressed lips.

Mic was shocked. She could hardly speak "Snake? The guy that tried to kill me and stabbed Angel?"

"Among other things," Slade said wryly. "Yes, him." Mic could imagine the scowl on his face, but she couldn't imagine why Snake would be on a cruise ship in the Mediterranean Sea.

"Why?" She asked, shock in her voice. "Why are two men we've been chasing forever on the same ship with Dottie and me and a bunch of hostile pharmaceutical types in the middle of the Mediterranean Sea?"

Slade contemplated her question and said, "Well, my best guess is they work together. We think Snake and St. Germaine are killers that work for an international crime syndicate. And, I think they're working for your favorite drug company, Blake Pharmaceutical."

Mic was shocked. "That's it. They do the dirty work for people. This time, it's Blake Pharmaceutical." She stopped, stunned for a moment, and then said, "So Blake Pharmaceutical hired Snake and Vadim to kill people who objected to Quelpro and believed it was a dirty drug."

"That's my best guess at the moment."

Michaela was quiet, lost in thought as she considered a relationship between St. Germaine and Snake. Then she was riveted by a memory. "You're right, Slade. I saw the two of them having drinks at the pool bar a few days ago."

"You did?" Slade was surprised.

Mic gulped and said, "I didn't realize who they were then. I missed it," she said sadly. "Perhaps I could have saved Dr. O'Leary's life and the Senator's life," she said sadly.

"Don't beat yourself up, Mic. We'll get them and we'll take these corporate assholes down," Slade said in a forceful voice.

"Yeah, you're right, Slade. We're gonna do it... In memory of Dr. O'Leary and Senator Bostitch. And people all over the world who are taking unsafe drugs."

A second later, Mic was fast asleep in the ambulance.

Epilogue

It had been the cruise from hell. But, from the laughter and good feelings around the table, it seemed the events on The Regina Mediterranean were only a distant memory. There was much to celebrate and many things to be thankful for. The Regina Mediterranean was in port in Mykonos, Greece, a lovely island in the Mediterranean with whitewashed cottages and blue roofs. Dottie loved Mykonos and she'd planned a lovely dinner on the island. The owner of the restaurant was an old friend and was the same age as Dottie. Mic was delighted to see Dottie actually flirting with the distinguished elderly gentlemen. Mic wasn't sure she'd ever seen Dottie 'flirt' but she was having a great time watching. She touched Slade on the leg and urged him to watch. She was pleased when Slade cracked a smile.

The group dined outside and consisted of Dottie, Michaela, Slade, Jack, Travis Stoner, and Ian and Alana Pennington, who were visiting the island. Everyone had enjoyed an incredible feast except for Michaela whose left jaw was wired and still terribly painful. She enjoyed an array of fruit juices. Her leg was wrapped in bandages, but was unbroken, just badly bruised.

"We did it," FBI Agent-in-Charge Stoner announced with a broad grin as he checked his phone for the message he'd been waiting for. "We've issued warrants for the arrests of the President, Chairman of the Board, Board Members, Officers, and Executives of Blake Pharmaceutical. They've been arrested on felony charges for conspiring to assault and assassinate a government official. We'll add felony murder charges for the murder of Dr. O'Leary if we find his remains," he said quietly.

Mic saw a flicker of pain cross Ian's face when his friend's name was mentioned. "Suppose we don't recover his body?" Ian asked.

Stoner nodded, his handsome face grave, "We'll need a body, Dr. Pennington. Captain Wodensen says there's still a possibility we'll find him," he added in a somber voice.

"When will the arrogant assholes be arrested?" Dottie asked, her face consumed with a smile. "Can we parade them on the ship? Could I make them walk the plank?" She joked. "I want to watch and cheer," she added with a conspiratorial wink. "I hope they rot in jail, the bastards."

Agent Stoner grinned at the Countess, "They've been arrested. You didn't think we'd let them continue on a posh Mediterranean cruise did you?" He asked with a raised eyebrow. "We got them a half an hour ago. The Greek port police picked them up from The Regina Mediterranean. They'll be flown to Athens, where they'll be met by a contingent of FBI agents and law enforcement officials who will escort them back to the United States," Stoner reported. "Captain Wodensen said the arrest went well," he said with a smile.

"I'll drink to that," Jack said as he raised his glass of Retsina. "Cheers," he said as everyone laughed and echoed his toast.

Mic, since she couldn't speak, held up a sign to Jack that said, "Sorry about St. Germaine. Next time… okay?"

Jack nodded as a small pop of anger passed across his face. "Yeah, Mic. Next time," he agreed. "Although, we did learn a few things this go around," he said a satisfied look on his face. "The information that St. Germaine and Snake work together is invaluable."

Slade nodded and said, "Yeah, it is. Now we know they're international assassins or killers for hire. We didn't know that until now, nor did we know they worked together."

Stoner interrupted and said, "The Bureau is looking into that. We think they work for an international crime syndicate. That's been our position since the terror attack in New Orleans. We know, or are reasonably sure, that St. Germaine is a part of one. We have him most likely as associated with Bratva."

"Yeah. That may work," Slade agreed. "We know the guy who masterminded the attack in Richmond was definitely Bratva."

Dottie gazed around the table and saw fear in Alana Pennington's eyes. "It's time to party. Attention everyone, let's save this talk for later, it's time for dessert and after dinner drinks. Everyone drink up. The night is still young," Dottie said gaily as she winked at the elderly restaurant owner who couldn't take his eyes off her.

Michaela looked over at Dottie and shook her head. The old girl was amazing and once again, she'd saved her life. Mic reached down and petted Angel. Then she raised her juice glass, pointed, and mouthed, "To Dottie."

Everyone cheered and Dottie wiped away her tears.

Life was good after all. They'd get the bad guys next time. The bad guys always lost, didn't they?

The End

To be contiued…

Want to read more about Mic, Dottie and Angel?

I hope you enjoyed reading ***The Case of the Man Overboard***.

The adventures of Mic, Dottie and hero dog Angel continue in, ***The Case of the Very Dead Lawyer*** when the body of Richmond's most despised plaintiff's attorney is found dead in his office. Foul play is evident and the city is turned upside down searching for the killer.

If you'd like to join my mailing list and receive updates on the latest news and releases visit: www.JudithLucci.com.

Do you like cozy mysteries? If so, try my **Artzy Chicks Cozy Mystery** series set in the Massanutten Resort in the Virginia Mountains. These humorous cozy mysteries surround the art gallery and feature the artists, Lily and LauraLea and the guests that visit the resort.